Also by Monica Bhide

Fiction and Short Stories

The Devil In Us (2014)

Singapore Noir, edited by Cheryl Lu-Lien Tan (Akashic Books, 2014)

Food Essays and Cookbooks

A Life of Spice (2015)

Modern Spice: Inspired Indian Flavors for the Contemporary Kitchen (Simon and Schuster. 2009; Random House India, 2010)

The Everything Indian Cookbook: 300 Tantalizing Recipes from Sizzling Tandoor Chicken to Fiery Lamb Vindaloo (Adams Media, 2004)

Monica's essays have been included in *Best Food Writing 2005, 2009, 2010,* and *2014*, edited by Holly Hughes (Da Capo Press)

Inspirational Books

The Write Colors: Motivation for Creative Minds (artwork by Deepa Patke; 2016)

In Conversation with Exceptional Women (ebook)

Monica's books are available through Amazon.com, BN.com, Kobo, iBooks and her website, MonicaBhide.com

Karma and the Art of Butter Chicken

A novel

Monica Bhide

ISBN-13: 978-0-9976624-1-2
ISBN-13: 978-0-9976624-2-9 (ebook)

Bodes Well Publishing
Please contact publisher@bodeswellpublishing.com about special discounts for bulk purchases

Disclaimer

Everything in this book is fiction, including all the characters and the monastery. The story about carrying the burning house is a tale I have heard many times. I do not know who the original author is, but I do know that many cultures have the same type of story: a story about how you leave your bygones in order to move forward. So I credit all the wise people who have taught me that lesson over the years.

"There is NOTHING as powerful as a changed mind."
Bishop T. D. Jakes

PROLOGUE

New Delhi, India
Present day

The stakes have never been higher.

The young man sees his name glittering as it flashes on the enormous digital screen outside the television studio. He instinctively moves his hand to his chest to calm his pounding heart. His entire life, he has felt unworthy, incapable, and yet, here he is today.

His dream is unfolding in front of his eyes: a chance at fame, fortune, and an unbelievable opportunity to make a difference, to leave a tiny positive mark in this world.

He smiles as he realizes he may possibly be the only person ever to enter a cooking studio with a monk by his side. Destiny, it seems to him, favors the leaders in the karmic game. He hopes perhaps the monks' karmic escrow will rub off on him.

But first things first: the TV crew thrusts him into a makeup van, and the monk is sent to the audience seating.

Two hours later, he emerges from the van, his old self

discarded like a tree shedding its dying leaves. He stops to look at himself in the mirror. His soft hair is spiked, the short-sleeved red shirt shows off his tattooed arms, and slight makeup accents his sharp jaw. He notices something in his amber eyes he has never seen before. Hope? Fear?

A quick photo shoot follows.

His assistant for the day ushers him onto the set.

The judges fire off the challenge for the day, "Give us the taste that defined your childhood."

Within seconds, the cooking show contestants rush around like mad scientists trying to create alchemy from ginger, cardamom, and fire.

The young man rushes to create his dish, a simple, spicy soup. The air around him smells of sizzling cumin, roasting chilies, fried garlic, lemony cilantro, and manifesting dreams.

"STOP, NOW! Time is up. Knives down, step back from your stations!" the director screams.

"Are you ready for us to taste?" the judge asks him in a snooty tone.

He hesitates.

The judge is getting impatient.

The young man eyes his soup again, then nods his head.

The judge moves forward and bends down to pick up a spoon.

But just as the judge is about to take a sip, the young man stops him.

He takes the bowl of soup he has just cooked and throws the contents into a large trashcan.

There is a stunned gasp from the audience.

The judge looks angry, befuddled.

Only the monk understands and is proud of the young man. Not many people can speak their truth when so much is at stake.

The young man points to the now bare bowl.

"This is really all I remember about my childhood: constant hunger and empty bowls."

With that, he removes his apron, tears rolling down his cheeks along with his dreams, and he quietly walks off the set of the show.

A few years ago

Eshaan Veer Singh's Journal

Death is cheap in my town
Life is cheaper
I stare out my window
The rotting livestock
The stray dogs covered in blood
The failings of my father
The faults of my fate

The sun burns the earth
The earth eats its own
Paradise or abyss
It is both, I am told

She is dying
No shroud
No fire
No sandalwood for her pyre
Hers was deemed an inconsequential life

I stare out my window
As the rain begins
Each drop embraces the earth
As it begs for less pain

She dies as she lived
Quiet and frail
Nothing owed, nothing gained

I look out my window
The rain is gone
The earth, it smells
Like it has hope again
An illusion or truth
Only time will tell

Her pyre still burns
Inside my heart's hell

A few months ago

Chapter 1

The brand-new coins, black and gold, were scattered across the hard wooden boards. With each hit of the striker, they smoothly whizzed past each other. Indian children's play. But everyone knew, today, this was war, and there was only one goal: to capture a beautiful magenta-colored coin dubbed the Queen.

"The one who wins this game will be crowned King of the Queen," one eighty-year-old competitor joked as loudly as he could. The other competitors, at different tables, laughed. Many of them had been playing this game, carrom, for as long as they could remember but the official rules had changed recently. Now one needed to score the most points by sending the highest number of his own color coins into the pockets. Since all the competitors were widowed or single, they decided that at this age, the only woman they would get would be the Queen coin on the carrom board. "Who cares about the highest score? I want to win the Queen!" was the consensus. So it was decided, much to the chagrin of official rule lovers, that the game winner would need the highest points *and* the Queen. No Queen, no win.

"Yes, yes, I will win and be King," another competitor

shouted out, leaning eagerly over the large wooden carrom board.

"A king, yes! But it will be a one-eyed king," Eshaan Veer Singh, standing guard at his tea pot as the official chai wallah for the event, remarked after noting a total lack of skill in most of the competitors.

"You know, it is as the saying goes: In the land of the blind, the one-eyed man is king," he said, but even as he joked, he knew this yearly event wasn't really about winning at a game of carrom. For the old men who were competing, it wasn't the carrom coins that zigzagged on the board with abandon; it was the memory of their youth. They exhibited their intellect and perceived power here, in this game, since society at large had written them off as old and useless.

The uncharacteristic blue morning sky, free of the daily smog, turned shades of orange as the sun opened its heart. The air was cool. The rains were delayed, running on the perpetually late Indian standard time. The sandy ground hosting the carrom competition was parched, dry, and brittle.

As the competition intensified, several people walking along the path stopped to watch. The sight of these old gentlemen, all dressed in their best whites, playing a child's game with childlike abandon at this ungodly hour of the morning, was quite endearing if not entertaining. The competitors were sitting on stools surrounding specially made tables. The brand-new carrom boards were placed atop the tables.

"Stop talking! You are distracting me," Dr. Sinha screeched as he turned his focus to the coins on the board. The largest disk, called a striker, was used to hit the coins in the center of the board and send them to the corners. The goal was to get the coins into the pockets at the four corners of the carrom board. The person with the most coins *and* the special coin—the Queen—won the game. There was an important rule, though: if a player got the Queen into the pocket, the player had to get another coin, called a cover, into the pocket to keep the Queen. No cover, no Queen, and the battle would continue.

"Your time is up, Dr. Sinha! You will lose this competition," called one competitor.

"Give up now! Time to show the world what a gracious loser you are," called another.

Dr. Sinha ignored them. He was the reigning champion, not having lost a contest in six years. And a few seconds later, just as he had anticipated, he got three coins in with just one strike.

"I am the champion! You see!" he laughed as he greedily pulled the coins out of the pockets of the carrom board. The group had specially purchased four new boards for the competition. Two men played per board, and right now, the competition at every table was getting fierce.

"Dr. *Ji*, your fingers are more powerful than your older competitors here. These poor old men have painful joints in their fingers and cannot really compete at your level. It doesn't really seem fair," Eshaan joked as he called out to Dr. Sinha.

"Eshaan Veer Singh," Dr. Sinha playfully mocked the young man, "even though you have been coming here with me for years, let me remind you that you have no idea about playing carrom. As my father used to say, 'How would a monkey know what ginger tastes like?' You are here *only* because I love your chai."

"Oh, I've learned a lot from watching you. I think I can win the Queen easier than you can," Eshaan teased and pulled out his phone to take a picture of the doctor and his carrom board.

Dr. Sinha flashed a big smile, and then added for good measure, "Now watch me defeat them all—then take another winning photograph!"

Eshaan immediately emailed the photo to Kitt, along with a note: *TODAY, IT IS OFFICIALLY A YEAR SINCE I'VE HEARD FROM YOU. I MISS YOU. BTW, YOUR FATHER IS STILL AN AMAZING CARROM PLAYER... JUST DON'T TELL HIM I SAID THAT.*

"The tea is ready," a young woman named Rani, Eshaan's assistant for all his catering events, called out to the motley crew.

Eshaan rushed over to check on the tea boiling in a deep saucepan. He swirled the liquid in the pot and bent down to smell the sweet aroma of cardamom emanating from the hot tea. A brief dizzy spell unnerved him, but he steadied himself by balancing one hand on the table.

"Are you okay, Eshaan? Can I go to set up the hookah now?" Rani asked him.

"I am fine. But please wait, Rani, I want to do something," Eshaan said to the young girl, whose full name always made him snicker: Radio Rani. "I want to add one more thing to the hookah tobacco."

He dug into the vegetable bag and took out a large chunk of brown root. Using the back of a spoon, he scraped away the skin, then grated the root, catching the juices in a small container. He poured the juices over tobacco.

"Now we are ready. Come for tea as soon as you are done," he called out to the group, but no one was listening.

The battle was fierce now, just Dr. Sinha had gathered most

of the coins and the Queen seemed within his reach.

Suddenly, Dr. Sinha's opponent called to Eshaan, "I have to go to the bathroom. My prostate is killing me. Take over! I am leading—but you need to get me the Queen for the win!" And with that he pushed Eshaan towards his stool and then rushed toward the woods.

Dr. Sinha mumbled something about Eshaan not being in the all-white outfit required to enter the contest. Eshaan was dressed in jeans and a bright red t-shirt that read WE ALL NEED AN EVIL PLAN.

"You, you will never beat me. Like I said earlier, what does a monkey know about ginger? Watch how a professional does this! Look, look," Dr. Sinha called out. In one deft move, he captured another coin, but then lost one.

Instructions were flying out the mouths of everyone gathered.

"Don't hit the striker so hard, you have to be slow."

"Put more Borax powder on the board, it will help the coins slide easier."

But the two men were oblivious to the crowds and focused on the board.

Earlier that morning, Dr. Sinha had ritualistically slipped a few rupee bills in a white envelope and stuck it in his pocket. He always gave that money to the winner but since he had won the last few times, he had boasted that morning that the money, just like always, would just come back home with him.

Eshaan used his forefinger to push the striker hard, and with a single strike, captured three coins. Then, with another swift move, he captured the Queen. He knew he wasn't done—in order to keep the Queen, he knew he needed the cover. He placed the striker on the board, positioned it, and steadied his hand. He hesitated when he looked at the forlorn expression on Dr. Sinha's face. He looked back down at the board: there was just one coin left and he needed it or he would have to put the Queen back on the table. Muttering something about women bringing him good luck, he gave the striker another push. The last remaining gold coin slid easily into the pocket at the edge of the board . . . and suddenly the contest was over.

Reluctantly, Dr. Sinha reached into his pocket and fished out the envelope with the money.

"Beginner's luck," Dr. Sinha mumbled as he handed the money to Eshaan who smiled.

Eshaan took the envelope with a smile. He folded his hands in front of Dr. Sinha and said, "I know you think I am not worthy, but you have to admit that I did beat you in a fair game!"

Dr. Sinha laughed. "You have no painful joints! That is why you won. It had nothing to do with skill!"

Eshaan joined in the laughter. He opened the envelope, took out the money and handed it over to one of the beggars who was standing on the sidelines, watching the carrom contest. Mission accomplished he thought to himself: a good deed early in the morning was always a good thing!

Taking a clean white handkerchief out of his pocket, Dr. Sinha wiped the sweat off his forehead and his hands. The sun was getting hot as the morning wore along. He then produced another clean handkerchief from his pocket and handed it to Eshaan. "I always carry two. You never know."

"This competition is officially over; the other three tables are done as well," declared the oldest of the crew, Mr. Merry Mehra.

Merry Mehra was a tenant in Dr. Sinha's lavish three-floor bungalow. Dr. Sinha stayed on the ground level of his home and supplemented his retirement income by renting out the middle level to Mehra, and the terrace level to a young, vibrant Punjabi girl named Loveleen Singh, who was, at the moment, very pregnant.

"You did well. I am surprised," Mehra said to Eshaan, who forced a smile in return. He despised Mehra for his outlandish beliefs about bad omens.

For instance, Mehra had been coming to the competition for years, but refused to actually play the game. He said he couldn't because sitting on a stool would kill his back. But the group had enough wrinkles and grey hair to know that Mehra's astrologer had told him that carrom would bring him bad luck, so while he came to the contests, Mehra stayed as far away from the carrom boards as he physically could.

The carrom competitors walked over to the large picnic table Eshaan had set for them outside the main garden. Each of the gentlemen handed him an envelope intended to be his payment for the meal. Despite Rani's insistence, Eshaan never checked the envelopes. There had been occasions when a few had been empty, but he never seemed to mind. It drove Rani crazy.

"What magnificent tea! I can drink this all day long," said Dr. Sinha as he poured the tea into a saucer and slurped the warm liquid.

"Oh, look at this breakfast. I am impressed, Eshaan. Sesame brittle and oh, what is this dish? I don't know it."

"It is a spicy soup with mustard greens, radish, onions, garlic, and shredded cabbage. The monks tell me it is a cure-all for anything that ails you, 'specially old age!" he replied with a big smile as he ladled the piping hot soup into large bowls.

"Child, at this age, the only cure-all is death," another octogenarian quipped. "I do hope those monks are feeding you, Eshaan. You are as thin as this stick."

The men, having eaten, all moved toward the shade of a large tree, where the two massive and colorful hookahs were set up.

"Well, at least this contest has one good thing. We can all smoke hookah here in peace," Dr. Sinha said and took a deep inhale from the tube. Then he called out to Eshaan, "Young man, tell me what you put in the hookah today. It's really delicious!"

"Oh, that? It has what your father said, you know, about the monkeys!" Eshaan's eyes gleamed in the afternoon sun.

"You are a rascal," Dr. Sinha said and laughed aloud as it dawned on him that the secret ingredient was ginger.

As Eshaan began to clean up, a small group of vagrants gathered around the table, begging for leftovers and crumbs.

"We are out of food. We only cooked for these carrom people. I've already given them all that was leftover. I saved a cup of tea for you, since you haven't had any breakfast yet," Rani said to Eshaan as she pointed to the empty bowls and the single full cup of tea.

As soon as she said the words out loud, she regretted them and wished she hadn't spoken up.

"Eshaan, don't," she whispered, as she knew what was going to happen next.

"How can I not?" he answered back with a smile, and then without a minute's hesitation, he picked up all the payment envelopes and rushed toward the far side of the park, where several local vendors were selling bananas and apples.

Rani stared helplessly as he zoomed off.

"Now, we can feed them!" he announced as he returned a few moments later with several bags of food, which he began to place on the table.

In the blink of an eye, chaos broke out as beggars began snatching the food from his hands and from the table. One pushed Radio Rani so hard she tumbled and fell on her side. Eshaan rushed over and covered her body with his. He knew from experience that he could not stop the chaos, but regretted he had not pulled her away earlier.

The commotion attracted more beggars, who came running from around the other areas of the park, pushing, shoving, and trying to grab what they could. They hit each other, older beggars pushing ahead of the children, and little children bit the adults in order to get ahead.

Just as quickly as the chaos had started, it ended. And instead of gratefulness, the beggars spewed anger at Eshaan and Rani as many of them left empty handed.

Eshaan was still crouched over Rani. He slowly got up and gave her his hand so she could stand up.

The carrom group came forward to help after the beggars left. They were smart enough not to interfere during the madness, as the beggars were very aggressive. The old gents asked Eshaan if he and Rani were okay, and when the duo nodded, the men went back to their hookahs. Drama was just a part of their everyday life.

As soon as they left, Rani began screaming at Eshaan in her

native tongue. He did not understand one word of what she was saying, except the expletives she used. She had taught him those years ago. He stood quietly and listened.

"Rani, they were hungry. How could we not help them?" he asked.

She shook her head. This was the same conversation they'd had several times now. "Giving them food like this is *not* helping them. It teaches them it is okay to beg," she said sternly as she dusted off all the dirt from her clothes.

"Come on, Rani, forgive me? Since neither of us is bleeding, I will plead to guilty as charged. But you still love me, right?" he said as he got down on both knees, clasped his hands together, and beamed her his biggest smile.

That made Rani laugh. Some days, she thought he needed to be granted sainthood. But then there were days like today. She knew Eshaan's heart was in the right place, but this man just refused to see what he was doing. He kept throwing his money away to help these people, and it was solving nothing, for them or for him.

She had to forgive him. She knew his secrets, the dark shadows and where they cast their spells. He was, at the moment, as far as he could possibly be from learning the lessons the shadows were trying to teach him.

Chapter 2

"I still don't have enough money. This is nothing," Eshaan said as he looked at the pathetic balance on his bank statement and the few wads of cash he had just placed on the table. He'd worked day and night over the past two years, trying to save up enough money toward his dream project. What he conveniently didn't mention was *why* there wasn't enough money in the account. But of course, the kind old monk who was his audience for this diatribe already knew that.

Lama Dorje, the monk who rescued Eshaan as a child, stood quietly in the doorway of the Welcoming Room of the Tibetan monastery where he and Eshaan lived. As he listened to Eshaan whine, the Lama recalled the night he had found him, a mere skeleton of a child, with hollowed eyes and a spirit just about to be extinguished. That child had come a long way, but the Lama wondered how long it would be before Eshaan really understood his big dreams needed to start with a small step.

But at this moment, it appeared Eshaan had thrown himself a pity party and all his fears had come in to help him complain.

"I don't have a fancy degree, Lama. I don't have any great

talent. Do you think the universe gave me this dream as a big joke?" he asked, knowing full well the Lama was too smart to step into the discussion.

Eshaan pursed his lips and folded his arms tightly across his chest. His amber eyes furrowed in despair. He moved his right hand over the very visible tattoo on his less-than-bulging left bicep. The tattoo read: *Rab Rakha.* It was a title given to him, years ago, by carrom champion and retried physician Dr. Sinha, who lived across the street from the monastery.

The old teaching monastery, *Karma Norba Ling*, was located just outside New Delhi. "Old does not mean decrepit," Lama Dorje, the monastery administrator, often reminded people who wanted to enlist for the monastery's classes on Buddhism. The progressive monastery was fully equipped with Wi-Fi, a digital and paper library, Skype broadcasts of all its courses, and, not to be left out of social media, a very active Facebook page. The main building, painted with a multitude of reds, yellows, and greens, overshadowed the neighborhood filled with plain white and beige bungalows. The building was flanked by lush gardens in the front, and vegetable gardens and monk-made lotus-filled ponds in the back. Banks of unassuming rooms on each side of the building housed Buddhism students from the world over.

In exchange for room and board, Eshaan helped where he could at the monastery and did everything from cleaning to cooking. Just this morning, he had set up equipment to paint the altar in the main prayer room. The altar, holding a brass statue of the Shakyamuni Buddha, a glorious statute of the deity Tara, several purple orchids, and gently glowing lotus-shaped butter-and-flour lamps, was Eshaan's favorite part of the entire monastery. It was the only place in the monastery where he was not afraid to be alone. His demons dared not enter the sacred space. He would often go in there in the middle of the night when his nightmares frightened him. Here, he would fall asleep at the base of the altar.

When Eshaan had first arrived at the monastery years ago, some monks kept referring to him as the child saved by his karma. But back then, for young Eshaan, the words that spoke to his heart were the words Dr. Sinha had used to address him: *Rab Rakha*, the one God whom protects. He had them tattooed on his arm a few years ago and they became his evil-eye refuter, a free pass to try crazy things, a constant reminder that faith was the answer to everything. Yet here he was, *Rab Rakha*, seated on an old rattan couch in the Welcoming Room at his monastery, complaining about his perpetual lack of cash.

He looked up at the Lama, who was still standing there and listening.

"Lama Dorje, everything is going wrong. No money. And Kitt isn't answering me back. What am I doing wrong?" Eshaan asked as he instinctively ran his hand over the hidden tattoo under his wristwatch. It was a tiny pink lotus with the name Kitt written under it.

The Lama gazed appreciatively at the morning sun casting soft-colored shadows on the floor of the Welcoming Room as it seeped through the tiny red and green stained-glass windows. He knew this child was not at a point where he was ready to absorb any truths the Lama had to share. Eshaan had always been big-hearted, even as a child. He would often share his food with stray dogs on the street, fill terra-cotta pots with water and set them out on the roadside for thirsty pedestrians, and volunteer at all-night food kitchens. His heart was in the right place, but his brain had yet to figure out what his heart really wanted.

Eshaan fidgeted uncomfortably as the Lama continued to stare and not say a word. Suddenly, the tiny beige room, with its cool, tiled floor, felt claustrophobic.

"Did you really think you could raise all the money you needed in such short a time?" the old monk's eyes glittered with mischief as he finally spoke and purposely baited his young friend.

Eshaan studied the face of his inquisitor. The creases and the folds in his face confirmed signs of an industrious life gone by. Lama Dorje's eyes, a gentle brown, were hidden behind his large silver-rimmed round glasses. Eshaan learned quickly as a child not to be fooled by Lama Dorje's frail looks. The man could lift weights, run (and win) marathons, and played some mean cricket.

"I know I spent some of the money I earned, but I was really hoping there was more in the account." Eshaan tried to avoid looking Lama Dorje in the eye. He knew exactly what the Lama would say, since he had said it many times over the years: *You are incapable of holding onto any amount of money for more than a day.*

"Okay. Answer me this question. When you take a train from, say, Mumbai to Delhi, you don't get down at Delhi and keep staring back to see where Mumbai is, right?" the old monk asked.

Eshaan looked confused.

"What I am trying to say is . . . what is done is done. You

need to move forward. Forget about yesterday," Lama Dorje said as he moved toward the table and picked up the bank statement to see how bad it was.

"Eshaan, this is not bad. There is enough money in here to get started. You are being silly for wanting everything in its place and paid for before you start."

"Do you think I am going to fail, Lama Dorje?"

"Yes," the monk replied with a smile as he put the bank statement down on the table.

"What? You don't have any faith in me? You told me you thought I would succeed," Eshaan said.

"Yes," the old monk laughed.

"Yes or no, which one is it?" Eshaan asked, and rolled his eyes. He knew perfectly well Lama Dorje loved to play the role of the wisecracking monk. It was his most endearing and most annoying habit.

The old man just grinned.

"I need a lot more money, and these small catering events just don't pay enough. I need more of the dinner theatre work. That pays a *lot,* but it is hard to come by. I don't know what to do," Eshaan sighed and mumbled.

It was about eight years ago that he had first talked to Lama Dorje about his dream project. He rushed back from school one day and waited impatiently outside the prayer room as Lama Dorje and all the other monks finished their afternoon prayers. Since teaching season was in full swing, the prayer hall was filled with Buddhism students whom Eshaan adored. He spotted his favorite Swiss lady praying in the back of the prayer room. She'd told him tales about her life atop a snowy mountain. He had never seen snow, and in Delhi's sweltering heat, he could not even imagine what snow felt like. He spotted another lady he admired, who sold ice cream and taught meditation on the beaches of south France. Usually, it was the students he sought out to speak to, as he loved their tales.

But at that moment, none of the students mattered.

At that moment, he *really* needed to share his big epiphany with Lama Dorje.

The prayers had seemed endless, so Eshaan decided it was time to interrupt. He ran to the kitchen, picked up the teakettle, and proceed to the prayer room at tea break. He walked in behind the young monk serving tea and had poured additional tea into each monk's cup in the prayer hall until he finally reached Lama Dorje.

"I know what I am going to do with my life," he had said.

The old monk was amused at the self-assurance of this now-handsome seventeen-year-old. "Not now, child. After prayers, now go."

Eshaan refused to budge and began to talk.

"No, not now," the monk insisted, so Eshaan had begrudgingly walked to the main entrance and waited. As he lingered, he began to do several prostrations on the hard temple floor. It was something he had grown up seeing many people do at the monastery every day. In his young mind, it seemed like a magical solution to gain bonus points with the Buddha.

"Okay, enough with the prostrations. What is going on?" Lama Dorje asked as soon as the prayers ended.

"I am going to open a kitchen for poor people. You know, a place where you will never be refused a meal. A place where no one will ever go hungry," Eshaan responded.

"Hmmm . . . I think you will need a lot of food for that. And that means you will need loads of money. Do you have a loot stashed away somewhere that I don't know about? Who will pay for this magical kitchen, child?" Lama Dorje asked with a sweet smile.

"Oh, that is easy. He will help me," the boy said, pointing to the large statue of Buddha at the prayer altar. "Oh, you know, you said all I get in my life is a result of my karma? I will call this Buddha's Karma Kitchen."

At the time, to young Eshaan, the idea had seemed like a stroke of sheer genius. But now, seated in the Welcoming Room, an older Eshaan was having a hard time believing in his own dream.

"Lama Dorje, the cash I have, I calculated. If we feed thirty people twice a day, even with simple dishes, we will run out of money in two days. Maybe less."

Chapter 3

The Lama listened to Eshaan for a few more minutes and then decided enough was enough. The young man needed a lesson in the reality of life.

"Eshaan, just come out with me. Get up," Lama Dorje said.

The monk gently closed the door to the Welcoming Room and took Eshaan by the hand. They passed through the monastery's gardens filled with jasmine, roses, and wildly colored bougainvillea. A walk in these gardens was like walking into a perfume shop in Old Delhi, where the sweet smells of fragrances intermingled with the scent of the souls who lived there.

Several of the young monks were outside cleaning the pathways, dusting the sides of the buildings, and clearing fallen twigs and leaves. The compound sparkled, not a bit of dust, dirt, or any trash anywhere.

As a child, Eshaan often asked Lama Dorje, "Why don't we keep the rest of Delhi clean? There are so many garbage heaps outside on the road."

Lama Dorje's response was always the same, "The rich don't have the need to clean. The poor don't have the drive to clean, and, of course, the government sees no urgent need to fix something it deems isn't broken. One has to acknowledge the mess first before something can be done about it."

Both men walked in silence until they were a couple of blocks away from the monastery and near a tiny slum area.

Lama Dorje pointed to a beggar sitting by the side of a worn-down cement wall. "Eshaan, do you know what ails him the most?" he asked.

"Is this a trick question? Of course, poverty," Eshaan answered as he readied himself for another Lama Dorje sermon, which he knew would go over his head.

"So you think if you give him a bit of money now, he will be fine?" Lama Dorje asked.

"Yes, of course! He is like this because he is poor." He worried that perhaps the old monk, as kind as he was, was becoming senile.

Lama Dorje went up to the man and held his hand for a minute, and the old beggar opened his eyes and smiled at the kind monk. No one would dare come near him, much less touch him for the fear of contracting whatever diseases ailed him.

"Think realistically, Eshaan. What is the chance he will get enough money to take him off the streets, to give him a home, to take care of his illness? Is that realistic?"

Eshaan looked at Lama Dorje with a confused expression. The senile theory was making more and more sense.

The beggar smiled at the Lama as he lay there in his own filth, smelling of urine. He had one hand extended out permanently, in the hope that someone, anyone, would help him.

"His spirit is broken. So he begs. That is the cycle that you have to break. Feed his spirit, his body, and nurture him. You need to help the likes of him, the forgotten, the ones shunned by society," Lama Dorje said quietly and looked toward Eshaan with the hope that the young man could understand what he was trying to show him.

Eshaan was perplexed. "But that is what I am trying to do, right?"

The Lama nodded. "Yes, your heart is in the right place."

One of the beggar kids called out to Eshaan, "Do you have anything for us today?" They were accustomed to seeing him handing out fruits on many mornings.

Eshaan habitually reached into his pocket, pulled out a few notes, and placed them in the child's hand. Soon, several other beggars surrounded him. Many called out to him by name, "Eshaan, *bhai* brother, Eshaan *bhai*, I haven't eaten in days. How about some money for me?"

Eshaan pulled out all the remaining money he had and passed it around. Yet, as always, many had to be turned away.

Lama Dorje sighed, shook his head, and pulled Eshaan away from the crowd, which was getting larger and more aggressive.

They began to walk back to the monastery as the beggars kept calling out to Eshaan and the Lama to help them, to bring more food, but then the cussing began, the vile words calling them horrible and unhelpful.

"I don't understand, Lama. I give them money and food, and yet they act like this," Eshaan said as he tried to block out the voices behind him.

"Child, you have a kind heart. But you seem to be looking for the noble poor who will give you their undying gratitude for helping them. When you understand what your real mission is, then you won't need their gratitude, and their approval or disapproval will not matter."

When they entered the monastery, it was buzzing with students, as the morning classes had let out and people were walking toward the cafeteria for tea.

"Eshaan, if this kitchen of yours feeds even one or two people a day, it will be a success. But, you will need money to sustain it. Think about it. Maybe you can ask people to pay for the food."

"Ask people to pay? But . . . but, I don't want it to be a restaurant," Eshaan protested as they walked back to the Welcoming Room.

The Lama debated whether to go on or stop. He decided to stop the discussion. "I have to go for prayers now. But before I forget, I have news for you. I talked with the other administrators, and we have decided to allow Tulku Tenzin to help in your kitchen," he said, and the very mention of the young monk, Tulku Tenzin, made Eshaan brighten up.

The ever-smiling Tenzin loved telling jokes, was a terrific cook, and enchanted everyone when he played his Tibetan singing bowls in the monastery gardens. His title, Tulku, meant reincarnation of an old lama as a child. It fit him perfectly; he truly was a young man with the soul of a wise old spirit.

"Lama Dorje, that is great," Eshaan mumbled as he sat back down on the couch. "But I still need to get a lot of money to start this kitchen."

"Okay. So how do you intend to do that? By playing Robin Hood like you did a while ago?" Lama Dorje asked.

Eshaan looked away and placed his head in his hands.

"Perhaps you need to get more tattoos? Or start doing the prostrations again?" The monk laughed heartily at his own joke and left Eshaan to reflect on the bank statement still lying open on the table.

Eshaan Veer Singh's Journal

My father
He ran
He never looked back
To see
The ruins of the lives
He left behind
He never looked back
He never once saw
The teeth that rotted and fell out of my mother's jaw
He praised the gods when I was born
Yet my face, he said, mirrored his wrongs
He was kind, I'm told by my memory banks
Or not, I'm told by the demons in my head
I smile like him, my mother often said
A curse that I bear
You hold my hand
You guide my way
Why do you do this?
Why do you pray?
For my well-being and for that of the world
You listen
You hear
You hold me dear

Who are you?
Why do you care?
You are no father of mine

Chapter 4

"Your chai, Eshaan," Radio Rani said and handed Eshaan a small cup of tea.

A warm, gentle morning breeze brushed their faces as they both sat beside the small pond located in the monastery's vegetable garden Rani had single-handedly planted and now maintained. Rani Park, as the monks sweetly called it, now produced enough to feed the entire monastery, the students, and even a guest or two.

The garden housed okra, large, plump tomatoes, lemony coriander, sweet-smelling cucumbers, mounds of mint, several pots of fragrant curry leaves, and a glorious row of cabbage and carrots. While Rani tended all the vegetables with love, she was especially drawn to the wild black roses that grew at the far end of the pond. She had never seen anything like them in her life. Some students at the monastery referred to them as evil, but not Rani. She found solace in the deep, dark, soft petals of the black rose. It stood out, bold, brave, different, and it survived.

Both Eshaan and Rani loved to sit by the manmade pond. Next to the pond was a large banyan tree with its gnarly roots encircling its main trunk. Lama Dorje said the tree had been there as far back as he could remember and that the monastery had been built around it. At least once a day, one of the teaching monks would bring his students to sit under the shade of the tree as they studied the sutras or listened to tales from the *Jataka*, legends about Shakyamuni Buddha and His unflinching commitment to serve the needy.

This garden covered almost a quarter of the monastery. The ground for the establishment was actually gifted to the famous monk Lama Karma by the Delhi government. Back then, the compound had just one building and the banyan tree. Now it was thriving with five buildings: the main prayer hall, the dorms for the students who lived on campus, the building where the monks stayed, a box of rooms that housed Eshaan and Rani ('The House of the Unwanteds,' Eshaan called it), and the small building that would now house Buddha's Karma Kitchen.

As a child, Eshaan spent most of his time in the prayer hall building, which had three floors. One of the floors housed a large library, a volunteer room equipped with computers, several teaching rooms with smart boards and large screens for viewing lectures from monks around the world, and a cafeteria. The top floor was an open terrace filled with large potted plants, which Rani maintained, of course, and several meditation pillows for those who wanted to meditate in a different setting.

The area around the pond echoed with sounds from the tiny green frogs that had made their home there.

"Are you ready for your tea?" Rani asked, and Eshaan smiled.

It had been a few days since the disaster at the carrom event. He knew no matter how angry she was at him, she was never angry enough not to bring him tea.

He sat down, picked up the teacup, and sipped the hot, creamy liquid. It tasted as though the milk and tea leaves had a disagreement about who was going to dominate the cup and neither won.

"You still don't like my tea?" she asked as she watched him intently.

"I . . . I love it, of course," he said as he twitched his nose and raised his eyebrows.

"I will get it right one of these days," she laughed.

They had both spent the last two days cleaning out the small building behind the monastery that was to become Buddha's Kitchen. It had electricity, running water, and an entrance that was separate from the entrance to the monastery. Tulku Tenzin had been instrumental in cleaning the gunk that had caked onto the decrepit walls of the building. Rani had given Eshaan the silent treatment during the cleaning process, but it now seemed like things were back to normal.

"Eshaan, the stoves are arriving again today—" Radio Rani stopped short of completing her sentence. What she really wanted to do was to shake him and yell at him for not paying for the stoves the first time they had arrived. She had begged and cajoled the driver to come back two days later with a promise that Eshaan would have the money by then.

"Don't look at me like that. I have the cash. In fact, I put it in the lock box at the Welcoming Room this morning. You can go and check," he said as she eyed him with doubt.

"Oh, and Rani, thank you for not telling Lama Dorje about what happened at the carrom event. He already thinks I cannot be trusted with any money." Eshaan smiled at the brightly dressed, tiny lady in front of him.

It was a few years ago Eshaan had found her wandering in the ruins of a small archeological park near the monastery. Her scruffy clothes, unkempt hair, and the foul odor emanating from her body would have scared off any other mere mortal, but Eshaan had a soft spot for the unlucky and unwanted. He knew what it was like to be at the receiving end of that avatar.

He had approached her slowly, not wanting to frighten her.

"Hello, I am Eshaan. I live over there. See that colorful building there? What is your name?" he inquired in his softest, kindest voice.

"Myself Radio Rani," she had said with a thick accent that made him think that perhaps she wasn't local.

"Radio Rani?" Eshaan had tried not to laugh. "What an interesting name you have! Where are you from?" He offered her an apple he was holding and she snatched it out of his hand.

"Thank you for you share . . . for apple. I am *MaWik* tribe from south . . . south, not from here," Radio Rani confided as she bit into the apple. She sat on the muddy ground and finished the apple in just a few bites. It was clear she had not eaten in a while.

"Wait here. Don't move. I will be right back," Eshaan told her as he ran back to the monastery and brought back some biscuits, a bottle of water, and another apple. He gave them all to her, and then sat down beside her as she ate and thanked him again and again. She looked so tiny, so frail. He wondered what she was doing walking around alone in the park. It wasn't the safest place to be.

He asked about her family.

"My mother made and sold flower necklaces. She die one day when she fell into a dry well. My father die when I was little baby," Rani said, wiping the apple juice from her lips with the back of her hand.

"Radio Rani, my mother died when I was very young, too. Anyway . . . I don't know anything about your tribe?" he prompted, gently moving away from the subject of dead parents.

Radio Rani explained they were a tribe just outside the city of Bangalore and now made a living by cultivating and selling vegetables, and making garlands instead of their traditional occupation of bird catching.

"How wonderful. You live to make the world a more beautiful place! Oh, and I love your name! It is so interesting!" Eshaan said.

"In my tribe, they name children after first word that comes to mind when the child is born. My mother told me the radio was playing when I was born, so my name is Radio Rani. My mother name was Coffee Rani, and my father was Hotel Raja," Radio Rani said, thrilled to share.

Then her smile disappeared. The food was over and she looked forlorn.

"What are you doing here, so far from home?" he asked.

She looked around to see if anyone was approaching then gently lifted her shirt, just enough to show her midriff.

"Oh, hell, what is that? What happened to you?" Eshaan stared at the scars on her stomach.

"When mother die, one old man wanted to buy me. I said no. He threw big bottle of acid. Missed my face. It burned stomach . . . I ran away."

What struck Eshaan more than the welts and barely healed burns on her stomach was the look of sheer determination in her eyes.

"This place is not safe for you. I mean . . . I hope no one has harmed you?" Eshaan asked in the softest tone he could muster.

It was a miracle she had survived in that dreadful park for the past few nights. She had seen the thugs harassing other girls and had found a dark spot behind one of the disintegrated monuments in the park that hid her well. She crawled inside when the sun went down, and only came out when the sun was up, there were other people walking around, and the Dogman was out. The Dogman even came in the night sometimes to check in on her and had been giving her food to eat.

"Oh, you mean Raju!" Eshaan said of his old friend. Often called names like thug or bastard, Raju lived deep inside one of the old ruined houses in the park along with about twenty-three stray dogs. Some thugs had harassed the Old Men's Carrom Club once, and the Dogman had stepped in to help. Since that day, Eshaan and Raju had become buddies. Now, every time the Old Men's Carrom Club met in the park, Eshaan would always bring a bag full of treats for Raju's dogs, various cooked vegetables, and a half-bottle of brandy for Raju.

"Rani, the Dogman, as you call him, is a good friend of mine. In fact, look there. See those bags of meat? I was on my way to give him that for his dogs when I saw you," Eshaan said.

Then, he asked her to come with him to the monastery. He left her in the prayer hall and went to convince Lama Dorje to allow Radio Rani to live in one of the smaller rooms in exchange for working in the kitchen. The kind Lama had agreed.

Within two days, however, they discovered she had little aptitude in the kitchen, so she was put on cleaning duty. Within a few months, they discovered she had the most amazing green thumb, and Rani Park was born.

Rani and Eshaan sipped their tea in quiet familiarity, with a sense of deep support that is rarely found in the modern world.

"What are you writing?" Rani asked, pointing to the journal on his lap. He turned it around and showed it to her.

Rani
Those burns on your skin
Are emblazoned blessings
As
I believe it is the curse
That protects us and guides our way
Good fortune comes, sometimes,
Wrapped in a bottle of acid
Good luck comes, sometimes,
Disguised as a slow, persistent, searing pain
Each agonizing moment
Reminding us we are alive
I envy you, my friend
You have found your purpose
As nature shares her secrets with you
And you share her bounty with us
I struggle
Your curse nurtures you
Mine destroys me

Rani looked away.

Why did he make her remind him again and again and again that she could not read? She saw the ink on the page and the interesting images his pen made, but that is all they were to her, images. She had explained to him why she did not want to read. The real world was hard enough to navigate, but then to purposely get into another world, Rani could never understand why anyone would do that.

All these monks with their chants, all the students with their books, and even Eshaan with this journal, it was all a waste of time. The blessed blooms held everything one could ever want to learn about life. The *tulsi,* for instance, could nurture your body and your spirit. *Neem* leaves were perfect for treating bites, and *neem* twigs for brushing your teeth. The harvest of Rani Park, the gorgeous flowers, the butterflies, the ever-present chirping mynah birds, and the little cadre of white rabbits could teach one everything they needed to know about life. Books and gods not required.

One of the things that bothered Rani the most about books was that people read them from beginning to end. *Why not read the end first? This would help you decide if reading the entire book is going to be worth your time,* she had said to Eshaan.

Eshaan got up and put his hand on her shoulder.

"We have been working on your reading for a year now, my friend, but unless you try to read, it will never happen."

She simply shook her head and pushed his hand away.

"Rain coming," Radio Rani said. "I am going to go take the clothes off the line. You did not even finish your tea. Only two sips?"

"I tell you what. You start reading, and I will start finishing my tea!" He laughed and hugged her as she left and started picking the vegetables he needed for cooking dinner that night, when he heard the screaming.

All hell was breaking loose outside.

Chapter 5

Loud, angry voices tore into the quiet morning air. Curses, in several different languages, flew like angry bees. Eshaan dropped the vegetables he had just picked and rushed out of the monastery's main gate.

Standing in the middle of the road, just outside Dr. Sinha's residence, was Loveleen Singh, dressed in all blue. Not the blue of the sky or the blue of the water, but the blue of the Indian cricket team. She was wearing a t-shirt that read: I BLEED IN BLUE. Cradled in her arms was a cat as black as the underside of an iron skillet.

Merry Mehra, wearing an outdated beige safari suit, was yelling so loud he was screeching, "You are a witch! A bloody witch! You put this . . . this *black* cat in my path as I leave for work! You are wretched."

Not one to back out of a fight, Loveleen screamed back, "It is my cat, and I will do what I like with it. It will live here with me. You can scream all you want, but you don't own this place. *You are a total loser*!"

She stomped her feet and her anklets jiggled, but their sound was drowned out by the chaotic screaming.

The two were standing in the outdoor, all-marble foyer of Dr. Sinha's home. The foyer was flanked on one side by waist-high walls and a small garden on the other. Merry Mehra rented the second floor, and Loveleen, and now her cat, rented the third floor of Dr. Sinha's bungalow. Neighbors on both sides were out watching the unfolding drama and offering a running commentary. At this very moment, more were rooting for Mehra and telling Loveleen to let the cat go.

A Mehra–Loveleen screaming match usually lasted a few minutes. It was almost a once-a-week ritual. They would scream and then part ways. Not so today. Today, it was a debate about evil harbingers of horrible luck, and everyone around had an opinion on that.

"You! No husband, but a baby on its way. A bastard child! *You* are the loser, *not* me. I actually have a *real* family!" he yelled back.

That did it.

Loveleen let the cat go, and in an instant, she moved forward and slapped the Mr. Not-so-Merry-now Mehra across the face.

"Don't you ever, *ever* call my child a bastard! You hear me? The next time, I will kill you."

The neighbors on each side screamed. *Hit her back! Don't hit her; she is pregnant! How dare you let her hit you? Her class shows. This is why women should not live on their own.* All comments intended to turn the already bitter battle into a full-fledged war.

Eshaan rushed into the foyer and firmly planted himself between Loveleen and Mr. Mehra. Loveleen shoved Eshaan out of the way and began to scream obscenities at the neighbors who are egging Merry on.

"What are you doing, Loveleen? Stop. Think of the baby. Mehra isn't worth it," Eshaan said as he tried with all his might to pull her back. "And all you people, don't you have anything better to do? Go home. You all have no business here," he shouted to the gathering crowds.

No one budged. In fact, more people came out. Now the maids and a few of the monks had come out to see what the commotion was about, and even a few of the homeless beggars walked over to watch the drama. Nothing quite as exciting as an epic battle between good and idiocy: reality television without the television.

Mr. Mehra, brimming with anger, raised his hand to slap her, but was stopped just in time by Dr. Sinha, who had also come out of his house after hearing all the commotion.

"Stop, what do you think you are doing? You are going to hit a lady? A pregnant lady! Mehra, you are a grown man, a respectable man. How can you do this?" Dr. Sinha said.

"Doctor Sinha, you stay out of this. This . . . this . . . *witch* is the cause of all my problems. First, she shows up whenever I have to go out. Do you know how inauspicious it is to see a widow's face first thing in the morning? And now she has this black cat. A *black cat*. She placed it in my path this morning. Do you have any idea how bad that is?" Mr. Mehra ranted on.

"I am *not* a widow. How dare you say that? What right do you have?" Loveleen shouted back.

"Eshaan, take Loveleen out of here. Now. Mr. Mehra, please come with me," Dr. Sinha said and then called out to him, "Oh, and Eshaan, I have to go to the airport soon. Will you be able to drive me? The driver hasn't come today either."

"I can," Eshaan responded and tugged at Loveleen's arm. "Stop this nonsense, Loveleen. He is not worth it." He waved to the crowd. "Okay, okay, everyone go back. All the drama here is done." The homeowners retreated to their air-conditioned mansions, the maids retreated to dusting, the monks to praying, and the beggars and homeless to just . . . being. The cat was nowhere in sight.

Chapter 6

Eshaan gently tugged at Loveleen's arm to keep her moving. Every few steps, she turned around and screamed out a few choice curses that would make even the trashiest street thug blush. As much as Mehra and his nonsense annoyed Eshaan, he really wished that Loveleen would stop reacting in such a rowdy way. He secretly hoped that once the baby arrived, all this daily drama would end. In fact, Mehra had been very neutral toward Loveleen until she starting showing.

"Loveleen, my sweet friend, you cannot go around like a rebel. What if he had hit you back?" Eshaan said as gently as he could.

He knew she was hot headed. Many a fruit vendor selling produce on this street owed their sanity to Eshaan when Loveleen insisted on arguing with them about their prices. They had met when she moved in and hit it off instantly. He loved to cook, she loved to eat; it was a match made in paradise. While Eshaan tended to be introspective, Loveleen's only thought was that thinking was overrated. "You bring me sanity," she told him, and laughed when he said she brought his boring life much-needed insanity.

But at the moment, she was being even more irrational than usual.

"I can take care of myself. You don't have to be my savior. I don't need any help." Tears began to well in her eyes and she stopped walking.

"Yes, I know you don't need me. But let me feel like a hero, okay? Why do you want to take away my ego?" he asked with a big smile.

She laughed and gave him a hug. "You know, I love you, but that Mehra drives me crazy. What is it to him if I am married or not, or pregnant or not? Why he is so worried?"

"Hey, did you see the cricket match last night? Wasn't Sachin amazing? That boy is a magician with his bat! I watched the highlights late last night," Eshaan tried to smoothly transition to Loveleen's favorite topic: cricket.

"It was an amazing match! I shouted so much I thought I would go into labor. Why did you miss it?" Loveleen asked.

"I was cooking in south Delhi all day yesterday. Some guy was getting married and decided to host a buffet for all the poor people in the area instead of inviting guests. Isn't that unique for south Delhi? The girl's parents were furious and refused to attend the wedding!"

"Wait, did they pay you, or did you do this for free, again, out of your golden yet bankrupt heart?" Loveleen stared him straight in the eye, then just shook her head. "How are you going to make a living if you work everywhere for free?"

"You know me. Money and I are like you and Mehra. Not compatible!"

Loveleen rolled her eyes.

They entered the monastery, and the rich, smooth tones of Tulku Tenzin's singing bowls stopped them in their tracks. Tenzin was seated in the small garden outside and meditating while playing the large metal bowls. Eshaan looked questioningly at Loveleen who nodded, and they walked back outside to the main road. She had always loved the sounds of the bowls, but after becoming pregnant, the tones disturbed her and she felt uneasy.

"I have a surprise for you, Eshaan. I was going to my car to get it when that idiot Mehra stopped me and started this fight. Come, come with me," she said as she led him to her new and shiny red BMW parked on the side of Dr. Sinha's bungalow.

She popped open the trunk and took out a wrapped, large, slim package. "You should put this picture up on the main wall of Buddha's Karma Kitchen. It will bring you good luck." She beamed a smile at her dear friend.

Eshaan eagerly took the package and ripped open the cover, fully expecting to find a photograph of the Sikh saint Guru Nanak. Loveleen, who was Sikh by religion, was an ardent devotee and often spent hours at the local Sikh temples, helping keep the place clean and, more importantly, playing matchmaker to anyone who even remotely appeared single. Eshaan pulled back the brown paper packaging, and instead of the saintly radiant face of Guru Nanak, there was a photo of the current cricket superstar and heartthrob, Virat Kohli.

At the bottom of the photo, Loveleen had penned "King Kohli blesses King of Khana."

"King of Khana? King of Food? I guess that means me? I will take it. I can use all the blessings I get." Eshaan laughed and gave Loveleen a big hug.

"This is India's future. One without morals, and the other one . . . who knows what trashcan the monks picked him out from." They both turned to see Mehra standing behind them. He was sitting on his motorcycle, with his red helmet, which was covered with pictures of every god known to him. He spat in their direction then rode off.

"Eshaan, stop staring at him. Look what I got you last night when you were cooking for that wedding, and you thought I was watching the cricket match. Come on. Forget him!" Loveleen said as they went toward the back entry of the monastery toward his dream kitchen.

Radio Rani was there, sweeping the floor. "Eshaan, I wanted to tell you about this when we were having tea, but did not want to spoil Loveleen's surprise," she said with a huge grin.

Eshaan stood there, stunned. Just outside the door of Buddha's Karma Kitchen, Loveleen had set up a large, sturdy, custom-made brown bamboo bowl.

"This is the donation bowl—you know, for alms—just like the monks have their small bowls and people can donate anything they want: food, money, flowers, coconuts," she said.

The red sign above the bowl read, *Anna Dāta Sukeebhava*—May the person who donated this food be blessed forever.

"Everyone can give what is dear to his or her heart," she said with great pride.

"This is fantastic. I never could have imagined—" Eshaan trailed off and was about to call Lama Dorje to come see the magnificent bowl, when his mobile rang. It was Dr. Sinha calling: *TIME TO GO TO THE AIRPORT.*

"You are taking Dr. Sinha to the airport? Did he mention

Kitt is coming today? I thought that would make your day!" Loveleen smiled, turned around, and left, jingling her anklets and waddling on her legs.

Chapter 7

Loveleen's words stopped Eshaan in his tracks.

I WILL TIE LOOSE ENDS THERE AND COME BACK. I PROMISE.

Kitt's last words were etched in his brain. They promised a future, but delivered betrayal.

Yes, beautiful, lovely, funny, energetic Kitt, whom he had fallen in love with, had lied. Even the very straightforward Dr. Sinha failed to mention it was Kitt they were going to the airport to pick up.

Eshaan placed his fingers over the tattoo of her name. Betrayal embedded in his skin.

In the heat of a drunken stupor, a few months ago, he had decided to slice the tattoo off his wrist. He had sat at the edge of his bed with a sharp army knife and inserted the knife into the lotus tattoo just above Kitt's name. His blood trickled, but he felt no pain. He remembered taking the knife again, this time to remove the name, to slice it off, to cut her off just as she had cut him off. His hand shook, his body quivered, and the pain in his heart was stronger than the pain on his wrist. Ironically, it was his memory of Kitt's favorite quote that made him stop incising the tattoo. They had both heard the quote together when they had watched a movie and the lead actor recited a famous love story, quoting the poet Nizami. "*If you knew what it means to be a lover, you would realize that one only has to scratch him and out falls the beloved.*" He stopped cutting. He could not let his beloved fall out of his body. He had gotten a clean handkerchief and gently tied it around his wrist. And then he wept. People he loved always seemed to leave him.

He just couldn't understand what it was about her that touched him so deeply. There had been other women, but he had never felt a deep stirring for any of them. With her, it was different. Her mere presence elevated his spirit.

Eshaan slowly walked to his tiny room at the monastery to pick up his wallet.

Hidden in one of the deeper pockets of the wallet was his favorite picture of Kitt, taken a year ago. Katrin "Kitt" Sinha was the most beautiful girl he had ever seen.

In the picture, she was wearing a long purple dress and a garland refashioned as a tiara. "I am queen of the marigolds," she had said and laughed as Eshaan captured her on his phone's camera. It had taken him a week to figure out how to print the photo so he could always have it with him. That was the night she had left to go back to Austria.

"Dr. Sinha is outside the gate waiting for you. Are you okay? Eshaan? Are you listening to me?" Radio Rani approached him and interrupted his thoughts. "Also, the stoves are here. I had them placed in the kitchen. Okay?"

Kitt was coming back.

Eshaan nodded and walked to the main gate, lost in thought

as he recalled the first time he saw her.

That first time was, in fact, a local legend of sorts. The entire monastery remembered the first time Eshaan saw Kitt. It had become the monks' favorite "funny Eshaan" story to tell. Dressed in a pair of light blue jeans with a long pink shirt, her golden blonde hair trailing down to her waist, and a tie-dye scarf around her neck, Kitt was standing at the door of the monastery's main hall. It had been prayer time, and several of the monks were sitting in the prayer hall chanting. Eshaan's job that day was to serve the monks tea during their prayer service. Just as Eshaan was pouring tea into the cups, he saw her. He kept pouring and kept staring at her. She looked uneasy and was scanning the room. The tea overflowed, and the monks called out to him, but he was oblivious, entranced. "Eshaan, watch the tea, not the girl," one of the young monks called to Eshaan, startling him so much that he dropped the entire kettle on the floor. The young monks laughed hard, and called him Chai Romeo for the longest time.

"How does her face glow like that?" Eshaan had asked Lama Dorje that night.

"It isn't her face. It is your eyes," Lama Dorje answered. "Now go sleep."

But Eshaan did not sleep that night, or for any of the nights she was in town. He could not remember seeing her as a child, although Dr. Sinha insisted that he had.

Each day Kitt was in town, Eshaan had gone to Dr. Sinha's house to deliver food—fresh mangos one day, guava another day. On the third day, Dr. Sinha warned him not to bring the entire fruit market into his house.

Not wanting to miss out on seeing her, Eshaan began taking dishes he cooked up just for her on the pretext of asking Dr. Sinha to taste his latest cooking creation.

Finally, it was Loveleen who made Eshaan's dream come true. She invited him and Kitt over for a Bollywood night, to watch old movies. Kitt loved to dance to Bollywood tunes, Loveleen loved to sing them, and Eshaan, he loved to do both. Shortly after the movie night, they invited him to go to Old Delhi with them to shop for shawls and spices. He agreed, and then became their coolie, as he called it, carrying their shopping bags as they traversed the history-filled lanes of Delhi.

Eshaan felt he was living a life that he had only seen in the movies. A beautiful girl with him as they strolled through the Garden of Five Senses, the mesmerizing moment when she first hugged him, and a memorable meal as she devoured his creations.

Then, one evening, his life changed. It all started with Dr. Walker.

He had gone to pick the girls up for a special night at a local interactive dinner theatre where he often cooked. Loveleen backed out, owing to what Kitt called "the result of gluttonous consumption of Delhi's amazing street food." Dr. Sinha was out of town for a family wedding, and Eshaan was waiting at Kitt's house for her to get dressed. He had been especially excited, as the theatre was showcasing his food that night. Kitt asked if he wanted to have a drink before they left. She poured him a scotch, her father's favorite brand: Johnnie Walker.

"Kitt, I want to tell you something," Eshaan had said after a few sips as she sat down next to him. He gulped down his liquid courage. "I . . . I need to tell you. I don't know . . . I have never done this before. I know everyone thinks it is madness—"

"I . . . I feel the same way." Just like him, she loved quoting poetry. "*When love is not madness, it is not love.*"

They did not make it to the theatre that night. He ignored all the calls coming in from the theatre owner, Gina, from Loveleen, and even from Lama Dorje. Real life just needed to take a backseat. Instead, he had focused on her—the scent of her hair, the softness of her body, her gentle touch, her racing heart. After they made love, his reaction surprised him. It was as though it was his first time; he had never felt this way with any other woman. Her embrace made him feel whole, unbroken.

Kitt left a few days later, vowing to come back to him.

It had been 436 days since he had last seen or heard from her. Perhaps love, marriage, kids, and all that were not part of the plan for his life. Perhaps her leaving was a sign from the universe that he needed to focus on Buddha's Karma Kitchen. It was the story he tried to tell himself each night for the past four hundred plus days. And yet, in the morning, he would long for her laugh.

"Maybe she has realized she is very educated and the daughter of a rich man, and I have nothing," he told Loveleen again and again.

"Dr. *Ji.* Who is flying in?" Eshaan worked up his courage to ask Dr. Sinha as they began their drive to Delhi's International Airport.

Dr. Sinha's driver, Ram, sporadically showed up for work these past few months. Dr. Sinha had stopped driving after his first stroke. Eshaan drove the doctor around whenever he needed it. It was Eshaan, in fact, who had taught Ram to drive, and all was going great until Ram fell back into his old drinking patterns.

"I hate all this bloody karma nonsense your monks talk about, Eshaan. What have I done to deserve this life in the gutters of Delhi? This city is full of whores, pimps, and politicians. They make the money. And people like me? Born only God knows where and left to die on sidewalks—" Ram would rant to Eshaan. Some days, Eshaan could pull him out of his slump. On other days, Ram would stare into a void for hours.

Eshaan looked at his rearview mirror. Dr. Sinha had not answered his question and appeared to be frowning.

"Dr. *Ji*. Are you okay? Loveleen told me we are going to pick up Kitt," Eshaan prompted.

Dr. Sinha responds with a frown, "Yes . . . she called two days ago. I guess I haven't seen you since that carrom competition to tell you."

Eshaan nodded.

"Kitt is coming here to get married."

Chapter 8

Married?

Eshaan slammed on the brakes of the car as his mind raced haphazardly through his memory banks.

Married? Did he miss the news? How could this happen?

And the timing of it all, just when he was starting to let thoughts about her leave his heart and mind so they could be absorbed by infinity, by God, by the universe, by ether. Just when he thought he was free from distressing memories of his love, the universe laughed and said, *Try again*.

"What happened? Why did you brake?" Dr. Sinha's body jerked at the sudden stop. The cars and motorcycles behind them honked in anger and annoyance. Eshaan released his foot from the pedal and accelerated slowly.

"Sorry about that. Dr. *Ji*, a marriage is such a fortunate occasion," Eshaan said, looking straight ahead. His chest twitched, and what was that in his right eye? A tear? A tear for a love that truly never had a likelihood of being whole?

This is reality, isn't it? You kept telling the universe that you weren't good enough for her, and the universe complied, Loveleen would have said, had she been in the car.

Why does fate always favor the rich?

The car inched along, slowly maneuvering the streets of Delhi. The soothing, green ashoka trees lining the overcrowded roads provided much-needed clean lungs to a city that was choking on its own creations.

"I don't know if it is fortunate or not," Dr. Sinha responded a few minutes later. "Do you know I speak to her every week on this video thing, and not once, *not once* has she mentioned him or the wedding." Clearly agitated, Dr. Sinha removed his glasses several times and tried to clean the lenses with his shirt. "Oh, and do you know what else, Eshaan? She wants a court marriage next week. No relatives, she says. What kind of a wedding would that be? I mean, if she is going to do what she wants to do, why come here? Why bother asking her old father anything?" the old man rambled on and on, not waiting for a response.

"My mother used to say that grand, expensive weddings are for the status seekers. So you see, Kitt is actually helping you not waste money." Eshaan tried to lighten the tension in the car. In his rearview mirror, he could see a forlorn look on Dr. Sinha's face, the look of a man who clearly felt he had outlived his purpose in life.

Eshaan felt his own face flushing at the man's obvious sadness. He offered a small green bottle filled with water to the anguished gentleman.

"Tell me the truth. Did your mother really say that?" Dr. Sinha asked as a faint smile crossed his lips.

"Truthfully? I don't really remember too many things she said. I've learned wisdom sounds a lot better when I begin with

'My mother used to say,'" Eshaan said as he laughed. Lama Dorje often told him he had big talk for a small mouth.

Both men laughed, and the unspoken bond of trust between them helped them hold back tears.

The rain came down suddenly, bursting through the heart of the sky, obscuring Eshaan's vision. He tried to maneuver the car, but the curtain of rain along with the overcrowded roads made for a nasty traffic jam.

"Go slowly. I am not in a rush. By the time they clear customs and come out, it will be well past noon," Dr. Sinha said.

All Eshaan heard was "they." What did he mean by they?

Oh . . . *they*. That meant only one thing. Eshaan had thought only Kitt was coming, but, of course, if the wedding was to be in a few days, that only meant one thing. *He*, whoever he was, was coming as well.

He was going to meet the reason she had not answered him over the past year.

"Why doesn't she write me back, Lama Dorje? What have I done?" Eshaan had repeatedly asked the monk this question over the year. The Lama had mostly ignored it.

Then one night, when Lama Dorje saw Eshaan staring at her photos, he had said very gently, "Eshaan, not everything is for everyone. Not every dream is to be realized."

"Lama Dorje, is this your ploy to get me to believe in rebirth and reincarnation? What should my karma be right now so I can marry the girl of my dreams in my next birth?" Eshaan had retorted sarcastically.

"You are assuming this is your karma, Eshaan. Perhaps it is hers?" Lama Dorje had countered, much to Eshaan's chagrin.

The traffic was now at a complete standstill, and street vendors selling everything from pirated copies of bestsellers, to coconuts, to windshield cleaners began bombarding the stopped vehicles.

DID YOU KNOW KITT IS GETTING MARRIED? Eshaan texted Loveleen as he waited impatiently in the bumper to—to bullock cart, to bicycle, to motorcycle, to scooter, to pedestrian—bumper traffic.

YEAH. DIDN'T TELL U. DID NOT WANT TO MAKE U MISERABLE FOR MONTHS. U KNOW NOW AND U R MISERABLE, RIGHT? was Loveleen's quick response.

The traffic began to move, and after an excruciatingly slow drive, the airport arrival area was finally in sight.

Eshaan pulled the car onto the crowded arrivals lane and Dr. Sinha stepped out. "Dr. *Ji*, I will drop you here and wait in the parking lot. Just give me a call when they arrive and I will drive back up here," he said, rolling down his window. The arrival area smelled like rotten eggs mixed with the latest Dior perfume.

To counteract the revolting smells assaulting his nose, Eshaan reached into his jacket pocket and took out a small bottle of his favorite *itar*. He dabbed a bit of the perfume on the inside of his wrist and on his handkerchief. The perfume man in Old Delhi who sold Eshaan the *itar* had told him about its magical power. "Smell this," the man had said. "What does it remind you of?"

"Hmmm . . . smells like the earth after it rains," Eshaan had responded.

"Yes, but do you know what the smell signifies?" Eshaan did not. "Hope! The rains assures the earth that it will bloom once again," the perfume maker had said as he beamed with pride at the *itar* he had crafted himself.

Yet, at this moment, seated in a car outside the airport and awaiting the love of his life to arrive with her new fiancé, despair, not hope, was what was on Eshaan's mind.

Chapter 9

"Papa!! Here, Papa."

Eshaan looked toward the terminal to see Kitt running toward her father.

It was a moment he had been dreaming of all year, a moment he had been begging the universe to grant him again, a moment he felt he could exchange his entire life for. She was here, and the very sight of her made him giddy. It was the exact same feeling as he had when he first saw her. His senses began reacting, once again to the sound of her soft, sweet voice. His heart remembered how his hands felt around her slender waist, her beautiful silky hair on his face.

Well, he thought, *so much for letting go.*

Eshaan got out of the car and popped the trunk.

"Kitt! My child. Where is he? Where is my to-be son-in-law?" Dr. Sinha gave his daughter a big hug then unceremoniously pushed her aside.

"Oh, Nikolas! He's right here." Kitt turned and pointed to a tall young man walking toward them. Dressed in a light blue t-shirt, white linen pants, and casual sandals, the man looked perfectly dressed for the Delhi heat.

Eshaan stole a look from behind the car. Nikolas was everything Eshaan did not wish him to be: a handsome man with a chiseled jaw, dark blond hair, and bulging biceps. He was as close to perfect as he could be. Seeing Nikolas walking with a help of a cane reminded Eshaan of an oft-quoted saying in Delhi that even the magnificent moon has a stain.

"I am Dr. Sinha, Kitt's dad. And what is your full name, young man?" Dr. Sinha extended his hand to the handsome man.

"Hello! I am Nikolas Ekman. It is a pleasure. Wow, Delhi is hot! This heat can be a killer," Nikolas joked as the three of them walked toward Eshaan and the waiting car.

"Hello, Eshaan. My goodness, you have lost so much weight! Nikolas, Eshaan is Dad's friend and lives with monks!" Kitt introduced the two young men. Eshaan looked her straight in the eye, but she deftly avoided looking back by turning her face to Nikolas.

"Nice to meet you! You are a monk? I've never met a monk." Nikolas extended his hand toward Eshaan and beamed a very friendly smile.

"Hello. No, no, sir, I am not a monk," Eshaan replied as he picked up their two small suitcases and loaded them into the trunk.

"No more bags? Only this?" he asked as he gripped the handle of the suitcase as hard as he could. What he really wanted to do was push Nikolas out of the way, hug her, hold her, shake her, and ask, *Why him? Why not me? Why? Why? Why?*

"Keep moving . . . please, keep moving. No standing here," a policeman wearing deep blue shorts said as he approached them.

"Oh, we do have more bags. The airline lost them. They said they would bring them when, or if, I guess, they find them," Kitt said, getting into the car.

"We flew here from Dubai. That is a direct flight. How can they lose bags on a direct flight?" Nikolas rolled his eyes.

Eshaan could see Nikolas in his rearview mirror, seated so close to Kitt. "Dubai? You live in Dubai? I thought you both lived in Austria," Eshaan blurted out as he maneuvered the car out of the arrivals lane and back onto the main artery headed toward Delhi.

"Eshaan, your English! You are so fluent now." Kitt smiled softly at him. During her last visit, he had a very difficult time with conversational English and often resorted to a strange mix of Hindi, English, Tibetan, and random words from French, German, and Greek, thanks to the trove of international students at the monastery.

"Oh, it is just like your Hindi. Do you remember last time? You repeatedly asked for a *pappi* when you wanted *pani*. You know, you asked for a sinner, when you really wanted water," Eshaan said softly as he glanced at her in the rearview mirror.

Kitt looked different somehow. It saddened him to see she had cut her beautiful, long blonde hair and it was just above her shoulders. Did she do that to spite him, he wondered? He had always loved her long hair. She was wearing a white shirt and purple skirt, and had several tattoos on her right arm. The last time he saw her, her eyes glittered when she laughed. Today, she seemed subdued, or perhaps that was what his mind wanted him to believe.

"I like that smell in the car. What is it?" Nikolas asked as he took a few deep breaths.

"That is Eshaan's cologne," Kitt said. Eshaan looked in the mirror and saw her inhale deeply.

"Ah, nice. You must tell me where I can get it. It smells wonderful. Also, can we please turn the air-conditioning up a little? I am a bit hot," Nikolas said, and Eshaan noticed he had moved even closer to Kitt.

"So this marriage . . . it is all of a sudden. You did not give me any time to prepare," Dr. Sinha, who was sitting up front with Eshaan, finally spoke. He formed his words carefully.

"I know, Papa. Everything happened so suddenly. I had an accident—" Kitt began to mumble.

"Wait, accident? What accident? You never told me you had an accident. When was this? Are you all right?" Dr. Sinha frowned as he turned around and looked at his beautiful but fiercely independent daughter.

"I am sorry, Dr. Sinha. She would not let me call you. She was in the hospital for a month, but of course, as you see now, she is how we say *perfekt,*" Nikolas answered.

"I, I . . . the accident was totally my fault. That accident ruined everything," Kitt mumbled.

"No, no, it was not anyone's fault. These things happen." Nikolas tried to brush off the incident but the anguish on Kitt's face clearly indicated that she held herself responsible for what happened to him.

Eshaan was stunned. His Kitt was in the hospital for a month and no one told him? He was going to have a serious conversation with Loveleen about this. Of course, at the moment, all he could think of was the fact that she was here, and in the car, and so close . . . and yet, so far.

"What accident? Kitt, you make me feel like I do not matter in your world anymore," Dr. Sinha said as he crossed his arms in front of him. Kitt assured him that she was fine and it wasn't a big deal, but now, Dr. Sinha was agitated.

"Nikolas, do you have a job? I don't even know what you do." Dr. Sinha was done being pleasant, and now his tone was terse, angry.

"Papa! Of course he has a job. What a question to ask," Kitt interrupted, and as if on cue, to settle a tense situation, Nikolas' phone began to ring.

"Oh, please excuse me. I must take this," Nikolas said then began talking in brusque German into the phone.

"Papa, I am sorry this is all of a sudden. But, you know, things happen," Kitt said as she reached out and touched her father's shoulder. Dr. Sinha pushed her hand away and pulled out a handkerchief from his pocket to wipe away his tears. "You are like your mother, Kitt. I know you want to do what you want to do and follow a path, like she followed hers, but sometimes you forget who you are leaving behind in your dust. Just as she forgot us."

Eshaan tried to follow the conversation, picking up as much as he could over the loud traffic outside and Nikolas talking loudly inside. But all the understanding of the language could not help him figure out why Kitt was marrying this man. Granted, he was handsome, probably rich, and maybe even loved her, but still. That was no excuse.

Delhi breezed by as the conversation in the car moved from

accidents and disappearing loved ones, to the impending wedding, to an uncomfortable silence as Nikolas asked them all to please be quiet as he finished his call with his office.

Chapter 10

Mercifully, the ride back to the house was fast despite the now water-clogged roads and slower traffic.

Eshaan drove quietly as he thought about all the things he wanted to say to her, but none of it mattered as he observed the two young lovers holding hands in the backseat of the car. Nikolas must have great karma. He tried not to keep looking at her. How could a beautiful face like that cause someone so much pain? Did she not even realize what she was doing to him?

"Which hotel is Nikolas going to stay at?" Dr. Sinha asked rather pointedly.

Kitt, embarrassed by her father and worried Eshaan might spill the beans about their former relationship, reacted rather rudely. "Papa, he is staying with us. I am not a child anymore!"

Dr. Sinha nodded, but not before giving Kitt a brief lecture about the proper behavior for a young woman who is about to get married.

Eshaan gripped the steering wheel harder. His Kitt—his love, his life, his dream—had been sleeping with another man. He had lost sleep for her, wept for her, worried about her, prayed for her.

And here she was, telling her father that she was sleeping with another man. Fucking karma. Perhaps the title he had given to his building at the monastery, The Unwanteds, was in fact even truer than he had imagined.

"Please go ahead and I will bring the bags," Eshaan said to his passengers as he parked the car outside Dr. Sinha's bungalow.

Thankfully, there was no sign of Mr. Mehra, Loveleen, or the newly resident black cat.

Dr. Sinha stepped out of the car and into the foyer of the bungalow. He had paid the maids an extra two hundred rupees to make sure the foyer gleamed, and not a piece of trash was in sight. The maids had been instructed to use Dettol, a family favorite antiseptic, to scrub the foyer twice and to use Dr. Sinha's own special concoction as a final rinse.

"Oh, this is such a magnificent house. Oh, and another sweet smell!!" Nikolas said, pointing to the large red roses growing in Dr. Sinha's postcard-sized garden.

Dr. Sinha smiled for the first time since leaving the airport. "You aren't smelling the roses. You are smelling the cleaner the maids used on the floor."

The garden had been planted by Kitt's mother and consisted of a delightful mix of wild tea roses and red roses. Dr. Sinha pointed to it. "My wife left me with two beautiful things: the soft scent of these roses and my Kitt."

"Dr. *Ji*, do you remember the lines you taught me last year? '*It wasn't the rose but its fragrance that made its home inside my heart*,'" Eshaan said as he placed a sympathetic hand on Dr. Sinha's shoulder.

"Ah, you are both poets at heart. I, alas, am a very boring

man. So, Kitt, don't expect poetry about roses from me!" Nikolas laughed.

Eshaan looked expectantly at Kitt, but she was looking down at her feet, fiddling with her skirt. Last time she was here, she had animatedly recited several lines from the poem Eshaan had just mentioned. But now, she did not seem to be engaged and stood aloof. Her body moved with tired energy, tense, as though she was conserving her energy for a battle of sorts.

They all entered the house through an elaborately handcrafted wooden door that Dr. Sinha purchased a few years ago from a local exhibition. He'd spent hours refurbishing the door and painting it with gloriously bright blues and reds.

"You have a marvelous eye for good workmanship. This door is one of the most beautiful things I have ever seen," Nikolas said as he walked into the house.

"You have good taste, I see," Dr. Sinha said as he proceeded to show Nikolas toward the rather elaborate living room. He then turned back to the door and called out, "Eshaan, bring the bags in and don't leave. I want you to have some tea with us. This is my peace offering to you, since I let you win the carrom contest."

Eshaan carried the bags in as Kitt trailed behind him. He walked slowly to be close to her, to feel her energy.

In the living room, the two servants were ready and waiting. A beautiful crystal tea service adorned the main table. The food platter was filled with all of Kitt's childhood favorite desserts: figs stuffed with sweet cheese, milk and flour dumplings in a syrup laced with saffron, and cashew nut brittle.

The four sat down together in uncomfortable silence.

"Turn the A/C up. It is hot in here," Dr. Sinha called out to one of the servants then immediately turned to Nikolas. "So, what is it you do, Nikolas? Are you in IT or business?" His tone was sharp and dripped with anxiety and tense anticipation.

Eshaan fidgeted awkwardly on the sofa. He knew James Bond here would have the perfect job to go with his perfect face, his perfect body, and yes, his perfect girl.

"Oh, Papa! I was going to tell you. Nikolas has his own social media consulting business. And he—"

Before she could add more, Nikolas interrupted her, "Dr. Sinha, I have a degree in marketing and have been running my own company for about ten years. We are quite profitable now, and I have a worldwide staff of about 400. I think I can take care of Kitt," he added with a wink.

Take care of Kitt? She can take care of herself! Eshaan wanted to scream out loud, but instead, he took a large sip of the tea. *Damn James Bond and his job.*

Dr. Sinha took a few sips of his tea as he stared directly at the young man his daughter had decided to marry. "What is wrong with your leg? Polio?"

"Papa, stop! It is *not* polio." Kitt stood up suddenly with her hands on her hips.

Nikolas immediately put down his tea and said, "No, sir. It was an accident. It happened during the accident, well, the one Kitt mentioned in the car. But those are all bygones now. Sir, I am sorry that we . . . Kitt has brought this on you so suddenly, but I really hope we can work this out. We are in love, Dr. Sinha, and I promise I will keep her happy."

Fucking karma.

Eshaan wanted to throw the cup of tea on the floor, wrestle this James Bond, and show him out the door. Why couldn't Kitt have picked a person who wasn't so nice? It would have been easier to hate a creep.

"Will your family be coming to join us for the wedding? I would love to meet your parents, and do you have any siblings?" Dr. Sinha's inquisition continued despite the cold stares from Kitt.

"I lost my *mutter* and *vater*—my mother and father—when I was a young man. I am an only child. But I have some good relatives who are close to me. Kitt and I plan on throwing a large reception back in Austria once the wedding is done here. So, it is just the two of us for now. And, of course, your family."

Eshaan laced his fingers together and squeezed them until his knuckles turned white. Here was a man who lost his parents and created this hugely successful company, and there he was, with no work, no money, and now, clearly, no girl. His entire life, he had pushed against feeling sorry for himself: Eshaan, the orphan boy. He had fought everyone who looked at him and expressed pity. He never wanted anyone's pity or sympathy. He wanted to make himself worthy of their love. Clearly, with Kitt, he had failed.

"I have to go now. Dr *Ji*, since you let me win, I owe you dinner, so don't cook this evening. I will bring by your favorite lamb curry and rice," Eshaan said as he got up to leave.

"Wait, Eshaan, wait," Kitt said. "I will walk you out."

Eshaan looked at her and their eyes met. His mouth felt dry, his body tense, and his heart was pounding as they walked toward the main door of the house.

"Loveleen told me that you are preparing to open Buddha's Kitchen soon. I am so happy for you. I know that has been your dream forever," Kitt said as they walked together. He simply nodded. "Eshaan, I'm sorry." She looked at the floor as she talked. "I hope you will forgive me."

"There is nothing to forgive. It's like the Sufis always say: 'A crushed rose still has its fragrance to share.' I am glad you are happy. I will be fine," he said hesitantly, as his heart prided him on not rushing forward to grab her and tell her how much he still loved her.

They both stood in the doorway for a few minutes, letting the awkward air around them settle.

"I want to tell you what—" Kitt stopped midsentence as she heard Nikolas talking on his phone again, his loud voice echoing from inside the house.

"Has she told you yet? She wants you to cook for her wedding!" Dr. Sinha interrupted their conversation.

"Oh, right, yes . . . that. Thanks, Papa. It won't be a big thing, as we will have just ten people. So if you do not want to, that is fine," Kitt said tenderly, as though trying to soften the blow.

"Ten? Kitt, that is not possible. We will have at least a few hundred. We just need to invite them. And, Eshaan can cook for that many easily. You are not having a Delhi wedding with ten people. I have friends and relatives that we must invite." Dr. Sinha looked angry.

Kitt shook her head.

Eshaan tried to stop the argument from getting worse. "I will cook for as many as you want me to, and it will be my honor.

But, right now, I have to go. It is my turn to cook for the monastery."

He turned to leave, when Kitt put her hand on his shoulder, then hugged him. "You are the sweetest, kindest man I know. Thank you for agreeing to do this."

He wanted to hug her back, hug her so tightly she would become one with him. Instead, he just stood there stiff. His feeling seesawed between deep love and seething anger. How could she?

The poets aren't always right, Eshaan thought as he left Dr. Sinha's house to go back to the monastery kitchen. *The crushed rose may still have a fragrance, but the point remains: the rose is crushed.*

Eshaan Veer Singh's Journal

I do not want to fade away
Your eyes may not see me
Your ears may not hear me
But I am here
I do not want to fade away
Into the oblivion of your old memories
Into the craters of elapsed times
I do not want to fade away
Into that dark part of your heart
That houses the wretched abyss of first love
I am here
See me
Hear me
Let me hold you
To be one again
As we were then
I am here
Come back
I am
Fading away

Chapter 11

Eshaan crossed the quiet street and headed toward the monastery. All the landmarks were in place: the six beggars at the right end of the lane, and the fried egg vendor cart on the left, with its owner now sleeping under the cart as he tried to hide from the sun.

Isn't it ironic how something that gives life can be so cruel? Eshaan pondered as he looked up toward the sun. He used his hand to shield his face from the fierce glare. He passed a few local hoodlums, who always seemed to be at war with something or someone, as they rested at the roadside. Summer did not suit Delhiites. Other places may hibernate in winter, but in Delhi, summer hibernation was the key to survival. A truck rolled by, picking up stray animals that had died of dehydration or perhaps just quit living as the earth ate its own. *Someday, they will pick up humans like that,* Eshaan thought.

The earth reflected the sun's heat and the air smelled of hopelessness and dung.

Eshaan reached the front gates of the monastery and felt the bile in his mouth. That last cup of tea he just drank was revolting against his stomach. He stopped for a moment to gain his composure. Perhaps the sweltering heat and the hot winds that were enveloping all of Delhi were getting to him as well. And, in under a second, he began to throw up as his body twisted and his emotions revolted against accepting what life was throwing at him. "It isn't the summer heat; it is her," he muttered to himself. *How could she do this to me?* he wondered. But looking at Nikolas, it was hard to imagine how she could not do this. Eshaan leaned onto the wall of the monastery for support then suddenly punched it as hard as he could. Pain always stopped tears. He was living proof of that theory.

Entering the brightly painted monastery usually uplifted Eshaan and made him grateful. It surprised him when visitors remarked on how quiet the monastery was. To Eshaan, it wasn't quiet at all. It was just that you needed to learn a different way to listen here—the soft chanting from the prayer halls, the muted sounds from the study rooms, the gentle taps of the monks' shoes as they walked, the rustling of the leaves. Yes, the monastery shared with those who were ready to listen.

His phone buzzed. Tulku Tenzin had texted. *UNLESS YOU ARE OUT SAVING THE WORLD, I NEED YOUR HELP IN THE KITCHEN.*

THE WORLD SAVED ITSELF. I AM BACK TO BEING USELESS! I WILL BE THERE IN A MINUTE, he texted back.

Eshaan rushed past the mango trees that bore a generous amount of fruit, the guava trees that were misers, and the orange trees that blossomed when they felt like it. He stopped for a moment at his favorite tree. When it blossomed, it produced quite possibly the most perfect fruit ever, a jamun. He plucked one and popped it in his mouth to remove the terrible taste the bile had left in his mouth.

The cool air of the prayer hall welcomed him as he stepped inside. It was the only air-conditioned room in the whole monastery. He was there every morning with Lama Dorje. In truth, he was supposed to be meditating during that time, but he never did. Instead, he would stare at the monks deep in silence and wonder where they hid their pain.

As soon as he stepped inside, the quiet air calmed his nerves. He walked over to the altar where people placed their food donations. He scanned the altar. Bottles of Coke, three boxes of Cadbury's chocolates, two large jars of ghee, several bags of garlic, and masala potato chips were in today's donations.

"You are supposed to offer what you love," Lama Dorje had explained to him one day when he found six bottles of Johnnie Walker whiskey placed near the altar. Eshaan had removed the bottles from the monastery and handed them to the guard outside the main doors. "Now, we are friends for life," the guard had beamed.

Today, Eshaan found what he really needed: a large bottle of donated rum, Old Monk brand. He laughed; the brand was so apt. He planned to store it in his room and then go out drinking with Raju the Dogman later. He picked up the bottle of rum, and crossed the prayer hall to head over to the kitchen to start preparations for dinner.

As Eshaan opened the back door, he heard Lama Dorje on the phone. "Yes, I will be there. No, you do not need to come get me. I can come. I will be there in an hour."

"Eshaan, is that you? Come in here!" Lama Dorje called out from his office.

Dressed in his deep burgundy robes, wearing bright red Adidas sneakers, and speaking on his new iPhone, Lama Dorje was pacing in his office. Eshaan admired the fact Lama Dorje, at his grand old age of seventy, still ran barefoot for four kilometers every morning before sunrise. When Loveleen first visited the monastery, she had questioned Eshaan about the usage of the iPhone by monks. She had encouraged him to ask the Lama about the seeming hypocrisy of a monk using one. Eshaan asked, and the Lama replied, "You should know this by now!"

Before Eshaan could answer, Loveleen had laughed and jumped in, "Eshaan, it is all about the attachment. If it can make his life easier, he will use it, but he isn't attached to it."

Several resident monks were all clearly attached, but perhaps spiritually detached, as they spent a lot of time on the phones. A few used them to spread teachings via video chats, and at least three had their own personal websites and Facebook pages and wrote interpretations of The Buddha's teachings. Tulku Tenzin used his phone to download recipes he shared with Eshaan. The recipes had to be simple and inexpensive. "We must make sure nobody gets attached to them, so we will tell them there will be no repeat performance of any dishes!" the young monk would joke.

Lama Dorje finished his phone call and turned to Eshaan. "I have to go to a family's house for a condolence service. Will you please tell Tenzin that I will be back in time for evening prayers?" Eshaan nodded. "Is something wrong? Why the long face? You are looking so pale. You worry me. And why are you hiding your hands?"

"I just came back from the airport. I picked up Dr. Sinha's

daughter. You remember . . . Kitt? She is getting married, you know," Eshaan responded as he stared down at his shoes and unsuccessfully tried to hide the bottle of rum behind his back.

Lama Dorje frowned. "Eshaan, if you want to make friends with elephants, make sure your ceiling is high enough. Besides, you have a mission in your life. You are going to start that restaurant! Speaking of which, you better go see what is happening back there in your kitchen. There is a surprise waiting!"

Eshaan perked up at Lama Dorje's words. "What surprise?"

Eshaan Veer Singh's Journal

The pain doesn't just hurt.
It sears.
It burns.
It rips a hole in my soul
Then fills it with acid.
The acid sinks in deeper and deeper.
It smolders, it chars, it annihilates
The pain doesn't just hurt.
The pain humbles me.
I used to fight back.
I don't now
It takes too much effort
The pain doesn't just hurt.
The more I fight
The worse it gets
I am like the elephant at the circus.
My spirit is tied with the strings of my imperfections.
I cannot be free.
The pain doesn't just hurt.
The pain destroys.

Chapter 12

Dr. Sinha's friends often referred to his large dining room, with its flawless glass table, state-of-the-art air conditioners, golden chairs, multicolored chandeliers, and several antique vases as a wannabe palace. At the moment, his line of servants had just begun to serve dinner with much gusto.

As pleased as Dr. Sinha was to have his daughter back home, he still wasn't sure about Nikolas. Of course, on the surface of it all, the man seemed fine. His daughter was going to marry an Austrian, just as he had. But the one big difference between his own wedding and his daughter's impending nuptials was that he had been so happy he wanted to invite the whole world to his wedding. Now, here they were seated around the dinner table. Eshaan had called to say he couldn't bring the food he had promised earlier. Kitt had totally overreacted by getting upset. Dr. Sinha did not understand why.

Anyway, that was not important at this moment. What was important was the wedding. So Dr. Sinha brazenly prodded Kitt again about the guest list.

Instead of responding, Kitt quickly changed the topic. "Papa, this *rajma* curry reminds me of Kimi *Bua*. When does Kimi *Bua* come back?"

She pretended to focus on the gently spiced red kidney beans on her plate. Kimi *Bua*, Dr. Sinha's younger sister, was one of Kitt's least favorite relatives, but a tremendous cook. Kimi lived with Dr. Sinha now that her own children were married and living abroad, and her favorite activity was, of course, using Facebook to spy on the children of relatives and then gossip about the same. Luckily, she had gone off to a spa retreat for a few weeks, and Kitt hoped the wedding would be over before Kimi *Bua* returned.

"She will be back soon. She has already called three times to speak with you. Why don't you call her back, Kitt?" Dr. Sinha was close to exasperation with his self-willed wild child. Kimi had done a lot for Kitt after his wife left them. Of course, he understood Kitt's resistance to a point; Kimi had no filter on her mouth. She spoke her mind and did not care whom it hurt.

Two of the servants returned to the table with piping hot *rotis*, Indian griddle bread, smeared with homemade butter.

"Wow, you have a lot of help here, Dr. Sinha," Nikolas said, and went on to describe his last visit to India when he toured the country on a luxury train, oblivious to the fact neither Dr. Sinha nor Kitt were paying any attention to him.

Dr. Sinha sighed deeply. It was hard to believe that this slight girl, barely five feet tall, had the iron will of an Olympic athlete, and a decidedly firm habit of never, ever wanting to be in one place for too long. A marvelous combination when it came to traveling the world, but a lethal combination when it came to focus. He had wanted her to study medicine. But no, she wanted to be a painter. So she had gone to art school and dropped out in three weeks, and then on to music school, and dropped out of there in two weeks. She had then wandered for a year then finally gone back to art school, and now she taught art at a local school in Austria. The one habit he hated was that she would randomly disappear and send him postcards from places he had never heard of. She was snorkeling off the Indonesian island of Raja Ampat, learning to cook ramen in Wakayama, taking flamenco lessons in Genalguacil, or learning to sky dive in Fiji—the only place he had heard of.

Kitt's mother came from one of the wealthiest families in Austria and had left Kitt a considerable amount of money in her trust fund. Dr. Sinha had repeatedly warned Kitt about paying for friends to accompany her on her trips. "You will run out of money. You are only withdrawing, Kitt. If you don't put anything back in—" And, of course, he had been right. Within two short years, the money ran out and she started her job as an art teacher. Her last visit, she had seemed so happy to be back home with him. In fact, he had never seen her happier than she was with Loveleen and Eshaan as they explored the depth and breadth of Delhi.

But today, as she sat across from him, his once happy-go-lucky daughter looked visibly distraught. Perhaps she was missing her mother at this time. A wedding, after all, is an important moment for mothers and daughters. Also, twice now, in the span of the past few hours, Dr. Sinha had noticed Nikolas reach out to hold Kitt's hand, and Kitt had pulled away.

Dr. Sinha tried to probe the wedding situation a little, and this time, it was Nikolas who responded. "Kitt, I am not sure why you are being so stubborn about this. I have watched some of those Bollywood movies with you, and to be honest, I would not mind a big, fat, Indian wedding. They look like fun!" Nikolas's words surprised and pleased Dr. Sinha. The groom was on his side.

"I just don't—" Kitt stopped midsentence as Nikolas tried a bit harder to push for a more opulent ceremony.

"Come on, Kitt! We are only going to do this once in our lifetime. Why not have a beautiful ceremony?" he asked in a tender tone.

Just as Dr. Sinha was about to ask Nikolas some more questions about the impending marriage, Nikolas's phone rang again. "You will have to excuse me. I have to take this call," he said as he got up from the table and headed toward the verandah of the house.

"Papa, the only person I want at the wedding is you. Okay?" Kitt prompted as she got up, kissed him on the forehead, and then went to her room on the pretext of taking a nap.

Dr. Sinha retreated to his living room, as he often did after lunch, for a short nap. He sat down on his favorite golden couches and looked up at the enormous paintings by M. F. Husain and the intricate Turkish tapestries on the wall. This room was his sanctuary and where he preferred to be when thoughts of his wife haunted him.

He reached over to the coffee table and picked up his little notebook. He had made a list of potential guests, a modest list of about two hundred and fifty or so. Now, he began to strike off the names. "How am I going to reduce this list to ten people? This is so embarrassing," he muttered as one of the servants brought him a cup of steaming hot ginger tea.

Dr. Sinha reluctantly struck out all the names except his sister, his brothers and their families, Loveleen, Mr. Mehra, Lama Dorje, and Eshaan. The list was down to fifteen, an unheard of number for an elite Delhi wedding. He knew his carrom club would be disappointed, but if anyone would understand, they would. *Kids these days don't follow traditions,* one of them had told him earlier that week at the competition. *They do what they want. We, in our golden years, have to adjust.*

Sipping his tea, he decided to call his brothers to invite them and to try to explain the situation. Dr. Sinha recalled the day his older brother's daughter got married. There were five major functions. Chefs had been flown in from all over the world to cook for the two thousand–odd guests. Each guest had received gold coins, and the main family members had each received an iPad.

"Dr. Sinha! India is proving lucky for me. Our company just signed its biggest deal ever!" Nikolas walked into the living room and announced. And then, he waved his hand and apologized once again as his mobile rang.

Dr. Sinha beamed. Well, this was good news. Perhaps he was just overreacting to the whole thing. This was a happy occasion, and if this is what Kitt wanted, he was going to give it to her in style. Dr. Sinha picked up his mobile and decided to call his brother first, and then realized he did not have the wedding date. He called out to Kitt, but did not get a response. He placed his tea, his mobile phone, and his little address book on the table and decided to go to her room to ask her about the date.

He found two of the female servants standing outside Kitt's

room, looking very concerned. “What is it? What is the problem?” he asked as softly as he could as to not make a scene.

“Kitt is inside. She is crying so much,” one of the servants murmured.

Chapter 13

Buddha's Karma Kitchen was just days away from opening its doors. Eshaan confided in Rani that he was focusing on the two truths of the day: Kitt was not yet married, and Karma Kitchen, despite the seriously lack of money, was opening soon.

"It is like the old saint said. Delhi is far off. I still have time to try to stop Kitt from marrying that man," Eshaan said.

Rani looked at him with confusion. "What does Delhi have to do with Kitt getting married? And what do you mean Delhi is far off. Aren't we living here?"

Eshaan had laughed; sometimes his whole life felt like it was lost in translation. He explained to Rani that years ago, when an arrogant emperor threatened to take over Delhi, a Sufi saint had correctly predicted the emperor would fail to even reach the city limits of Delhi, much less rule it. The saint had used the words, "Delhi is far off." Rani just shook her head, rolled her eyes, and walked away, muttering something about what reading too many books does to sane minds.

Now, here they were. "The bride is getting her jewelry," Rani had remarked as the kitchen signage was being set up.

"A little to the left, a little higher," Eshaan yelled as he directed two young monks, who were helping in setting up the sign for the kitchen. The sign was glorious, each letter crafted and painted as a different colored lotus flower. Underneath the letters were symbols of every religion that Eshaan could think of. *Everyone needed to feel welcome here*, he thought and beamed with pride when the sign was almost in place.

"Eshaan. We have moved this sign four times. It is fine now," Tulku Tenzin said, wiping the sweat off his forehead.

Eshaan bowed to Tenzin, who had singlehandedly created the beautiful sign. Lama Dorje was right when he said Eshaan would be surprised.

"Okay, it is fine now. Maybe we can move it again later?"

The little kitchen now had some makeup on, as Lama Dorje put it. The large bamboo bowl with a sign thanking donors had already been installed outside, thanks to Loveleen, and now a sign announcing the name of the kitchen, thanks to Tenzin, and again, thanks to Loveleen, a larger-than-life portrait of Virat Kohli, the famed cricketer, hung on one of the inside walls.

Oh, and yes, there were three large stoves that had been paid for, one antiquated ceiling fan Eshaan had purchased off the streets, and an old-fashioned box room cooler that one of the carrom club members had generously donated to keep the kitchen cool.

"You want the food to be cooked and roasted, not your guests!" the elder gentleman had remarked as his driver helped deliver the unsightly cooler.

"You know, Eshaan, the lines are going to be long. Do you think we will have enough food to feed everyone?" Tulku Tenzin asked Eshaan as he stepped down from the ladder.

"Hmm . . . I guess when we run out for the day, these people can always come back. Right?"

Tulku Tenzin shook his head; he wasn't convinced this would work. He had seen poverty, a lot of it as a child, and he knew that eventually people's generosity ran out. He had begged as a child, and the humiliation of it still woke him up many nights. The deep desire for a morsel was a great motivator and a great deterrent at the same time.

"There are too many who are hungry, and not enough of those who want to feed them," Tenzin declared, but instantly felt bad about his negative attitude. "At least you are trying. I will support you, Eshaan."

Eshaan smiled. The sign was up, and one of their most pressing problems was about to be solved later in the day. A few days ago, the kind Lama Dorje had casually asked, "What are you going to serve the food on?" The crew had been upset at the question, as they had failed at finding a reasonable solution.

Radio Rani had tried to come to Eshaan's rescue. She wanted to find banana leaves to use as plates. The leaves were large, clean, hygienic, inexpensive, and easily disposable as compost. However, finding banana leaf trees in Delhi had been near impossible, and when she did find some, the owners had told her to get lost.

The previous morning, Lama Dorje had offered a simple suggestion regarding the dinner plates: Ask someone who has the resources to help. So Eshaan had done just that. He routinely volunteered at a famous Sikh temple in Old Delhi. His favorite way to help out was not in the kitchen, but at the counter, where people dropped off their shoes before entering the temple. He would take the shoes of the devotees and clean them while the devotees prayed. These types of actions, meant to serve other people, were referred to as *seva.* Cleaning the shoes was an ongoing lesson in humility, reminding Eshaan, and all those who did the work there, that material ego is worthless and harmful.

It was at the shoe-cleaning booth that Eshaan had met several wealthy and prosperous Sikh gentlemen, all of whom volunteered to clean shoes for any devotee who came in to pray. One of the wealthy gentlemen had been impressed by Eshaan's volunteer spirit and had helped him with bags of spices and rice. So, taking Lama Dorje's advice, he had gone back to the same temple and asked the gentlemen again for their help. It was an instant yes, and now a hundred round, shiny, traditional steel dinner plates would be arriving any minute.

"Eshaan, I am coming down! I am done!" Tulku Tenzin called out from the top of the ladder. Eshaan nodded again and began to sweep the entrance to remove any debris that had fallen from the wall as they hammered the sign in.

"The sign looks amazing, Tenzin. We are official," he said, and turned when he heard clapping. Standing behind him and clapping were Loveleen and Kitt.

Kitt, dressed in all white, her favorite color, looked radiant. Eshaan could not help but notice she still would not look at him. Loveleen was, of course, wearing the blue of the Indian cricket team. He pushed his feet down and dug his heels into the ground, as though he wanted to cement them into the earth, lest he run toward Kitt and envelope her in his arms forever. He pushed his hands deep into his pockets.

"Hello! To what do I owe this pleasure? Oh, Loveleen, who is this?" Eshaan said, looking to the young boy standing next to Loveleen. The kid, about fifteen, was wearing a ragged old pair of pants and a white t-shirt with the Indian flag on it. He was holding several cloth bags filled with wheat, rice, and lentils.

"This is Om," Loveleen said, introducing her guest. "He is going to be your food guard."

Eshaan looked confused. "Food guard? What are you talking about? The monastery already has a security guard for their students. What do I need a guard for? I own absolutely nothing of value to anyone."

"My dear, if people are going to come and donate food in this big bowl out here, how long do you think it will be before people start stealing? Seriously? You don't think about how this crazy city works. You will be inside cooking, and the monks will be praying, but no one will be keeping an eye on your food stack outside."

The monks, now done with the sign, smiled politely at Loveleen then left quietly.

Somehow, they haven't warmed up to her, Eshaan often thought. The only one who seemed even remotely warm toward Loveleen was Tenzin, but then, he would probably offer to clean the knife of anyone who stabbed him.

Loveleen proceeded to tell the boy to place all the big bags of food into the bowl outside the kitchen. Her unpredictability always surprised Eshaan. Yet, questioning her about her choices had never, ever resulted in a meaningful discussion. If he asked her why she did something, her answer was always, "Because." One loaded word that dared you to try and ask again.

"You bought more food? Also, this guard . . . I understand, but you know I have no money to pay him, and where will he live?" Eshaan whispered while watching Kitt help the young boy unload the bagged grains into the bowl.

The young boy then sat down on the large patch of grass right next to the bowl. "I'm here now. No one will steal," he said, beaming a smile.

Eshaan waited for her rehearsed response of, "Because." But this time, she surprised him.

"Who asked you for money? Did I? Did I say, 'Eshaan, give me money?' You are my friend, and this is my investment in Karma Kitchen. So I have done my part. Now, will you please show us inside and make me something to drink? This heat plus the pregnancy hormones are making me very uncomfortable. Also, he can stay at my house. I have a servants' quarter that is empty," she said, and then turned to take Kitt's hand and headed toward Karma Kitchen.

The three friends entered the kitchen together.

There were ten tables inside, with about five plastic chairs at each table. On the left side of the kitchen was a large floor mat for those who could no longer sit on chairs.

"Lama Dorje, Tulku Tenzin, and I built those tables. We went to Old Thieves Bazaar, you know, the place that sells junk, and bought some old planks and tables and used them to make these." Eshaan beamed as Kitt sat down at one of the tables and ran her hand over the smooth wooden tabletop. He still couldn't believe she was here, sitting in his kitchen, at a table he had made.

Loveleen pointed out the picture of her idol, cricketer Virat Kohli, and launched into a huge tirade against the cricketer's current choice of girlfriend.

"The table, Kitt? You are looking at the table? Look at the wall. There he is, the King of Cricket. He should have picked someone at his level. She is just an actress! This man is cricketing royalty. He needs a queen, a *rani*!"

"I am here and ready whenever he is," Radio Rani said as loudly as she could.

The entire room erupted with laughter. Radio Rani hugged everyone then headed off to the main kitchen to make something cool for Loveleen, who was now fanning herself with one of the few plastic plates in the room.

"So, Kitt, where is Nikolas? I haven't seen him around for the past two days," Eshaan asked a bit too casually.

Before Kitt answered, Loveleen butted in, "*Where* have you been for the past two days? You haven't come to see either of us. Nikolas flew back to Dubai. Work emergency and all. So now, here is this poor girl, who has to get ready for her wedding and has no groom. So sad, right?"

Eshaan knew Loveleen well enough to recognize the sarcasm in her tone, and the glint in her eyes gave a whole other naughtiness to her intentions.

"Oh, so that is why you are looking sad, Kitt?" Eshaan joked, and added, "Your Romeo is out of town. Loveleen, how about we take her to where all the sad lovers go? You know, where they can pray for their love to return?"

Radio Rani returned, carrying a large tray with a few glass tumblers on it.

"Tenzin told me to bring this to you," she said, walking toward Loveleen. "He has prepared it for you with the honey from his own honeybees. He must really think you are special. He never offers that to anyone!" She offered a tumbler to Loveleen and one to Kitt, and then looked at Eshaan. "I don't suppose you want a chilled lemonade, do you?" she asked him, and without waiting for an answer, left to give the last tumbler to the new guard outside, Om, and to also get Om an umbrella so he wouldn't melt under the hot Delhi sun.

"What is Radio Rani's problem with you, Eshaan? This is the third time this month that I have noticed her rolling her eyes at you," Loveleen asked as she drank the chilled liquid.

"She is a bit upset at me, since I am fasting," he said. He forgot to mention he had been fasting for about three days now, only drinking water or tea. He had reasoned with Rani that this type of fasting would make him stronger and more determined. She was not convinced.

"Yes, Eshaan, please do fast. It does the world a lot of good when *you* don't eat," Loveleen replied sarcastically and moved on to the topic of going out in the evening to cheer Kitt up.

They made plans to meet later that evening, and an elated Eshaan walked them out. As he neared the main gate of the monastery, he noticed a stout gentleman push pass them and rush toward the monastery office.

"Eshaan, I am really so worn out answering all of Dad's questions about Nikolas and the wedding. I could really use a break," Kitt said as she reached out to hold his hand.

"I . . . I . . . yes, we can go," Eshaan muttered as he stood there, admiring her radiant face. He pulled away suddenly, worried she would notice her name tattooed on his hand. The deep cut he had made there still throbbed each time he thought of her. He said goodbye and watched them as they walked away.

His phone began to beep. It was a text from Loveleen, and she was barely two hundred feet away.

WEAR YOUR CUTEST SHIRT THIS EVENING. REMEMBER, SHE ISN'T MARRIED YET.

He smiled at the message. Perhaps this day was going to turn out to be terrific after all.

Chapter 14

Eshaan returned to Karma Kitchen, still smiling, when he saw the short, stout man he had seen rushing in a few moments ago was standing outside the entrance. He appeared to be talking rudely to Tulku Tenzin. Eshaan rushed over.

"What is going on here? Can I help you, sir?" he asked, positioning himself between the man and Tenzin.

Eshaan surveyed the man from head to toe. He was wearing navy blue pants, a starched white shirt, and flat, beige rubber sandals. His hair, full of oil, was slicked back, and he was chewing betel leaf, which he then proceeded to spit right outside the door of the Kitchen.

Tenzin gently touched Eshaan's right hand and whispered, "Do not reflect his behavior."

"Who am I? Oh, yes. I will tell who I am. I am from the Food and Safety Board of Delhi. Who are you? You cannot just open a restaurant here. That is against the rules. This area is for the monastery. And the monastery doesn't have the right to open a restaurant. You are breaking the law. With whose permission are you doing this?" the man said as he spat again.

This time, it was Om who responded, "Hey, mister. Are you a *junglee*? This is The Buddha's house, and you are spitting here? Eshaan *bhai* and these monks may have patience, but I know how to deal with people like you."

Eshaan stood there in disbelief at what was happening.

The man retreated a few steps. "Oh, so now you hire thugs to scare me? You will see. I will come back with a formal notice. I will make you close this place down."

Eshaan tried to get a word in edgeways. "Sir, wait, sir, this is not a restaurant. Let me explain. But first, can I offer you something to drink? It is such a hot day. Please, come inside. We will sit down and discuss this. Come, sir, please. Excuse this little boy. He is just young."

The man was reluctant and spouted out words that made Eshaan want to break both his legs. But instead, under the vigilant eyes of Tulku Tenzin, Eshaan remained patient, coaxing the man a little more to come in.

"Why are you so scared of him? I can take him out!" Om said loudly.

"Be quiet, please. This is your first day here, so I am letting this go, but do this again and I will throw you out," Eshaan responded sharply to Om. "Please, sir, come in. Let us talk about this." Eshaan gently guided the man into the kitchen. He turned on the ceiling fan and called out to Radio Rani to bring some chilled lemonade. Then he sat down facing the man and noticed a group of monks had gathered outside the door. Instantly, he felt safer. They always had his back, literally, figuratively, spiritually . . . always.

The man accepted the lemonade from Radio Rani. "Look,

young man, this area is for the monks. You cannot open a restaurant on these grounds. It is just not allowed. I will have to close this up and fine you."

Radio Rani tried to catch Eshaan's eye, but he was too busy trying to figure out how to get this menace to calm down.

"Oh, and let's look around here. Even if you could legally open a restaurant, I can see so many things that will not pass a formal review. Where is the refrigerator? Where is the area for washing dishes? How will you charge without a cash counter? This looks like a child designed it. Having a picture of a big cricketer on the wall doesn't make you an instant star, you know," the man droned on as he pointed out several other flaws, holes, and requirements-not-met type issues that existed in the small kitchen.

Eshaan quietly assessed his options. What he really wanted to do was take Om up on his words and kick this guy out. His mobile started to vibrate. It was a text message from Tulku Tenzin.

RADIO RANI TELLS ME SHE SAW THIS GUY TALKING TO MR. MEHRA A FEW TIMES THIS WEEK. MEHRA MUST'VE TOLD HIM ABOUT YOUR KITCHEN.

The man noticed Eshaan checking his phone and became abusive. "You young people have no respect for anyone. Here I am talking to you, and all you want to do is check your phone? Have you no sense of respect or etiquette? Did your parents not teach you how to behave, young man? I find your attitude very disrespectful."

"I am so sorry, sir. It is just the monks sending messages. They are concerned. First, my name is Eshaan Veer Singh. I welcome you to this kitchen. But let me explain. See, we are not planning on charging the customers a single *paisa*. It is just a place for the poor to come and eat for free. It will be run on donations and elbow grease. So you see, what we are doing is a form of charity and we are not a restaurant," Eshaan tried to explain in his most kind, soft, nonconfrontational voice. Tulku Tenzin often teased Eshaan that he sounded like he was trying, and failing, to channel Lama Dorje.

The man stood up, clearly more agitated. "You are challenging me? You think I am stupid? Who opens a kitchen for free in this day and age? *You* are a fool to think *I* am a fool and that I will believe all this nonsense. Here is my card. My name is Naresh Gupta. It is a name you will remember. I *will* shut this place down. You have no right to do this here. Find a different place. Now get out of my way."

With that, the very cranky Mr. Naresh Gupta walked out the door, waited for Eshaan and Rani to come out, and then pushed all the monks aside. Gupta pulled the doors shut. He took out a large padlock from his suitcase, hooked it onto the two handles of the door, and locked it.

"You young people of today have no respect for the law. You think you can do what you want and when you want. Well, not in Delhi. In Delhi, we do things by the book and follow the law. This place is now closed."

The monks look bewildered. Eshaan, still trying to convince the man, looked forlorn, and then muttered, "I've failed before I even started."

Chapter 15

Loveleen's kitchen was simple yet eclectic. One small stove with large burners, a couple of large cupboards, and a whole line of painted terracotta planters filled with mint, curry leaves, coriander, and *tulsi*, all lush and green.

"Wow! What happened here? Last time I visited, all your plants were dying or dead," Kitt commented as she plucked a tiny mint leaf and placed it in her mouth. "This tastes like mint, but smells a bit like . . . chocolate?!"

"Oh, it isn't me. I can kill a cactus just by being in the same vicinity as it. This is all Radio Rani. She saves plants! She started helping me plant them, and Eshaan began singing to them. And now I have chocolate mint. No idea what to do with it, but, you know, Eshaan insists I need it." Loveleen laughed as she heated two small pots, one with a small amount of milk thinned with some water, and the other with whole milk.

She then added a heaped spoon of instant coffee, a few generous tablespoons of sugar, and the thinned, warm milk into a small bowl.

"Here is where the magic happens, and we whip, and whip,

and we whip," she remarked in a singsong tone to an old Bollywood melody as she used a whisk to dissolve the coffee into the milk.

Within a few minutes, the contents of the bowl become a syrupy, thick, pale brown liquid. She then poured a little bit of the liquid into two small cups and topped off each one with the hot milk. As if by magic, froth appeared on top of each cup. "That is what all that whipping does!" she quipped. "And now, I channel Eshaan," she said, "The piece-de-resistance: *eliachi*. Oh, sorry, I forget sometimes that you are not from here. Cardamom!"

Loveleen opened a cupboard and took two cardamom pods out of a small jar. She crushed them gently with her fingers and opened them. The pods revealed their sticky little brownish-black seeds. She popped them into a mortar and pestle and ground them while singing, "And we crush, and we crush, and we crush," and then sprinkled them on one of the finished coffee cups.

"Oh, that smells wonderful. You know my Austrian mum used to drink cardamom tea all the time," Kitt said softly.

"Ah, Indians! We love to make everyone Indian, but then we want to be like everyone else." Loveleen laughed. "Why don't you take this one with the cardamom and go sit in the balcony, and I will bring my coffee and some bites."

Loveleen called her maid, who was sweeping the bedroom, and began to fire off some instructions on what needed to be prepared for dinner.

The rich, toasty, warm smell of cardamom usually made her mouth water, but with the pregnancy, the aroma made Loveleen very nauseous. The scent dissipated as she walked, or as Kitt had aptly pointed out, waddled, to the tiny garden she had created on her balcony. The sun had disappeared behind some rather large clouds. Loveleen looked up at the sky. Her mother always said that moving clouds never rained, but today, it looked like the sky was about to have a good and hearty cry.

Kitt was already out on the balcony, which overlooked the monastery, staring into the distance. Her phone beeped and she picked it up. It was her father's sister, Kimi *Bua*, this was the fourth time she had called. Kitt put the phone back down. It was hard enough to explain to her father why she was rushing to get this wedding over with, but explaining it to Kimi required a whole other level of patience. Her phone beeped again, and this time, it was a text from Kimi.

ARE YOU PREGNANT? IS THAT WHY YOU ARE RUSHING?

Kitt looked at the message and rolled her eyes. The woman was relentless, shameless, and really hard to shake off.

"So, now I finally get you to myself. Let's talk, lady," Loveleen said, sitting down on the white rattan chair. She picked up her cup, poured a bit of the coffee into the saucer, and proceeded to blow gently on the liquid to cool it down.

"What are those statues on top of the monastery? Those? What is that big circle thing in the center? I've never noticed that before," Kitt said, pointing to statues of two large deer that sat elegantly atop the building.

"Oh, that, yes, Eshaan told me once that the central golden sculpture is the wheel of dharma. It represents Buddha's teachings. I think it has eight spokes that are the eightfold path to enlightenment. Buddha's first sermon, which the wheel represents, took place in the Deer Park at Varanasi in India. The deer are there to represent that."

Both women continued to drink coffee as they watched rainclouds form at a distance as the warm rays of the sun continued to the caress the golden deer and the wheel of dharma.

"So, miss, you never once mentioned to me that you are pregnant! In all those messages, calls . . . never. Pregnant? How and when? I did not know you have a boyfriend, a secret lover. You cannot stand most men! So what is the secret of this immaculate conception?" Kitt smiled as she began her own inquisition, clearly not anxious to answer any of Loveleen's predictable questions. It was such a relief to sit here and not be under her father's constant vigilance. "Well, are you going to tell me, or should I ask Mr. Merry Mehra if he knows?" Kitt teased, as her father had filled her in on all the building gossip.

Loveleen wondered how much to share. While she and Kitt were friends, she was still not sure her friend was ready to hear the reality.

Loveleen and Kitt had met, quite coincidentally, at a spa a few years ago. They started chatting over a chilled mint tea, and Loveleen mentioned she was looking for a place to live in Delhi. As it turned out, Kitt's dad, Dr. Sinha, happened to have a place to rent. Loveleen had moved in almost immediately, and she and Kitt spent a lot of time together.

The women could not have been more different. Kitt had a wealthy Austrian mother, a highly educated Indian father, and was raised in one of the most privileged places in the world, Austria.

A couple in a remote village in Punjab had adopted Loveleen, an orphan. She was two at the time of her adoption, and her adoptive parents were in their sixties. They also had a son. She was barely eighteen when both of them passed away in an unfortunate bus accident. After their demise, she left the village and moved to Delhi to try to start a life. She moved from job to job, a secretary (she couldn't type), a salesgirl (she couldn't have cared less if someone bought something or not), a call-center operator (well, the clients did not take to her verbal tirades when they refused to buy what she was selling), and there were a few more disasters. She moved from women's hostels, to cheap hotels, to paying guest places, never quite finding a fit.

Just when she had given up all hope, Loveleen's brother called her. The land her parents had left for them had sold for an outrageous amount of money to a private investor, who was going to build a hotel in that area. Her brother sent her a check for her half. She never heard from him again. They hadn't been close as children, but she thought for sure he would want to stay in touch. Clearly, he didn't. She was grateful to him, for now she no longer needed to work. And, after meeting Kitt, she found a home in Dr. Sinha's bungalow.

"How did I get pregnant? You do know how that happens, or are you just 'good friends' with your Nikki *baba*?" Loveleen asked as she sipped her drink.

They both laughed. Loveleen's maid came out holding a small steel bowl filled with warmed almond oil.

"Can I massage now?" she asked, and Loveleen nodded. The young maid poured a bit of the oil on Loveleen's scalp and began a gentle massage. For a few minutes, it was quiet and tranquil on the balcony-turned-makeshift-spa.

The maid exited as softly as she had arrived.

"Come on, now. Inquiring minds want to know. Who is the daddy, darling? And please don't call Nikolas 'Nikki *baba*.' He'll be pissed! He doesn't take well to what he calls 'Indianizing.'" Kitt's tone was flat, her face expressionless.

The palm leaf–style fan on the balcony's ceiling wasn't doing much to ward off the heat. In the distance, Loveleen could see the dark clouds as they approached the building. There was a time when rain used to annoy her, and then she met Eshaan. He always waited for it to rain, insisted on playing cricket outside when it was pouring down like hell, loved to sit on the street corner and get soaking wet when it rained.

"Please tell me you know who got you pregnant, Ms. Loveleen. This silence is telling a crazy story!" Kitt managed a faint smile and prodded her friend some more.

Loveleen shifted in her chair, a bit uncomfortable now with her growing girth. The baby had been kicking a lot lately, making it hard for her to sleep. But what a feeling! All the nurses at the doctor's office had been placing their hands on her belly and introducing themselves to the baby.

"It is a girl. I can tell you," the local vegetable vendor told her repeatedly. "It is a girl. Girls take away their mother's beauty, and boys make their mothers glow," she'd added. Every single time the vendor lady said that, Loveleen would look hurt. "You are beautiful, Loveleen," the vendor would assure. "But, see, you are not glowing, so this means there is a girl in your tummy. This is the way nature is." Finally, Loveleen learned to take it as a compliment and smiled as she thought of a beautiful little girl growing inside her.

"I will tell you, of course, but then you have to promise you are going to tell me what the hell is going on with you and that Nikki *baba* of yours. Hell, I have seen people happier at funerals than you are about your wedding!"

Before Kitt could answer, Loveleen's maid came back onto the balcony. "Madam, madam, madam . . . it is Om from the monastery. He is calling you to come down."

Chapter 16

"I will call you about this evening. I need to go see what is going on," Loveleen said before she left to go talk to Om.

Kitt debated following Loveleen to see what was going on, but then decided just to go back to her room. The past few days had been draining. Truth be told, she could not wait to see Eshaan, and even steal a moment alone with him to tell him what was going on. She hoped he would understand. She had longed for him in the dark nights, in the bright days, in crowds, and when she was alone. She slept with his name on her lips, his face in her dreams. She woke to his smell, that haunting scent of his *itar* that seemed to have taken a root in her spirit. And yet, here she was, getting ready to marry another man.

Back in her room, she opened her closet and instinctively picked out the red dress she knew Eshaan loved. Then, with some regret, she hung it back. She reminded herself that this struggle would end with the wedding. That would be her burden to bear.

BE READY BY SIX TO GO TO THE DARGAH. *NO SKIN SHOWING,* read a text from Loveleen.

K, Kitt responded, and dressed in her most conservative outfit. She wanted to ask if Eshaan was okay, but thought better of it. She would be seeing him soon and she could ask him herself.

Then she went to the living room, where her father was reading on the brand new e-reader Nikolas had gifted him. Beside him, on his coffee table, was his wedding album. He looked through it, she knew, at least once in the morning. *I don't want to forget,* he always told Kitt. But, sometimes, she wondered if he was trying to remember what she was like.

For the first time in her life, she thought her father appeared frail. The stroke had made the left side of his body weaker, and she noticed he leaned to one side now when he walked or sat down. As if the ravages of emotion weren't enough for him, now the ravages of the body were trying to destroy him. *This is what happens when those who are supposed to nurture you betray you,* she thought.

"Papa, Loveleen and Eshaan are taking me to something called a *dargah*. What is that?"

Dr. Sinha took off his reading glasses, blew onto the lenses, and began to clean them with the bottom of his long, white *kurta,* an old habit, still there, still the same, serenity in ritualistic routines.

When she was younger, Kitt remembered him lovingly cleaning his eyeglasses on her mother's clothes.

"Oh, a *dargah.* Do you know who the Sufis were? Yes? A *dargah* is the shrine that is built in reverence to a Sufi saint." He went on to explain that the *dargah* was built over the tombs of the saints. The Sufis followed a mystic form of Islam. In their eyes, the way to God was through love.

"Wow, I had no idea!" Kitt said, and wondered why Loveleen, who was a Hindu, Eshaan, who was a Buddhist, and she, who was not religious, were going to a Muslim shrine for an evening out. She wondered if she should just drop out. Honestly, a night at the bar sounded like what she really needed, not a night listening to sermons.

"Isn't today Thursday? I think they will take you to the *dargah* in Nizammuddin. The shrine of Nizammuddin Auylia is there," Dr. Sinha said as he ran his hands through his well-oiled white hair.

Kitt smiled. Her mother used to call her father's ritualistic habits "the constant soothers." Cleaning his glasses, running his hand through his hair, and when he was really upset, he would use one hand to massage the other, pressing down on all the mounds of his palms, trying to find his serenity, his center, to bring back peace to his heart.

Dr. Sinha continued to share all he knew about the area he thought she was going to. He animatedly explained that the daughter of the king who built the Taj Mahal was buried in the area. He stopped when he noticed his daughter looking confused. "I'm sorry. I am rambling. Tonight will be special at the *dargah*. It is Thursday, and you will hear troupes who sing the spiritual music of the Indian Sufi saints. Mesmerizing, I tell you."

He sang a few lines from his favorite Sufi tune and translated it for her benefit, "The Sufi saints say that you have to drown in the sea of love and only the ones who drown make it across."

"I love you, Papa. And yes, before you ask, Nikolas called,

and he will be back within a few days, so we now have some time to arrange the wedding, okay?"

Dr. Sinha smiled at her then picked up his diary, opened it up, and told her to take a look. It had a list of florists, priests, tent and outdoor equipment, henna artists, and makeup people.

"Papa, you already called all these people?"

"You know your mother always wanted a Bollywood wedding. I couldn't give her one, but I will try to give you one. Also, at some point you will need to return Kimi's calls. She is upset you are avoiding her and thinks Nikolas has done some black magic on you."

"I will call her tonight. I promise." Kitt bent down and kissed his forehead.

"You know, your mother and I have always been proud of you. I wish she was here for your marriage."

Kitt cringed at her father's acceptance of her mother's betrayal. And, yes, as much as he believed it was a choice, she believed it was a betrayal of the worst kind.

The day it happened was etched in Kitt's heart. It was a memory so vivid that each time she replayed it, it felt like a part of her died. She was a tiny kid. She had been sitting at the kitchen island, eating her banana, and getting ready to go to school.

"Mama, where are you? I need my lunch!" she had called out to her mother.

A few minutes later, her mother had appeared with a large suitcase. She was wearing some sort of a black gown.

Kitt put the banana down and laughed. "Mama, you look silly in that gown! Why is Papa looking so upset?"

Dr. Sinha had appeared behind her mother and was wiping his tears.

"Kitt, my child. I want you to know I love you very much. I am so sorry I have to leave you, but I have to go." That was it. With those simple words that shredded her whole world, Kitt's mother walked out on her family.

"Papa, what does she mean? Is she going on vacation? When will she be back? I want to go with her." Kitt had cried and cried.

Her father had explained that her mother had discovered some meditating group during her last visit to Bali and had decided to move there, to join them in praying for world peace. Her mother was never religious, and as far as Kitt could remember, had never even set foot in a church.

"We have to let her go with a smile. She is doing what she feels she has been called to do and we cannot fight that," her father had said.

They thought they would never see her again.

Kitt cried for so many nights that she lost count. Eventually, she and her father settled into a quiet pattern, but she never stopped praying and asking God to send her mother back.

Some prayers, Kitt learned, are better not answered.

It was a few weeks before Kitt's sixteenth birthday. Her aunt had gone to Bali for a trip and emailed Kitt photos from there. And there was her mother in those photographs, beaming, looking happy, laughing, and smiling. Kitt had smashed her computer screen with her coffee mug.

A text message from Loveleen brought Kitt back to the moment.

LET'S GO, KITT. I AM IN THE CAR. COME ON.

Chapter 17

The Nizammuddin area was one of the oldest in Delhi. By some estimates, the area had a seven-hundred-year-old history. Home to shrines and tombs of many great saints and poets, it was always flooded with locals, religious visitors, foodies who loved kebabs, and shoppers looking for deals on handcrafted perfumes and locally made wooden utensils.

Loveleen could not stop talking about the man who had locked up Eshaan's kitchen. She was angry and spewing expletives in Punjabi, English, and God knows what other language. Kitt felt her heart sink. That kitchen was his dream. She knew he would be devastated. In her heart, she felt grateful she could be there for him tonight.

Kitt held onto Loveleen's hand as they entered the Nizammuddin community through a very small, open gate.

"Why is the gate so tiny? I am not tall, and even I have to bend," Kitt muttered to Loveleen.

"Oh, these gates used to be huge, but then the people kept adding layers of concrete, sand, you name it, to repair the roads below, and now the road is very high, making the entrance seem low. Now we have to crouch!"

Kitt hoped Eshaan would join them as promised, but so far, there was no sign of him. And now, here she was, in this strange and highly congested part of town, wondering what the hell Loveleen was taking her to do or see.

"Be sure to keep your head covered. They don't like it here when foreigners disrespect their traditions," Loveleen warned rather grimly.

Kitt adjusted her headscarf to make sure her hair wasn't peeking through. She still felt the eyes of some men sizing her up, making her feel very uncomfortable. Loveleen was dressed in a bright pink outfit, and had covered her head with an even brighter pink and purple bandana. Kitt felt very self-conscious in her long black shirt and her dark blue jeans. She touched her scarf for reassurance. The crimson silk scarf with paintings of a lotus was the only gift Eshaan had ever given her.

Kitt noticed several foreigners buying vegetables in the market.

"These people live here? Why? This really isn't a modern area."

Loveleen pointed to an old building. "Yep, in that building there. It is cheap! Most of these folks are here with some nonprofit, and they want to be able to afford Delhi, so they live here. As long as they abide by the laws here, things stay pretty peaceful."

Together, the duo navigated the crowded lanes as they made their way to the *dargah* in the heart of the area. As they got closer to the main *dargah*, vendors began to call out to them to buy all kinds of offerings needed for prayer, everything from flowers, to amulets with prayers tucked inside them.

Loveleen stopped at a few shops.

"You know everyone here!" Kitt exclaimed.

"No, no, not everyone, but I come by so often that I have formed some friendships, like that guy there, the one with that open fire in front of him. He is my *kalai wala* . . . the English word for them . . . ummmm . . . re-tinners? I bring my brass and copper bowls to him so he can line them with tin. That way the copper doesn't taint the food. Poor guy is losing work, as most people are moving to stainless steel or the American Teflon thing."

As the shrine got closer, the crowds increased, and amidst it all, Loveleen was still providing a guided tour. "That *itar* perfume shop handcrafts Clinique's Happy perfume for me, so I don't have to buy it at the mall. Eshaan told me about this guy. That is where he gets his perfume from, you know, the one that makes him smell like his beloved mother earth after the rains," she said as she rolled her eyes. "Oh, and that one there, see that guy with the large, big copper bowls? He makes the best biryanis. Oh, now I am getting hungry!"

Kitt began to feel claustrophobic as the lanes got tighter and the crowds swelled. Why had she agreed to this? She hated everything about every religion. And this place was dingy, overcrowded, and, in her opinion, all these people selling religious paraphernalia were just trying to fool people into believing that a God did exist.

"Madam, please, please buy this card, for 10, 20, 1000, 2000, or 1, or whatever you want," a scraggly old man said as he thrust a note into Kitt's face, startling her.

"Yes, give me one for a hundred people, *Baba*. I hope you are well!" Loveleen took the card from the man's hand and handed him a fistful of notes. He grabbed the money then scribbled something on the card and gave it to her, along with chanting several blessings for her unborn baby. "Tell Eshaan he needs to come by soon. I could use some help," the vendor added as he smiled at Loveleen. Eshaan usually showed up here most Thursday evenings to help the old man cook for the throngs that lined the lanes.

"Wait, wait, Loveleen, what did you buy?" Kitt was curious.

"This is the tragedy of our country. We cannot feed our own. I bought a simple dinner for a hundred people, and do you know what I paid for it? Less money than I would spend on getting my nails done."

Both the women stood and watched as the vendor began to hand out small leaf plates filled with rice, curried vegetables, and sliced onions.

The hundred plates were served in less than two minutes.

The line was still there, hoping, waiting for the next gracious soul to come by and feed them. Despite the harsh heat, the claustrophobic lane, the stench of a thousand people sweating, the thirst for a sip of anything, there was no resentment on the faces of those who were still in line. They knew there would be food. Today on Earth, or tomorrow in Heaven.

"I bought it from one vendor, and now twenty people will try to sell me another one. Come on, walk faster!" Loveleen said to Kitt, pulling her arm to lead her forward.

"A gift of food, so nice. It saves people from begging, yes?" Kitt asked, eyeing all the small children running to several vendors for their plate of food.

"You know, all people beg, just that these guys do it on the street in plain view. Many of us do it in the privacy of our homes, our shrines, our temples, and in our hearts. We are all beggars," Loveleen said, wiping an errant tear from her eyes.

"YOU ARE EVIL. I KNOW YOU. I SEE YOU!" A young man in tatters, frothing at the mouth, appeared out of nowhere and charged toward Kitt and Loveleen. The old vendor who sold Loveleen the ticket jumped up from his chair and rushed over to get between the women and the madman. As soon as the man saw the old vendor, he stopped then turned around and ran.

"Sorry. That is my son. He is now lost to a different world," the old man said in a soft voice as he walked away.

Kitt stood still, startled.

"Come, Kitt. This is the irony of the world, isn't it? His father's job helps him feed the needy, yet he cannot do anything for his own son. I've seen this guy before. He just walks around shouting at everyone, but that is about it. He is harmless."

They continued to walk in silence as Kitt kept looking back to see if the madman was coming their way again.

"What is so special about this place, Loveleen?" asked Kitt, as the spectacular shrine came into view. It had a dome-shaped top, vibrant colors on its walls, lattice surrounding some windows, and religious scripts painted on some parts. It was still early in the evening, and only a few hundred people were inside. But Loveleen warned that as the evening went on, the place would be jam-packed with hundreds of thousands of people coming to pray and pay their respects.

"When Eshaan first brought me here, he told me to sit quietly in a corner and close my eyes if I wanted to experience true spirituality. It took me a while—many, many visits, I have to admit. I would keep opening one eye to see what the heck was going on," Loveleen said as she smiled. "Not anymore. Now I am here to pray for this baby, and if closed eyes is what it takes, then just watch me."

Once inside, they found a spot on a dark vermillion carpet close to the singers. They were all dressed in deep green silk outfits and warming up. Three of the men were checking the sound of their harmonium.

"Where is Eshaan? I thought you said he would be coming." Kitt could no longer contain herself.

Loveleen laughed so loudly that people turned to stare and give her the "be quiet or leave" look.

"Hmmm, why so much interest in my Eshaan? What I thought you were going to say is that if Nikki *baba* was here, he would really enjoy this."

Kitt moved closer to Loveleen as a woman pushed her way in and sat down next to Kitt. The shrine seemed to suddenly vibrate as the singers began to belt out tales of love and peace. The hall was packed with people from wall to wall, without even an inch of empty space.

"Loveleen, I don't understand a word they are saying. What language are they singing in? What are they singing about?" Kitt whispered as she looked around.

Several people around her moved their hands up toward the sky as though asking for prayers to be granted. Some were crying, some telling their loud children to be quiet. This supposedly magical place was making her increasingly uncomfortable. The resident chaos, strangely, calmed the energy in the room.

The woman, who had squeezed in earlier, leaned over to Kitt and whispered, "I heard what you said to your friend. They are singing in Urdu, but you know this isn't something you understand. It is something you feel. Breathe in the spirit of the saint and you will forever be healed."

Kitt turned her face to Loveleen and rolled her eyes. The only thing she was breathing in was the smell of sweat mixed with incense and fried garlic from the food vendors outside.

Loveleen put her arm around Kitt. "The sounds you are hearing is the universal voice of prayer. Just close your eyes and say your own prayers."

The singers got louder. People began to sway, the rhythm palpable, the beat seeming to go in tandem with the beats of the heart, and the entire room buzzed with a pulsating spirit.

"I have found that people generally pray for money, health, and love. Pick which one you want and pretend they are singing about it," Loveleen added, noting the annoyed look on Kitt's face. She then closed her eyes, placing both her hands on her stomach.

Kitt closed her eyes. She tried to tune out the noise of the children, the people around her. She focused her mind on the voice of the singer, but she found herself getting anxious. She thought of leaving, but then she heard a vibrant melodious voice singing in Hindi. It was an intoxicating male voice singing about his lost love and praying to God to give him strength.

The voice sounded so familiar. It was more vibrant than the other singers she had heard earlier in the night.

Kitt remembered her mother telling her about a legendary

Indian singer, Tansen, who sang in Mughal emperor Akbar's court. Folklore had it that Tansen's voice was so powerful that once during a singing competition, the sound of his voice melted marble slabs. Kitt had always laughed at that old tale, but today, sitting in this *dargah*, listening to this powerful voice vibrating through the air, Kitt reconsidered it. Perhaps the melting of the marble was figurative for the ability to touch the innermost part of your heart and caress it with sweet vibrations.

Kitt opened her eyes to see who it was. There were so many people surrounding the singer. They were singing with him, swaying with him. Then she saw him, singing and dancing in his own world, oblivious to the people around.

"Oh, my God, it is Eshaan! I had no idea. He sings?!" Kitt asked as she felt her entire body tense and then relax.

She didn't understand how he could be so happy. He was dancing and singing, and his kitchen, his dream, had just been shut down. Then his words from earlier in the week rang in her mind. "*A crushed rose still has its fragrance to share.*"

She wanted to push the crowds away, to go to him, to touch him, one time . . . just one more time.

He swayed and sang as though he was in a trance, his body moving to the music, his eyes closed, his palms pointing skyward. The crowds, captivated by his singing, followed in his footsteps.

Kitt wondered suddenly if her assumption that he was a Buddhist was right. Here he was singing Sufi songs. Then she recalled that her dad had told her once that he had heard Eshaan singing amazing tributes to Lord Krishna at a local Hindu temple.

"Not that it matters, really, Loveleen, but I am curious . . .

what is his religion?" Kitt turned to ask.

Loveleen opened her eyes and beamed a big smile at her friend. "My dear, this happens only in India. All paradoxes are reality. He feels he belongs to all of them. And, wherever he goes, all the people, of different religions, think he belongs solely to them. This is what I love about him." Loveleen smiled at Kitt, and then her friend Eshaan, who had finished singing and was sitting next to an old woman.

The singers were on a break, and Kitt could see that the old woman was crying and Eshaan was trying to comfort her. He was holding a cup and saucer. Kitt saw him pour a little of the liquid from the cup onto the saucer and then feed it to the woman. He kept nodding his head to whatever she was saying and continued to give her, what Kitt assumed, was hot tea.

There was a line forming behind him. It seemed like everyone wanted a piece of him, to talk to him. *He is mine!* Kitt wanted to yell when she saw some beautiful young women approaching him. He smiled at them as they chatted with him. Kitt looked on despondently. Her rose, her crushed rose, magnificent and glorious, wasn't hers anymore.

"He sings, he cooks, he is gorgeous, he is kind, and he is nurturing. Is there anything this man cannot do?" Kitt whispered to Loveleen as she continued to gaze at him.

"Yes, there is one thing he cannot seem to do. He cannot forgive himself for his mother's death," Loveleen whispered back with tears in her eyes. Then she added, "So why aren't you marrying him, Kitt? I know he worships you. Is it because he is a poor, ordinary man? He is a thousand times better than any rich man I know."

The crowds began to thin out. The air was lighter, the smells softer. Eshaan was still sitting with the old lady. A young man brought them a few plastic bags. The lady's face had lit up and she placed her hand on top of Eshaan's head. Kitt knew the culture enough to understand that the old woman was blessing him.

"I am already getting married, Loveleen. You just said you love him. What about you?" Kitt tried her best to be matter-of-fact and avoid answering Loveleen's pointed questions.

"Me? Marry Eshaan? If I could, I would marry him over and over . . . but there is a problem, my dear." Loveleen chuckled.

Eshaan was now at the grave of the Sufi saint buried in the *dargah*. Kitt could only see his back as he bent down in reverence.

"I cannot imagine what that is," Kitt said as she placed her hand on her fast-beating heart.

Loveleen stood up, straightened her shirt, and then replied in a hushed voice, "I cannot lie in the house of God. You see, I cannot marry him, because I am gay."

Eshaan Veer Singh's Journal

I dance all night
To the rhythm of faith
In a place of worship
In a place of grace
The words, they pour out
They mean nothing to me
I am looking for God
Where is he?
He is here, they say, as I dance all night
To their songs of faith and their beat of right
I close my eyes as the music seeps in
I am in a trance
I just want to come alive
Be faithful & He will find, you says the Qazi
Be giving & He will find you, says the priest
Be loving & He will find you, says the saint
Where are you, my God, I seek and don't find
I look for Him high and low
In every step I take
In every place I fall
In every smile I smile
In every song I sing
In every grain I share

In every tear I cry
In every bruise I bear
Then, one night, He appears in my dreams
and laughs and asks
Why do you seek what you've already got?

Chapter 18

The soft light coming into the kitchen cast shadows along the floor that reminded Eshaan of his immense dislike of the whole concept of shadows. It seemed like a betrayal of sorts to him when he was a young child.

"It is mine, so why it is on the ground? I don't want a part of me on the ground like that. Why does this happen?" he'd often ask the monks. Of course, the only answers he ever got were either amused looks or detailed lectures on illusions, and both went over his head.

Today, he wished he could melt into the ground with his shadow. Kitt had texted him the night he sang at the *dargah* to tell him she loved his voice. He had repeatedly sent her responses asking her to talk to him, to come see him, to just respond to his text. She never responded. He kept wavering between wanting to kidnap her and elope, and just plain leaving her forever. His heart made the decision, as he found himself standing outside her bungalow every night and just staring at her window and waiting.

At least all was not lost; Eshaan had finally managed to open the padlocked kitchen. It had been closed for almost two days by that crazy inspector. But it had been open for three days now, and he was doing all he could to get it in shape for the opening. He had been up since five in the morning, trying to refocus his attention on Karma Kitchen. He had swept the floor, and made sure the lentils were cleaned and ready to be cooked. He had also installed a basin right outside the entrance so people could wash their hands and feet before coming in to cook in the kitchen. The students at the monastery, so excited about the birth of this self-funding kitchen, had donated several boxes of liquid hand soap, cloth napkins, and even aprons. It was nice to be in the kitchen that felt warm. Eshaan hadn't slept most of the night; he'd tossed and turned as he tried to warm himself up. He had been feeling unreasonably cold, even in this sweltering Delhi heat.

Eshaan looked around and smiled. The kitchen now seemed remarkably well stocked for a free kitchen. His friends from Nizammuddin had managed to gather enough funds to buy him a large fridge and a deep freezer. All the donations coming in had been enough to fill four large shelves with flour, coffee, rice, and lentils. A mean-looking coconut grater that Tulku Tenzin had drilled into the side of the entrance wall had fallen off and was now fixed in a slightly safer place.

Dr. Sinha had come in two days ago to inspect the kitchen, since he felt it needed an experienced hand. He had not been impressed and had insisted that the kitchen be emptied. Then he brought in painters and a plumber to actually make sure the basin outside (and inside) did not leak. The cream paint opened up the space. Finally, he brought in carpenters who spent a day redoing the shelves and setting up cupboards for the spices. During the renovation of the kitchen, Eshaan tried to avoid asking about Kitt, as much as he wanted to.

"No point in getting close to her. She is getting married, you know," he repeatedly told Lama Dorje and Tulku Tenzin. It got to the point that the two monks teased Eshaan, threatening to break their vow of nonviolence and shake him up a little.

Tomorrow would be the first day they would cook in the new kitchen before opening it up to the public. The thought of that made Eshaan smile. His dream was on the verge of coming true.

All those hours he had worked, cooking at people's homes, the carrom contests, the birthday parties, volunteering at as many free kitchens as he could, everything had been worth it. Every dish he had burned, every time he had run out of food because he could not estimate, every time he had used the wrong ingredient, every time his food had tasted like it was revolting against him, every failure had been worth it. Now he would be able to run his own kitchen and feed people. His mother would have been so proud.

"Where have you been, Eshaan? Have you checked your phone? Lama Dorje has been texting and calling you." Radio Rani entered the kitchen with her hands on her hips and raised her eyebrows.

"Oh!" Eshaan went to one of the tables and picked up his phone.

"The battery is dead. I did not hear him. Thanks. I will go now to see him. Is everything okay?"

Rani just shrugged her shoulders in response.

Eshaan rushed out. Must be important. The old monk had

never sent for him before. He knocked softly on Lama Dorje's closed door.

"Come in," the Lama's firm voice answered.

Lama Dorje's modest office had a table he had built himself, a vase holding a single pink lotus, and then, the wall . . . the wall was what made the room. Lama Dorje, quite the artist, had painted a large Buddha on the wall. The golden Buddha had a gentle golden arc around him. The arc was filled with pictures of fish. "The fish is one of the eight auspicious symbols of Buddhism and represents the soul of an enlightened being, jumping like a fish out of the circular river of *samsara,* the cyclic existence," he had explained to Eshaan.

The painted wall faced the east window, and the rays of the rising sun would make the picture twinkle. The glittering painting was accompanied by the words of the Buddha: WHAT WE THINK, WE BECOME.

"You wanted to see me? All's well?" Eshaan felt the sweat on his brow as he worried that Radio Rani might have spilled his secret. She looked quite cranky when she had come to summon him.

Lama Dorje was seated at his desk. Eshaan sensed there was trouble as the ever-smiling monk frowned.

"Eshaan, please sit down." Lama Dorje pointed to a small chair then walked over to Eshaan and handed him a small book.

"Oh, this is my bank checkbook. Why are you giving it to me?" Eshaan took the book and instantly realized he had been busted. In a way, this was a relief, since it meant Radio Rani kept quiet. This was a matter he could handle.

"Wipe that silly grin off your face, child. Do you know what happened this morning, when I went to the bank to deposit the check for your work here?" Lama Dorje was upset.

Eshaan tried to answer in as soft a voice as he can muster. He hated it when the man he equated to God got angry with him. It wasn't very often. In fact, it had happened only once before, the day he had tried on Tenzin's robe for fun.

"Lama, I've told you I don't want to be paid for working in the monastery. This is my home. Anyway, what happened at the bank?" Eshaan knew the Lama could see right through his lies.

Lama Dorje handed him a note that he received at the bank.

Eshaan's account was empty except for the check deposited this morning.

"That account had over forty thousand rupees, money you have been saving for Karma Kitchen. Money that you need now to pay for some of the things we, or *you*, have ordered. Where is it? What did you do with it, Eshaan? Please tell me you did not play the savior again."

Eshaan stood up and walked to the window so he would not have to face the Lama as he answered. "I am sorry, Lama. I will make it up! I will work some extra hours. I guess I did not realize it was all gone. I thought I only spent some of it. I have work coming up at Gina's dinner theatre, and you know she pays me really well," Eshaan said.

"I know you are a grown man now and that what you do is your business, but—?"

Eshaan reached into his pocket and took out a large key, turned around, and placed it on the Lama's palm.

"What is this?" Lama Dorje looked on quizzically at the key.

"This is what I spent the money on," Eshaan whispered.

The Lama's eyes welled up as he realized the young man had taken his life's savings to "buy" the key that opened the padlocked kitchen.

Chapter 19

Tulku Tenzin had learned to pickle by the time he was ten. Perhaps it was becoming homeless at an early age that made him want to preserve what he could. He always cooked, as the Lama pointed out so eloquently, as he prayed: with reverence and respect. His dedication had nothing to with eating. In fact, much like Eshaan, Tenzin ate very little, but to him, food had the capacity to do something that nothing else could; it provided a bridge, a bond, a way to connect with the spirit of others at the table.

He was on the terrace of the monastery gathering the red chilies he had laid out on the roof. They had dried and become brittle. It was a worthy lesson, he thought. This brittle red skin had more power to light a fire in someone's palate than any of the other spices drying on the roof, which physically appeared more robust and powerful.

He walked around checking the pickling jars that were filled with raw sliced mangos, mustard oil, and the very stinky asafetida, or as Eshaan referred to it, the "smell from hell."

The large terrace was the perfect place for preserving, as it offered the two things his pickles craved: heat and loneliness. The sun provided the heat, and that heat assured that no one in their right mind would come to the terrace and disturb the pickles.

"Tenzin, I want to say sorry," Radio Rani said as she wrung her hands together.

Tenzin turned around, a little startled to see someone on the terrace.

"Sorry? For what? Is everything okay?"

She fidgeted, tugged at her hair, and averted her eyes.

"I have ruined your pickles."

"Wait? What? How did you ruin the pickles? I sealed all the jars . . . and I just checked. None of them has been opened. What happened?" Tenzin asked as gently as he could. His heart ached for this young girl. Eshaan had confided in Tenzin about Rani's acid burns. They had then begged a doctor who used to come to the meditation hall to help Rani. But in the end, the cost of plastic surgery was too much and they could not do anything. Eshaan had vowed to keep trying. Once his kitchen was open, he had said the next round of money would be for her.

Tenzin wondered what she could have possibly done to come all the way up and apologize to him.

Rani, who was never short of an opinion or a long rant, appeared to be having a difficult time finding the words. Tenzin gently prodded her again.

"I have my menses. I came to look for some chilies for Eshaan and then walked near your pickles. In my village, they say a girl with menses can spoil the pickles. I am so sorry. I know how much you care about these."

Tenzin started laughing, and Rani immediately went from

being ashamed to looking horrified.

"Rani, you of all people? Only Merry Mehra says superstitious things like that. You have done nothing, and your personal situation has nothing to do with the pickles. If anything, you bless them by coming up here."

It was clear to him that she wasn't buying what he was selling, but she did offer to help him carry the pickles down the stairs to Karma Kitchen. Opening day was coming up, and they had to be ready.

"You know, Tenzin, if we sold some of these pickles, we could make money to help the kitchen. 'Specially since Eshaan spent most of his savings in bribing that crazy man who locked the kitchen," Rani said as she panted on her way down the stairs.

"You always come up with such practical ideas, but I have never sold anything in my life. How will we sell this?" He was fascinated by this young girl, who seemed to be more business-minded than the entire monastery put together.

"It is simple. You know that store down the street from the new temple? Eshaan was telling me they are making a name for themselves by selling things that are made locally here. You are local, and your pickle is local and delicious . . . maybe . . . you can ask them?"

Chapter 20

The cool breeze woke Eshaan from his restless sleep. He hopped off the bed to go close the window. But instead of rushing back under the covers, he found himself staring out the window at the luscious green of the gardens, a large *tulsi* plant Rani had nurtured to great health, and blossoming jasmine. It had rained all night, and finally, the air seems lighter, as though it has rid itself of the burden of keeping the earth abundant. That sweet smell always reminded him of better days with his mother.

He wished he had a photo of his mother, or something that was hers.

"I've forgotten her face," he told Lama Dorje when he turned thirteen. "I can no longer see her. Do you think the image will ever come back?"

Lama Dorje had hugged him in response. Then he had presented him two Tibetan bracelets made of yak bone and corals. "These will bring peace to your heart." Eshaan had never taken them off.

He could not remember her face, but some days he remembered her words, her voice.

"The *tulsi* nurtures our spirit, Eshaan, so be sure to eat one leaf every day." His mother, Kavya, used to explain each plant to her son as they'd walk the length and breadth of their abundant field. Each petal, each leaf, each twig, it seemed to him, had something to offer. His mother would pick random flowers and announce that they were tasty to eat, or show him strange twigs and tell him that a tea brewed with them could heal broken hearts. But the most magical thing in the field wasn't the harvest, the gorgeous flowers, the butterflies fluttering, the ever-present chirping mynah birds, or the little cadre of white rabbits.

"Smell this? What do you smell?" she asked him once as she thrust a handful of wet dirt under his nose.

"Ma, it's dirt, and smells like dirt!" he'd exclaim.

"This is where the magic lies. This is what makes everything you see here possible," she said and thrust it under his nose again, and he'd roll his young eyes at her.

Eshaan's father, Papa Prakash, worked the fields at the time with other men. During the day, Eshaan's preferred activity was to follow his father around. "When will you learn to use the tractor, Eshaan? You are a young man of five. I think you are ready now," his father often teased him.

Mama Kavya joined them on special days, when Papa Prakash cooked. He could still see his father seasoning, massaging a whole chicken with a very smelly oil. As a child, he failed to understand why the chicken *and* he would be massaged with the same oil, since Mama Kavya massaged that oil into his head at least three times a week. Although his memory of the dish was fading, he did remember his father would throw in different colored powdered spices and large amounts of red chilies onto the chicken, then seal it in flour dough. Then came the best part, the part Eshaan loved as a child. Papa Prakash would give him several newspapers and tell him to wrap the chicken as best as he could. They would dig a deep hole, place in some smoldering coals, and then add in the covered chicken. Eshaan and his mother would help cover it with dirt. "It is all about the fire. Good cooking has everything to do with controlling the fire," Papa Prakash often said.

As if by magic, at dinnertime, when they removed the dirt, the newspaper would be burned off, and the dough and the chicken inside it would be fully cooked.

"To cook well, always respect the earth and remember where your food came from," was the mantra in the house.

Their land seemed particularly blessed that summer. While the other farmers struggled to grow anything, Prakash's land blossomed. Their forefathers had worked hard to create a massive pond in the center of the farm, and now that pond irrigated all ten acres, even during the worst monsoon season of the decade.

"Each grain needs to be worshipped. Each flower needs to be respected. Each blade of grass is the promise of life," Papa Prakash, used to tell him.

As he stood in his room, letting the wind caress his face, Eshaan moved his hand to touch his tattoo. *Rab Rakha.*

The sweet memories faded, and the memories of the horror of his childhood came rushing back. Tears rolled down his cheeks as he recalled how quickly things declined. Once his father left them, the small abundant farm began to fall apart. He did not remember why his father left, only that his mother kept promising Eshaan that Prakash would return. He remembered crying for water as he tried to turn on the rusted metal tap and a few drips of black liquid pushed themselves out through the rusted spout.

In less than a year of his father's leaving, they began to run out of food. Since they could not afford to pay anyone, there was no one to work on the farm, no tools to work with, and nothing left to feed the livestock.

To survive, Mama Kavya had taken a job cooking and cleaning the house for the local doctor. Eshaan accompanied her on her long trek to work and back, his gentle face blistering in the summer heat. Each day, the walk took several hours.

"Oh, how I curse this big field now. Why us? Why is this happening to us? What have we done wrong?" Kavya cried as she hugged her seven-year-old, who now resembled a skeleton more than a little boy.

For the few months she worked there, it appeared things would be fine. The doctor's family let Kavya and Eshaan eat one small meal a day there. Warm breads, a bowl of gingered lentils, and a small raw onion was their princely treat. Once, the lady of the house let him try a chicken nestled in a deep crimson butter and tomato curry, a new dish Kavya had learned to prepare.

"This is the best dish ever, Ma. Why can't you cook like this at home? I am sick of the rice water for dinner."

Mama Kavya had just smiled. "We will eat like this again soon. When your father returns, all will be well."

Soon, the monsoons came, and walking to work became near impossible, so Kavya lost her job. And worse, she refused to leave the house and look for more work.

"We have to wait for your father. He told me to stay here. He told me he would come for us."

Mother and son began to shrivel away inside the closed room with no food or drinkable water. Kavya would not eat anything, but insisted that little Eshaan eat what he could. She hugged him, sang to him, and reminded him again and again to be grateful for each morsel, each drop that passed his lips.

Then one day, as predictable as the rising sun, the disaster that had been looming in the near distance struck hard.

"It is so hot in this room, Ma. Why is your arm so cold? Let me get you a blanket." Eshaan remembered those were the last words he ever said to his mother. She was limp and not moving at all. She was lying on her cot, staring up at the ceiling and not blinking at all.

Sensing something was wrong with her, the little boy had run out to find help. After running for as long as his little feet would carry him, Eshaan reached the end of the field. The road was now in sight. His head hurt, his lips were parched, everything around him was spinning, and he collapsed.

He opened his eyes to see a large red shape bending over him. His hazy eyes couldn't tell if it was a person or an animal. The red shape reached out to him, and Eshaan uttered, "My mother—"

A gust of wind brought some rain in through the window and splashed Eshaan's face. He wiped his tears, closed the window, and turned to his altar. He folded his hands then uttered the prayer he had been waiting to do since the day he turned eleven. *Thank you, God. Today we are having prayers to bless the kitchen and then, tomorrow, we open for the world. Please guide my way.*"

Chapter 21

"Eshaan, come on. We are already here!" Eshaan heard Radio Rani's loud and shrill voice calling out to him as he walked toward Karma Kitchen for the prayer ceremony.

Radio Rani had dressed in a new outfit for the day, a beautiful pink dress. Om had bathed!

Eshaan was touched to see Lama Dorje, several other senior monks, and a handful of monastery students were at the door of the kitchen already.

"Sorry I am a bit late," he said and bowed to the monks as a sign of respect.

Each monk washed his hands and feet at the brand-new basin outside the kitchen. Om repeatedly pointed out that the basins had specifically been designed to have two different types of spouts, one for the hands and the other for the feet. After the monks were done, Eshaan washed his hands and feet, then splashed cold water in his face, hoping it would stop his nausea.

Radio Rani pushed the kitchen door open, and the sight inside was just heartwarming. Each table held flat bowls filled with scores of freshly picked jasmine flowers, marigolds, and even a few pink lotus blooms.

"Oh, this is fantastic. Who did this?" Eshaan turned to the group as he resisted the urge to double down. His stomach had begun to cramp again, and he could feel the world spinning. Instead, he just stood as still as he could and waited for all the monks to enter the kitchen.

He entered the kitchen last and was stunned to see it was already filled with brightly lit *tormas,* homemade lamps crafted with butter and flour. After everyone settled in, the monks began to chant prayers and a vibrant energy filled the room. Each monk walked up to Eshaan and placed a white scarf around his neck, blessing him on his new journey.

"I have something for all of you," Eshaan said as he walked slowly toward the newly installed fridge.

At three in the morning, he had come in and prepared rice *kheer*, the magical dish of blessing and comfort, a combination of rice, milk, sugar, and his homemade rose petal syrup.

He carefully spooned a bit of the *kheer* onto small leaf-bowls. Radio Rani added a flat wooden spoon to each bowl, then handed them out to everyone.

"This is just delightful, Eshaan," one of the older monks remarked, and then added, "Where is your bowl?"

"Oh, I will eat later! I just wanted to thank you all first," said Eshaan.

"Look, look at what Dr. Sinha is bringing!" Rani's shrill voice pierced the peaceful air.

Dr. Sinha, dressed in a bright white starched shirt and khaki pants, was at the entrance of the kitchen, slowly pushing a large cart filled with cauliflowers, okra, potatoes, onions, bell peppers, and what looked like a crate overflowing with fiery green chilies.

"Eshaan, Lama Dorje told me that you are starting up tomorrow. We must have food ready! So I bought the whole cart of vegetables. Now, let's cook," Dr. Sinha beamed.

Everyone in the room clapped.

Dr. Sinha's love of cooking had become legendary in these parts. Of course, no one except him could actually eat anything he cooked. His idea of a mild dish was one that had at least ten super-hot green chilies, and he insisted that every dish prepared for him needed to be tempered with heated ghee, crushed garlic, green chilies, cumin, and yes, more deep red chilies. He added the tempering to pretty much any dish cooked in the house, including, but not limited to, Indian curries, Italian pastas, Austrian schnitzel, and even the already spicy Thai curries.

"Dr. *Ji*, you have already spent so much on redoing this kitchen. I am already in your debt." Eshaan looked at the large cart in disbelief. Was he really worthy of all this generosity that people showered on him? He took a deep breath and reminded himself that this generous gift was not for him; it was for the kitchen. And yes, those who would come to the kitchen *did* deserve a good meal.

"You have a donation bowl outside. Shall I just turn around and go put everything in that?!" Dr. Sinha laughed and called out to Radio Rani to help him take the vegetables off the cart and onto the main cooking area.

Everyone jumped in. Tulku Tenzin took over washing the vegetables, while Lama Dorje and Radio Rani began to chop. Loveleen entered the room a few minutes later and began firing off instructions to anyone and everyone about anything and everything.

Eshaan noticed Kitt had come too, but was standing at the door, hesitating to come in.

"Kitt, come in and bless this lovely kitchen," Lama Dorje said. She smiled and nervously entered.

The whole room hummed with grace, and even Mother Nature cooperated, sending in cool breezes and soft sunshine. The gentle aroma of the sun-kissed flowers in the room, the sharper aroma of the frying onions, and Eshaan's own *itar* of the wet earth all mixed together.

Eshaan centered himself, closed his eyes, and took a few deep breaths. This was the scent of abundance, the scent of being nurtured, the scent he hoped he could share and pass on to as many people as possible.

"Eshaan, what do you want me to do with all this cauliflower?" Radio Rani called out to him.

"Oh, ask Tulku Tenzin. He is going to make a dish with cauliflower and the *tulsi* holy basil leaves." Eshaan stepped forward, gave her a hug, and whispered into her ear, "I love you, Rani, for not telling Lama Dorje my . . . my problem."

Radio Rani shrugged away from him and was about to say something, when Eshaan placed a finger on her lips.

"Later, okay?"

Tulku Tenzin was now chopping onions and tomatoes. Radio Rani diced the cauliflower. Dr. Sinha was instructing Om on how to store the large amount of produce he had so enthusiastically purchased.

"What are we cooking? These guys are already working, and I have no idea what you even want to cook!" Loveleen asked Eshaan.

"We all decided the first meal we cook today will be for you and the baby. None of this would have been possible without you. You sit down here and just relax, and we will do the work," Eshaan responded.

"Eshaan, you have *failed* on your first day! Isn't this Karma Kitchen? Isn't this where people are supposed to work to earn their food? If I just sit here, how will I drum up any karma?" Loveleen smiled, picked up a large steel bowl, and then added a hefty amount of flour into it. "I will make the dough for the bread. You all cook with the spices. I just cannot deal with those smells right now."

The kitchen began buzzing with energy as each person helped bring Eshaan's dream to life.

One of the students from the monastery complained about the lack of quality spices in the kitchen and rolled her eyes at the modest amounts of rice and flour in the kitchen.

"May I just say something? I know we don't have enough, but we have to be grateful for what we do have," Eshaan said to the student, who looked skeptical.

"In fact, I say a prayer for the spices, sparse as they may be, to help heal the person who eats the food. That reminds me. I have only one rule in this kitchen. The cooks' energy gets passed into the dishes. Only food prepared with love will nurture. If not, it will just be another meal," he said, placing his hand on his heart.

"You are becoming like Lama Dorje, Eshaan. Soon, only you will understand all your philosophies," joked Loveleen, much to the delight of those in the room.

"What are you making, Eshaan?" asked Kitt. She was

standing next to him as he shimmered some pure ghee and added whole black cardamom, cinnamon, dark black cloves, and green cardamom to the pot. He leaned in to smell the spices. Then he turned the stove off and strained the oil into a bowl.

"This seasoned oil will be used to dress the white rice. A drop of this and the rice turns from plain to divine."

Kitt leaned over to smell it, and he could feel her breath on his arm. He gently edged away.

"We are not just cooking for today, but remember we are preparing for tomorrow," he announced without looking at her.

"Eshaan, I want to ask you something," Kitt leaned over and whispered to him.

He stopped chopping the eggplant and looked up at her. "Yes, what is it? Is it about catering for the wedding?" His words were laced with sarcasm.

Kitt shook her head. "Loveleen told me she is gay. I am sure you know, right? I just read a story on the plane that homosexuality is considered an offence in India. Does she know that? Is she safe here?" Kitt whispered so only he could hear her.

Eshaan stopped chopping and looked Kitt in the eye. "Yes. I worry about her sometimes, especially with hate-mongers like that Mr. Mehra who stays in your building."

Kitt tapped on the table. "How is she pregnant??"

"She went to some baby-making clinic in South Extension. Saachi is planning to move in soon. Saachi is her partner."

Then he added in a very quiet voice, "You never returned my calls or messages. And now, you are getting married?"

Kitt turned her head so she would not have to look at him. "I owe him a lot, Eshaan. He cared for me so much after my accident."

"Loveleen told me about your accident. Looks like you recovered," Eshaan said as he massacred the already chopped eggplants. He wanted to yell at her, to push her away, to pull her close, to hurt her feelings, to love her forever. But the monks were in the room, and Eshaan tried to keep his hand moving, his mouth shut, and his eyes averted.

"Eshaan, I don't mind helping and all, but it is really hot in here. Is it too much to ask to get some fans in here? I don't think we can work in this heat." Loveleen rolled her eyes in mock anger and pointed to the sweat stains on everyone's shirts.

"All you have to do is ask," came the loud and cheery response.

Everyone turned to see Lama Dorje at the entrance. He had left a while ago and was now back, holding four small table fans. "I know you have that old cooler there, but it is no match for this heat."

Eshaan looked surprised. "Lama Dorje, where did you get those from? I know the account—"

"Ah, you know. Sometimes it pays to be nice to people who sell junk at the Chore Bazaar. This kid I know, who comes in here every once in a while to meditate, told me about these fans. I got them very cheap, but you still have to pay me. I bring you fans. That is my contribution to your bowl. My fee: a full plate of food."

Eshaan walked over to Lama Dorje and bowed in gratitude.

"You don't need my blessings, my child. You have the Buddha in your heart. He will always guide your way. I only give you this advice. Just remember the snake must shed its old skin in order to get a new one."

Eshaan wanted to ask the Lama what that meant, but at the moment, he needed to return to his station to finish cooking the eggplant.

Kitt was still standing there. "Eshaan, I hope you know how proud I am of you. It is really commendable that you are doing this," Kitt tried to talk to him again. She touched his shoulder and whispered her words in a soft, loving voice.

"Please don't patronize me. I've already agreed to cook for your wedding. Happy?" he said in a pained voice, reached up to his shoulder, and harshly pushed her hand away.

Unable to contain herself, Kitt stormed out of the kitchen with tears in her eyes.

Eshaan Veer Singh's Journal

How can a promise never made
A love never affirmed
The shattering of an unspoken bond
Be upsetting
My broken heart
Seeks refuge
My mind says my fate lies in the cracks
In the wounds
A crafted life isn't mine
There is no solace in tears
There is no peace in serenity
There is only me and
the unmade promise
I search in the wrong places
I hurt in the right ones

Chapter 22

"What new hell is this?" Kitt said, as loud screaming startled her out of her chair.

She had been looking through the various albums that Dr. Sinha had insisted she review. Four of the five albums belonged to wedding florists, and one belonged to a local henna artist. Dr. Sinha had another set, featuring live bands and dance troupes for weddings, which he wanted her to review.

Kitt put the album down and listened to the loud voices again. Yes, it was Loveleen.

The previous night had been hard.

Eshaan just did not understand why she was getting married. And neither did Loveleen.

"Kitt, my love, Saachi, will come live here with me as soon as the baby comes. We will be together. We will be happy. *You,* on the other hand, will be with a guy whom I know you don't love," Loveleen had said. "Eshaan is madly in love with you, but he thinks he isn't worthy. You have to take the first step. He won't do it. 'Specially since he believes your Nikki *baba* can give you a better life than he can."

Kitt had tossed and turned all night looking for reassurance from the skies above, from her dreams, from anything or anyone, that she had indeed made the right decision.

Early in the morning, several large bouquets of roses had shown up at her doorstep with a note from Nikolas saying how sorry he was that he had to leave, but he knew she understood that the big deal he was about to sign would take care of them for a long time.

"I know how to take care of the likes of you," Loveleen's loud, screeching voice brought Kitt back to the moment. She habitually sent a text message to Eshaan letting him know a new battle seemed to be brewing. She hit send, then wondered if she had made a mistake. Then she reminded herself this was not about her. It was about Loveleen.

Kitt rushed to the door. Loveleen had switched from English to her native Punjabi, as she often did when she was really angry. Kitt could not make out a word of what she was saying, so she asked one of the servants who was standing by the door and listening.

"She is complaining about rice," was the response.

Rice? At eight-thirty in the morning?

Kitt rushed out of the house and into the open courtyard.

Loveleen was standing in the center of the courtyard, one hand firmly planted on her hip, and with her other hand, and she was pointing to a bag of rice in front of her and screaming.

"Oh, Kitt, I am so glad you are awake. Look at this, look," she squawked. "That mad Mehra left this at my door. Do you know what a bad omen it is to leave uncooked rice at someone's door?"

Loveleen was not one to be easily frightened, and Kitt was taken aback at her friend's strong reaction. "Loveleen, you know this means nothing. Nothing at all, right? Come on, come inside and let me make you something to drink," she offered then realized she had spoken too soon.

A black snake came wriggling out of the bag of rice.

Loveleen screamed, turned around, and ran out of the courtyard. Kitt stood there frozen as the snake slithered out.

Radio Rani, who had heard the commotion, was at the main gate already. "That is a bad omen for a lady who is expecting," she said, pointing to the snake.

"Rani, pick it up and throw it away," Eshaan said in a loud and stern voice from the gate. Rani swung into action and swooped up the snake by its head.

"Don't look so worried. Rani is an expert at catching snakes. Also, this snake is not poisonous," Eshaan said to the terrified crowd looking on.

"Why would Mehra do this?" Kitt was stunned. "Loveleen thought rice brought bad luck? But, why the snake? I don't understand."

"In these parts, it is considered bad luck for a pregnant woman to see a snake. I think that bastard Mehra is just getting back at her, because she walks around with that black cat in her arms." Eshaan was shaking his head, but Kitt noticed he still wasn't looking at her.

"We need to stop this. She won't let go, and neither will he. I worry what will happen after the baby comes," Eshaan said as an afterthought then left to go find Loveleen.

"Eshaan, wait. I will come with you," Kitt said, hoping to talk to him. They made their way outside in silence and walked slowly, really slowly. She walked close to him, just so their arms touched. He smelled of his morning run, a habit she knew well. She used to run with him. Now, they walked, content in each other's silence, at least for this one moment. Instinctively, his hand slipped into hers.

"I open Karma Kitchen today . . . in about an hour," he said.

"I know. It will be a success. You have put your heart into it," she replied.

"Yes, indeed, my heart is in it," he said as he brought her hand to his lips. He squeezed it so tightly she was almost afraid he would break it.

"Do you love him, Kitt?" he asked in a soft voice, but got no answer. Instead, she just squeezed his hand.

They saw Loveleen sitting out on the bench in the monastery gardens, crying. Radio Rani was standing at her side, and Lama Dorje was there as well, with his hand on her shoulder. Her body shook as she sobbed.

"How could he do this, Lama Dorje? A snake? What if I had been bitten? What if—"

"Child, now stop crying. He is a fool, but you are no less. Why do you *interact* with him? You instigate him, and he retaliates. Look at you. You ran out of that courtyard so fast. What if you had fallen?" Lama Dorje asked in a soft voice. He patted Loveleen on the head then headed back into the monastery for morning prayers.

Radio Rani was busy belting out new ways to annoy Mehra, and Om, who had just come in, joined her tirade.

Eshaan sat down next to Loveleen on the bench and put his

arm around her shoulders.

"I promise that after the baby comes, you and I can do something big together to annoy him! But right now, no more pranks with Mehra, okay?" Eshaan whispered with such gentle kindness that despite her hate for Mehra, Loveleen nodded in agreement. And then suddenly began smiling and giggling.

"Eshaan, put your hand on my belly! The baby is kicking! I can feel it!"

As much as he loved Loveleen, he hesitated to touch her belly. He was, he feared, too tarnished.

Eshaan Veer Singh's Journal

Don't come so close
I sense a dream
I sense an awakening
A new life
One that will fulfill
The promises that were made
To you
A new life of laughter
Of smiles and love
A new life of promises
Of precious moments to behold
Don't come so close
I fear my touch
May tarnish your womb
My energy may seep in
And destroy the bloom
You keep coming so close
That I am tempted to believe
Whom God protects
No one can harm
Or so my mother would tell

Chapter 23

Buddha's Karma Kitchen was now on its third day and open to the public.

The first day of the opening, there was a kilometer-long line of people wanting to come in and eat.

"You want us to cook?" some asked Eshaan.

"I haven't had a single morsel in two days, and you want me to cook? What kind of charity is this?" asked another.

Asking some of the people to wash their hands and feet before coming into the kitchen was, apparently, akin to asking them to part with their soul.

Yet there were others who decided to bathe in the sink, others decided the water was cleaner than any water they had ever seen, so they started drinking it. Still others complained of wasting water to wash, when it should be preserved for drinking.

Then there were the few who decided they could sit in the kitchen the entire day to be first in line for the next meal.

Radio Rani repeatedly hounded Eshaan about the hygiene of those coming in to eat.

"Their clothes, their hair are all laced with lice. They need water, a home, a livelihood . . . What is a free meal going to do for them?" Her concern, he knew, reflected her own position a few years ago, when he had found her. As cynical as she pretended to be, he knew Rani's heart was filled with compassion and sadness that they weren't able to help these people dealing with the most wretched of human conditions.

What surprised Eshaan the most was not the fact they were quickly running out of food, but that the line of beggars was inside the monastery, and it was disturbing and even destroying the serenity and sacredness of the complex. One man had actually urinated in the line during his waiting time. Another woman kept sending her child back for more food, and the child was barely two, if not younger. A young man kept smoking cheap cigarettes and throwing them on the sacred grounds.

And then there were the local thugs. The useless few who made their living by creating a fear in the local community.

Eshaan and Om had argued about whether to let these thugs in for a free meal. Eshaan wanted to feed them for the sake of keeping peace, but Om was adamant the thugs should not be let in, as they were fully capable of finding work and making money. In the end, at least for that day, Eshaan won that argument.

Only two people, a young man with a bad leg and a very old man with a hunched back, actually helped. The young man swept the kitchen and learned how to chop an onion. The old man did not want anything to eat, but just sat there, peeled and chopped potatoes, and drank all the cold water they offered him.

One young child had come in, and after taking in all the smells, said, "I will bring my mother here. She can work here instead of outside in the heat at the construction site." Eshaan waited and waited, hoping to save at least someone's mother, but the child never returned.

Today, the line was comprised of a few beggars, but mostly those working at a local construction site. They told Eshaan they didn't make enough money in a day to prepare even one meal. Most of them lived in a small makeshift tent next to the construction site. Their babies crawled around in the dirt of the bricks and boulders, being used to create magnificent towers.

Eshaan wanted to ask them to work in the kitchen, as per his original plan, and then he saw their hands, calloused, bleeding, with sand and stones that appeared embedded within their palms. He thought of his mother almost immediately, then said, "Please eat as much and when you want. No need to do anything here." So now, with his blessings, the construction workers ate at Karma Kitchen in the morning to have strength to work with boulders and stones all day. And then they ate there at night, so they could sleep with a full stomach.

"How do we take care of the babies outside?" he had asked Tenzin, and they realized that anything they wanted to do was going to cost them money they did not have. "Perhaps this dream is just too big for me, for us. I have failed before even starting out," he lamented.

During his early morning run, he had tried to focus on the babies and to figure out how he could help them. It bothered him that he, the one who wanted to be the helper of the poor, the champion of the downtrodden, the healer, had failed to notice the babies before. How could he be that blind? Had his vision obscured the reality so much that he now only saw what he wanted to see? The run had worn him out and caused him to throw up as some serious nausea made a home in his chest. Again. He blamed the unrelenting heat.

Now, as he watched the line of people coming to eat, his dream of a self-funding kitchen was looking more like the beginning of a nightmare, and there appeared to be no practical solution in sight.

Eshaan went to check the big bamboo bowl outside the kitchen to see what people had donated this morning. He found the bowl to be mostly bare, three bags of rice, two bags of lentils, and a few bottles of milk.

"Eshaan, the man who came to drop this off was telling me this is the last time he will come, because no one else is coming." Om rolled his eyes as he helped Eshaan take the ingredients into the kitchen. The milk was going to go to the small babies outside. Rani had been tasked with finding small baby bottles at the junk market.

As the men arranged the meager ingredients on the shelf, Eshaan noticed that Om's shirt was torn and ripped in many places. Om explained that while Eshaan was cooking inside last night, a small fight had broken out in front of Karma Kitchen. People in line had begun to brawl with each other to get in before the kitchen closed. He had tried to stop the craziness, and in return, an old woman had ripped his shirt.

Eshaan told Om to continue to line the shelves as he disappeared into the inner core of the monastery. He returned five minutes later with a clean white shirt.

"Please wear this, and I am sorry about the fight yesterday. We will just have to figure out how to solve this problem," he said, handing the shirt to Om.

The young boy took it. "It is the biggest problem in our country, you know."

"What is? Hunger?" Eshaan asked.

Om laughed.

"No. Not hunger. Lack. Lack is the problem. You know the saying, 'There is one pomegranate, and hundred people who want it.'"

He then took the shirt and said, "Oh, and thank you for this. I have never owned a new shirt before. Now I have two shirts!" Om thanked him again and rushed back out, as the line outside the door was already long and he knew people would start getting impatient.

Breakfast at the kitchen today was some griddle breads topped with home-churned butter and a few drops of honey.

Eshaan and Tenzin cooked as fast as they could while Rani served the food. Not one single person in line offered to help, or even wanted to make eye contact. They simply ate and left.

Tenzin wiped his sweat with a large towel that he kept handy. The kitchen, even with its fans and cooler, was really hot to work in. He did not mind though.

When Tenzin had first arrived at the monastery, he wasn't sure he would stay. He had been one of several refugees coming in from Tibet. His family had been dispersed, and only he and his brother were in the group that was sent to Delhi. His brother, who was much older than him, had moved to Dharmsala to study directly under the Dalai Lama. Tenzin was upset at first, but then happy when he learned he would have kitchen duty and could cook if he stayed in the monastery in Delhi. His duties now combined the two ways he wanted to help people: one by feeding them, and the second by helping them meditate when he played his heart meditations on his Tibetan bowls.

But at the moment, the Tibetan singing bowls were the furthest thing from his mind. He worried Eshaan was being too impatient and looking for success too quickly. Also, he rarely seemed well these days. Eshaan, it seemed to him, wanted everyone who came in to be filled with gratitude, to have the motivation to be a part of the kitchen, to earn instant karma—many of which were going to be very difficult if not unfeasible propositions. Regardless, Tenzin vowed to help his friend, and that is what he would do.

The breakfast crowd was gone, and Rani, Eshaan, and Tenzin cooked in the kitchen's quiet belly for two hours until they were ready to open for lunch.

The lunch line, as with breakfast, was out the door, and the minute the door opened, a flood of people walked in to have the chance to get a fully cooked, clean, hygienic meal.

"Eshaan, I've never tasted anything quite so sweet. You are a good man."

Eshaan looked up from the stove to see who was talking to him. It was the old man who had been peeling potatoes for the past three days. Radio Rani was sitting next to him, breaking pieces of bread and placing them in his hand. The man had not eaten anything for the past few days, only asking for chilled water.

"This is the first time in my entire life that someone has fed me as a human being and not as a dog," he said as a tear rolled down his cheek.

Eshaan went up to the old man and sat next to him. "What

is your name?" he asked as he offered the old man another glass of water.

The man took the glass and gulped the chilled liquid. "I don't know. I am sure I have a name, but I don't remember it," he said as he took another piece of bread from Rani's outstretched hand.

"That is okay. What shall we call you?" Eshaan asked with a tender smile.

"Potato *Baba*!" Rani said with a smile. "Just like my tribe would do!" The old man looked confused, but then Rani explained the strange custom of her tribe. He smiled. The first smile they had seen in the kitchen.

"Yes, give me more potatoes and I will peel them. I'm the Potato *Baba*!" the man said.

Tenzin called out to him to come over. "We are out of food now, Eshaan. What do you want to do?"

And it took under a few seconds for those words to cause chaos inside the kitchen. Tenzin quickly realized what he had done and apologized profusely for making the announcement out loud. People in line pushed each other out of the way to get in as Eshaan rushed over to the door to try to settle them down.

"Sorry, we cannot take any more now," Eshaan said to those trying to get in as he attempted to close the door.

"Please, listen to me," he pleaded. "Come back for dinner. We are out of food for lunch."

Amidst all the curses that began to be hurled at him, a woman in line walked up to him and spat in his face for giving her false hope. Two of the older beggars began to weep and fell at Eshaan's feet.

"Please, don't say no to us. We came here from the other side of the city. We were told you would feed us." Eshaan bent down to pull them up and looked helplessly at Tenzin, who looked pained.

Eshaan stood still and tried to block out the noises in his head, the sounds of breaking dreams and the crumbling of unfulfilled promises.

"Give them whatever we have that they can eat," he said to his crew. Rani began handing out cucumbers, small tomatoes, a few pieces of old bread, and whatever else she could find. Tenzin ran to the monastery kitchen to see if there were leftovers he could use.

They served the crowd what they could, and when the kitchen cleared, the three of them looked at each other wondering what to do. Radio Rani began to sweep the floor. Tenzin washed the utensils to get ready for the next round, knowing full well all they had on hand was a bag of rice and a few peeled potatoes.

Eshaan debated what to do, then shook off the questions and set his mind to the task at hand: to roast and grind the spices that would be used to cook dinner. He started with the coriander, cumin, and fennel seed mixture that was his favorite. He placed all the seeds on a warm skillet, and instantly a toasty aroma filled the room. He closed his eyes and inhaled. Could the smell of roasting spices heal a worried heart? Today was the first day the smell hadn't made him run toward the woods wanting to throw up.

"Oh, that smells so good," Rani said, looking up from her sweeping.

Eshaan stirred the spices with a wooden spoon. He lifted the skillet, transferred the spices to a deep marble mortar, and brought out his personal and prized pestle to grind them. The mortar and pestle were his only personal purchase, ever. He had bought the set on his sixteenth birthday with money he had earned from working at the monastery. He had placed it on an altar near his bed.

"It does smell good, but it is worthless. We have nothing left to cook. How are we going to make a bag of rice feed hundreds of people?" Eshaan sighed.

Chapter 24

"Rani? Rani?" Tenzin looked around for his helper.

"Oh, Tulku Tenzin, can you come here please?" she responded, calling him to a secret conversation she was having with Om. With nothing to guard in the donation bowl, Om had come inside to get some respite from the heat. Potato *Baba* was sound asleep in one corner of the kitchen.

Eshaan's phone had been ringing off the hook all afternoon, and he had finally stepped outside the kitchen to return the calls, as the mobile signal inside was terrible.

"What is it?" Tenzin asked after joining the conversation.

"Well, something really stinks. I have been standing guard outside, as you know, and I have been watching these people come in. They behave so badly in here, and yet, when they leave, I see them laughing and being normal. Something isn't right," Om repeated what he had just told Radio Rani.

Tenzin laughed.

"You are thinking there is some conspiracy here?"

They both nodded.

"You cannot be serious!" Tenzin said, looking rather

concerned. He refused to indulge in any gossip and began to walk back to the stove. There was much work to be done for the next meal, as meager as it was going to be.

"Wait, wait, okay, maybe we are wrong about the conspiracy part, but this thing is failing, and when it finally crashes, which it will very soon, it will kill Eshaan. Isn't there anyway we can help him?" Om asked.

"I will change my name if the vendors outside the monastery aren't behind this. Eshaan doesn't realize he is hurting their business," Rani said then explained that she had seen the egg-cart guy getting really upset when he saw the construction workers come into the monastery to eat for free. "They were his regular bread and butter, and now for three days, no one is buying anything from him and he is really upset."

That made a lot of sense to Tenzin, but he had to tell Om repeatedly that beating up the egg-cart vendor and others was not the answer.

"So what do we do? Nothing?" Rani said as she sat down on one of the chairs.

"Well, we cannot do nothing. We have to get ready for dinner," Tenzin started to look uneasy.

Om shook his head.

"Dinner? It will be another disaster. Have you seen the line outside? They all look hungrier and more annoyed than they did this morning."

"Wait, I have an idea. I am going to go out. Rani, can you take over the kitchen? We are only making rice and lentils, so you can handle that, right?" Tenzin looked quizzically at Rani.

"I can. You know how to help?"

Tenzin smiled and dashed out of the kitchen, with Om cheering him on, and Rani and Om wondering what he would do.

Eshaan passed Tenzin flying out at lightning speed.

"Where did you get all that?" Rani and Om both said as they rushed to help Eshaan bring in the armload of vegetables he was carrying in.

Eshaan smiled radiantly.

"You know my friend Gina, right? She runs the fancy dinner theatre, Bollywood Ballads? I learned to cook there. Well, I told her we were running low on food, so she sent her driver to bring us vegetables from her farm. Om, there are more boxes outside," Eshaan said proudly. He deftly avoided Radio Rani's eyes, because he knew she would insist this was just another Band-Aid on a badly bleeding wound.

His thoughts turned back to Gina. Most of the calls he had missed that morning were from her. He adored her boisterous nature; her ability to make people laugh and her prowess in bed were probably things that legends were made of. Gina was Italian by birth, but had lived in Delhi most of her life and could give any Delhi-ite a run for their money, as far as loving the city was concerned. She walked her talk, celebrating Delhi's colorful history at her dinner theatre that ran to sold-out crowds. Eshaan loved the highly trained chefs Gina always hired for her events. Every single chef taught him something new. He learned how to use a knife (and to not leave it lying around), he learned how to roast kebabs in a tandoor (and not complain about burning the hairs on his arms in the process), he became an expert at combining spices (and learned not to ignore roasting spices for even a second), and he learned that the power of the food was not just in the taste, but in the presentation. At the dinner theatre he could cook what he wanted, as the monastery had strict rules: meats and alcohol were not permitted on the premises and Eshaan respected that.

Ah, Gina. She had even forgiven him for the night, now a lifetime ago, when he had just not shown up for an event where he was to be the sous chef. It was that night when he and Kitt had discovered how much they loved each other. It was the first time he had made love to her.

It had taken weeks of apologizing, but Gina had finally forgiven him for bailing on her. She truly was one of the most generous souls he had ever met. He felt bad taking advantage of the fact she loved him, instead telling himself all this was for the greater good of the people he was trying to help.

"Wow, these vegetables are fantastic!" Rani clapped, and Om ran out to get more of the vegetables.

Eshaan hadn't eaten all day and decided to brew some tea for all of them.

"Oh, it smells wonderful in here, Eshaan. It is as though the blessings are swirling in here, posing as these soft smells and ready to embrace anyone who enters," Lama Dorje said as he stepped inside. Eshaan was delighted to see the Lama, who had been away for three days now. It was his first visit to the working kitchen.

"Please come have some tea," Eshaan offered and poured the brewing tea into two cups. He added a touch of sugar, a dash of ground cinnamon, and then handed one cup to the Lama.

"Lama, this kitchen is not running as I imagined. I could just as well go down the street and give filled plates to the beggars sitting in front of the temple."

Lama Dorje's eyes lit up and he smiled. "And what is wrong with that?" he asked.

Eshaan was visibly irritated. His entire body tensed up, he cocked his head to one side, and he asked in a sharper voice, "What do you mean? This is different. This is not a handout. I want them to come in here and work for a meal. I am not sure why you are implying this is nothing more than a free-food place."

Lama Dorje sipped his tea as he let the wave of irritation wash over Eshaan.

"Anyway, you are going to have another headache soon," the Lama said and went on to explain that in three days, the free kitchen had consumed more water than the monastery did in a month, and that their already measly water supply would run out soon. Eshaan would need to find an alternate way to serve the food, as it was the dishwashing that was taking up most of the water.

"How am I going to solve that on top of everything else?" Eshaan said, holding his head in his hands and pursing his lips.

Lama Dorje's phone rang. "I have to leave now. I may need to head back to Dharamsala for ten days. In the meantime, do you know where you can find the answer to your questions?"

Eshaan cracked a small smile. "Yes, I know where, Lama. I should meditate and go into silence. Right?"

"Well, you can do that, if you like. But I was going to suggest Google," the old man said.

"Yes, Lama Dorje," Eshaan said, rather unconvincingly, as

the monk laughed all the way out the door.

This day was going from frustrating to aggravating. To top it all off, Loveleen had texted him a few minutes ago to let him know that Nikolas was coming back earlier than planned.

"When all else fails, cook!" Tenzin had once told Eshaan.

So he decided to follow his friend's advice and do the only thing he could: he began chopping the okra. The mynah bird outside the windowsill sang a sweet song as the summer sun settled down. Eshaan walked over to the entrance of the kitchen every once in a while and tried to keep his composure as he saw the line outside getting longer and longer.

He was so lost in his ingredients that he didn't notice Loveleen and Kitt come in.

"It smells divine in here. What are you cooking, *Jaan*?" Loveleen asked, addressing him, as she often did, with a term of endearment meaning life.

Kitt chimed in, "It is my favorite okra dish! He made it for me a few times when I was here last time. Don't you remember? I ate almost all of it, and he freaked out because there was nothing left for anyone else."

The girls came up to him and tried to distract him as he fried the okra in a large wok filled with hot oil.

"You ladies need to leave right now. I have work to do. Did you not see the line outside?" he said, trying to fake some anger. The last thing he needed right now was Kitt standing there telling him how much she loved his cooking. It was like what Tulku Tenzin always said about putting butter on a burn. It hurt.

The girls ignored his rude remarks and walked over to the cutting boards.

"What can we do to help so we can eat here?" Kitt asked as she picked up two tomatoes. Loveleen busied herself with picking the leaves of several stalks of cilantro.

"Come on, spit it out, Eshaan. What is bothering you? You look like hell today," Loveleen muttered as she sat down on a large stool and continued to pick the leaves.

At first, Eshaan wanted to tell them to leave again, but then one look at Kitt and his resolve melted. She was wearing a red dress. Actually, she was wearing *the* red dress. It could be a coincidence. It was what she was wearing the first time he kissed her. The soft dress had rubbed against his rough arms. That kiss, his first ever, was nothing like he had dreamed it would be like. Except, he reminded himself, she was now another man's dream and he needed to stop dreaming about her. He stomped on his left foot using his right, a physical reminder that he should not dare go up and hug her, and hold her, and—

Besides, he was upset that the two of them had disappeared over the past two days after the snake incident and had not come in to see him. A bit of spying, asking Om, and interrogating Radio Rani had revealed that Loveleen had taken Kitt to meet Saachi at some faraway resort, away from prying eyes and interfering relatives.

Eshaan continued to fry the okra and began to explain, yet again, the issues of the kitchen.

"So this kitchen has caused you a lot of pain," Kitt said, and then looked at Loveleen, who added, "So what are you going to do about it? Are you just going to stay in pain, or are you actually going to do something to fix this place?"

"Well, ladies, if it was that easy, don't you think I would have fixed it by now?" Eshaan asked as he slammed his hand on the table.

"Oh, don't be so sensitive. Everyone told you this would be hard. But instead of rising to the challenge, you are becoming a victim. Of course it is easier than actually, you know, becoming a hero," Loveleen said.

Om and Rani joined in as well. "Yes, Eshaan, what are you going to do?"

"Well, since I have no money, no way of making money, and at this point, no help, I think I will go find my friend Raju and drink."

The girls giggled.

"I am so glad that I am amusing you," Eshaan said with a smirk as he used a slotted spoon to take the fried okra out of the hot oil and place it on a tray.

"Oh, stop being so oversensitive. We are here, because we have a way to solve all your problems. Here, take a look at this," Kitt said, handing Eshaan a large piece of paper.

Chapter 25

Eshaan checked his hair one last time in the mirror. His trousers barely clung to his waist, and the belt did not help too much. He cinched the belt and promised himself that he would start taking better care of his clothes. His lavender-colored shirt was a gift from Kitt. She had come by late last night to give him six different shirts that she had picked out for him. She made him model each one and then finally gave her verdict. The lavender made his face look brighter and, coincidentally, was the only shirt that fit his very slender frame.

"You aren't going for the size-zero thing, are you?" Kitt had asked playfully as she sat on his bed.

"Yes, that is it. Size zero!" He had managed a fake laugh. "Forget my size. What I want to know is how the two of you talked me into doing this. I don't stand a chance!"

"You are going to do this, because you are one of the best cooks in the world. You will win this thing and become a household name. People will line up to give money to run Karma Kitchen." Kitt had unexpectedly walked up to him and given him a big hug. Her embrace had been warm and sweet, just as he remembered it. She always smelled like jasmine. If time could stop, if his heart would stop beating instead of racing, if they simply froze in time, these were the moments to live by. He breathed in her smell. It would, he knew, be the only reminder of this night, the smell of love unfulfilled. He wanted to hug her. Instead, he had clenched his fists, digging his nails deep into his palms. He waited for her to stop hugging him.

"I'll see you in the morning, okay?" she had whispered in his ears.

Don't go. Don't leave. Please stay . . . The words in his heart stayed inside.

She had left, and Tenzin had arrived to check in on him.

"I was waiting 'til I saw her leave," Tenzin teased. "Anyway, I have a gift for you. Here, open it," he added, handing Eshaan a large white envelope.

"What is this?" Eshaan said as he opened it and was stunned to see a large amount of cash.

"Where did you get this?"

"Don't worry about that. This is for your, well, *our* kitchen. We need cash, and I found a way to make it. Don't look at me like that. I may be a naïve monk, but I know how to make money!"

"You? You are worse than I am when it comes to business!" Eshaan laughed.

"Well, fine. I cannot lie. Rani had this idea that I could sell my pickles to the local store. So I went there—"

"Wait, no! Those pickles are for the monastery. You are already giving me your time. We cannot sell those," Eshaan interrupted, and stood ready to return the envelope.

Tenzin laughed as he sat down on the small chair in the room. "At least hear me out! She was wrong. No one wanted to buy my pickles . . . even though, I have to say, they taste rather good."

Eshaan eyed him with confusion.

"Well, I donated all this blood this morning," Tenzin responded, and pointed to a bandage on his arm. "But that wasn't enough, so, Eshaan, last night, I gave up my right kidney."

"I'm telling you, Tenzin, if you were not a monk and if you were not my friend, I would've just killed you right now." Eshaan laughed. "So what did you do? Don't tell me one of the students gave you this money to give them your body for science?"

"Ha! No. I was returning from the store along with my pickles, when a young man came up to me. I have seen him here in the prayer hall so many times. He always has his camera with him." Tenzin went on to explain that the man loved the Tibetan bowls that Tenzin played.

"Oh, God, no. Please tell me you did not sell those bowls, Tenzin. They are priceless!"

Tenzin just smiled.

"My friend, one thing I have learned from Radio Rani is to never, ever, ever sell the cow. I did not sell the bowls. He wanted to record me playing those, and I played a sample. He gave me an advance for recording more. This is just the start!"

Eshaan bowed to his friend, in gratitude and in awe.

"Thank you but, honestly, I cannot just take this. Everyone is giving me so much, and I have no way to repay it."

"I am a monk. What am I going to do with all this money? We will use it together to make a difference in this world. But first, seriously, are you planning on wearing that shirt for tomorrow?"

Tenzin's generosity had made Eshaan feel even more determined. And now, here he was wearing a lavender shirt and ready to test his luck.

"Eshaan, are you ready? Loveleen and Kitt are waiting for you outside!" Radio Rani continued banging loudly on his door.

"I'm coming! Tell them to wait for one minute." Eshaan tucked his shirt in and took one last look in the mirror. He then walked over to the small altar in his room and bowed his head. He took one deep breath and then opened the door of his room.

"How do I look?" he asked Radio Rani.

She frowned.

"It is too pink? Pink is making you look, well, not so good. Why not white? But, anyway, I think they will be more interested in your food. Where is the food that you have to take?"

"Oh, I forgot; it is in the kitchen." Eshaan ran toward Karma Kitchen.

Om was standing outside, guarding the mostly empty donation bowl.

"The girls already took your food to the car."

Loveleen's BMW was waiting at the gate of the monastery. Eshaan saw her tapping her fingers furiously on the steering wheel. Kitt was in the passenger side, so Eshaan opened the door and got into the back of the car.

"I am here. Let's go do this before I change my mind."

The trio zipped through the empty streets, a rarity. It was 6:00 A.M. on a Sunday morning, and most of Delhi was still slumbering.

Chapter 26

"My name is Eshaan Singh. I am twenty-five years old. I run a small kitchen to help feed the needy," Eshaan said as he stood behind a large golden island placed in a huge replica kitchen on the sets of *India's Best Home Chef.*

A young assistant standing across from him held up a placard that read WHY ARE YOU HERE?

"I am here today—" Eshaan stopped. He wasn't prepared for this. "Oh, so sorry, I am not sure." He looked apologetically at the director.

"Kid, just try one more time. Haven't you seen any of the beauty pageants? Think of how those girls answer the questions so quickly. Come on, we don't have all day." The director was smug, stern, running on coffee, and out of patience.

"I am here today, because some friends think I should compete. My personal goal is to bring attention to the issue of hunger in our world," Eshaan said with less conviction than before, and the director immediately asked for a retake.

"If you cannot even stand and tell me why you *want* to compete, how in the hell are you *going to* compete? Now come on, with some heart this time."

Eshaan finally got it right on the fourth take.

The set was filled with gaudy but glittering chandeliers, several large cooking stations, about fifty or so hopeful candidates, and two superstar chefs who would be vetting the contestants from this part of Delhi. The room overflowed with cameramen, makeup artists, food stylists, chefs, and a live audience.

Eshaan could see Loveleen and Kitt waving to him from the back of the room. He took out a handkerchief and wiped his forehead, as the superbright lights made him sweat. The tissue was covered with a layer of foundation.

"Someone fix his head before we start again!" the director yelled, and a makeup artist ran to Eshaan.

"Now, let's try this again, and Eshaan, stop touching your face!" The director was beginning to lose his cool. They weren't paying him enough to deal with these amateurs.

"So we are told the dish you prepared for the qualifying round is a coconut soup?" superstar Chef Ram Singh, one of the lead judges, asked Eshaan.

Eshaan fidgeted and looked around then looked up at the camera and said,

"Yes. The basic part of this dish is a soup I often prepare for the monks at the monastery where I live. They enjoy it very much."

"Wait, I thought you said you run a kitchen? Are you a monk?" The cameraman immediately zoomed in to focus on the yak bone bracelets Eshaan was wearing.

The whole room was quiet as the director cut the shot.

"Eshaan, when you answer this, I want you to look at camera one, okay? Makeup. I need someone to fix his face *now*. He wiped his face *again*, and now the color is uneven," the director shouted a few more directions to the interviewers.

An old man with a large makeup box rushed to Eshaan and dabbed on more foundation to his forehead, and then whispered, "Don't worry. I will fix it if you rub it again!"

The director turned to Eshaan. "Do you have anyone here with you today?"

Eshaan nodded and pointed to Loveleen and Kitt in the audience, and they both waved to the director. The director nodded and told one of the cameramen to shoot the girls' reactions to Eshaan's actions.

"Let's focus on his dish please, and then we will go to the monk question. Don't worry. I will fix the sequence later," the director said to Judge Chef Ram Singh.

"The camera loves this kid. I've got a feeling about this one," the director then whispered into Chef Ram's earpiece.

The dish Eshaan had prepared for this audition was rolled out on a large cart. The assistant parked the cart right next to the island where Eshaan was standing.

"So, Eshaan, tell us what you have made today for us. As you know, today is the day we are picking the twenty people who will advance to the next round. If you get picked, you will appear in the live competition for *India's Best Home Chef*, brought to you by Spicetiques, India's premier spice company," Chef Ram Singh said, and had to do several retakes, because he could not pronounce the name of the company just right. At least three retakes were solely because of the chef's bad language and cursing at the name.

The director jumped in and cut the scene again. Eshaan rolled the large trolley in front of the island and tried to make sure his dish looked good as the camera came in to do a glamour shot of the dish.

"Okay, everyone, places, we are ready to go. Eshaan, we will start with you now, so go ahead, look straight at the camera, and answer his question."

The director rushed to get behind the camera then shouted, "Action!" followed by a quick cut when a cat ran across the stage and the audience burst into laughter. The director screamed something about firing someone at the end of the day and then looked at Eshaan. "You. Talk. Now."

"This dish, this dish is about experimenting with my favorite flavors. I enjoy adding unexpected touches to food and seeing how the taste changes. So today, I have prepared for you a chilled coconut and saffron soup with cashew nut bread sticks, a special griddle bread—" He was interrupted before he completed his description.

Chef Ram Singh was standing close to the trolley. He looked sternly at Eshaan as he interrupted the young man's description, "I am curious how you came up with this dish. Says here on your application that you were an orphan and that you run a charity kitchen. These are expensive tastes for someone like you, no?"

Instantly, Eshaan straightened up. He knew the routine. He had just seen it with people who had auditioned before him. The chef tried to rile them up; it made for great reality TV.

"Chef Ram Singh, we all want things that make us feel special. I begged and borrowed from my friends to create this dish, and then your cooking studio people helped me by placing my dish in these fancy plates."

"Well, let me see if the taste of this dish is as impressive as your attitude."

Judge Chef Singh used a large spoon and slurped up a bit of the soup. He then picked up a bread stick and bit into it. His expression changed in a second.

Eshaan looked helplessly at Loveleen and Kitt to see if they knew what the look meant. Kitt gave him a thumbs-up and mouthed, *You rock.*

Chef Singh turned to the other judge. "You need to come and taste this outrageous dish." The tone was mocking, piercing, sarcastic. Eshaan wiped the sweat off his forehead again.

I still have Karma Kitchen, he thought to himself. *At least I tried. It's fine. I am not one of them. I should not have come. I am not one of the cabal. These people are all trained chefs. I learned to cook by just messing around in the kitchen. What was I thinking?*

The second judge, Chef Navin Patel, came up and equally dramatically took a sip of the soup and a bite of the breadstick. His face remained expressionless.

"Eshaan, do you know what it takes to become a great cook? It takes hours in the kitchen, it takes a lot of study of technique and ingredients, and it takes an amazing imagination to come up with flavor and texture combinations. Do you know that?"

Eshaan looked down at the island and nodded. "Yes, Chef."

The director screamed to cut and then looked at Eshaan. "Now tell us about the monk part. Don't look confused. We will edit. Chef Singh and Chef Patel, as soon as he finishes talking, you need to give your verdict. You ready?

They all nodded. Everyone was ready.

"I live in a monastery, but I am not a monk," he said as one of his hands sought his *Rab Rakha* tattoo. He took a deep breath, stood tall, and pushed his shoulders up.

"I am one of the lucky ones. If the monks had not saved me, I would have died like my mother did, of hunger," he said as he pressed his finger deeper into the tattoo. "As I grew older, my calling, my purpose, started to become clear: to feed other people so no one, *no one* ever dies of hunger. I don't want another child to see their mother die because of the lack of a few grains of rice." Despite his best attempt, a few tears trickled down his cheeks. Then he looked up and saw the monitor focused on the audience. The camera for that monitor was on Kitt's face and her tears were glittering on the screen.

"Well, I know my decision, Chef Patel. Do you have yours?" Chef Singh turned to the other judge, who nodded.

"Eshaan, I have been a chef for twenty-five years. I have traveled the world. I have studied in the best of schools and cooked in the best of kitchens, mind you, with the best of chefs. If I hadn't seen you preparing this dish in the back, I would have sworn that some highly talented and trained chef had prepared this. My first thought when I tasted your soup was this: If this is what he is creating without any formal training, can you imagine what he would do *with* some formal training? So it is a yes from me, and you are in!" Chef Singh clapped as he announced his decision.

Loveleen screamed so loudly that the director turned and told her to do it again. "That is the kind of enthusiasm we need from our audience," he said.

Chef Patel went back to his chair, picked up a large rolling pin, and walked over to Eshaan. "You know what this is, right? This is the pin that says you are in!"

The director shouted, "Cut, pack up for the day." The support staff rushed on to the set to clean up and get ready for the next day.

Eshaan was still standing at the island. He held the pin close to his heart and closed his eyes. And then he heard Kitt's voice, "I told you! I told you, you could do it." She placed her hand on his arm, and instinctively, he turned and hugged her tightly.

"Lucky guy, he is in the competition *and* he gets a great girl," someone in the room said out loud. The director heard him and signaled to the cameraman to shoot the lovers' embrace.

Chapter 27

"Eshaan, I told you that you would make it! I've seen so many episodes of that show, and you just fit their mold so beautifully. All the aunties will want to adopt you, and all the young ladies will want to marry you." Loveleen smiled at her own statement.

They were in the car driving back to the monastery. Just before leaving the studio, the director had come up to speak to Eshaan to inform him that he had made it into the next round.

"Next time, try to show more of your personality," was the advice offered, and it had bristled Eshaan, who kept quiet at the time, but then complained to the girls in the car.

"What the hell does he mean by show more personality? I thought this was a food show! Shouldn't my dish be the focus?"

"Come on, Eshaan, you cannot be that naïve," Loveleen countered. Eshaan just shook his head.

"The first prize is your own cooking show. But that is not where you will make the money. *You* will get endorsements. That is where the money will come from, and then you take all that and retire. I mean, run the kitchen, and *not* run after rich people to help you out," Loveleen said.

"I am not running after rich people, Loveleen. I am trying to raise money and interest, and poor people have no money to give me." Eshaan hated that Loveleen could hit below the belt so very easily.

"I'm not suggesting you are doing something wrong. I am just saying the endorsements will help you." Loveleen softened her tone.

Eshaan managed a feeble smile as he looked in the rearview mirror. He could see Kitt in the back, staring blankly out the window. That embrace had been real. She had stayed so close to him. She still loved him. He knew it.

The roads were jam-packed as harried Delhiites rushed back home to TV serials, dinners, and family time. What should have been a thirty-minute drive was already into the second hour.

"Are you all hungry? They didn't serve a decent meal there all day," Eshaan asked Loveleen and Kitt.

"Yes," was the loud response from Loveleen, and Kitt simply nodded. Eshaan picked up his mobile phone and made a call.

"Can we come tonight? There are three of us. Yes, yes, I know you need notice. Sorry . . . yes, yes, that is the one. Okay. We will be there in five minutes. We are around the corner. No, I am not kidding. Seriously," he said on the phone as Loveleen tried to interrupt to figure out who he was talking to and what all this meant.

"Be patient. You guys will love this place. I can assure you this is something you have never seen before."

Eshaan cautiously maneuvered the car around the swarm of cyclists peddling on the side of the road. He then turned into a small lane with a cobblestone path. The lane had small homes on both sides. There were a few streetlights casting a feeble glow onto the street. A couple of young boys were playing cricket at the far end of the alley.

He stopped the car in front of a house with no sign, no number. The building had a very ornate wooden door, with a large brass doorknob in the shape of a woman's hand over a knob.

Loveleen looked quizzically at him. "Are we planning to break into someone's house for a meal?"

Eshaan winked. He then got out of the car and opened the door to help Loveleen out.

"This looks like an interesting place, Eshaan." Kitt managed a smile, and then at his urging, used the beautiful knocker to knock on the door.

A young man appeared from the left side of the street.

"Eshaan! How are you? I haven't seen you here for a long time," the man said and held out his hand.

Eshaan gave him the key to the car. "I know! It has been a while! Thanks for parking the car for me. Full night here?"

The young man nodded and took the keys.

The door opened, and an elegant woman dressed in a red silk gown stepped out. Even in the feeble light, it was easy to tell she was strikingly beautiful. Her dark long hair flowed down to her waist. She was wearing a gold belt around her slim waist, and both her wrists were adorned with golden and red bangles.

"Eshaan, if I did not love you so much, I would be so mad. I haven't seen you in months," she said and moved forward to hug him, very tightly. She kissed him fondly on each check as she took his face in her hands.

Loveleen looked at Kitt, who appeared stunned. This woman was clearly not "just a friend."

"Who is she?" Kitt whispered to Loveleen, who shrugged her shoulders.

"I have missed you, Eshaan. Now, who have you brought with you? Introduce me to your friends!"

Loveleen extended her hand. "I'm Loveleen, and you are?"

"My name is Gina. It is nice to meet you, Loveleen! When is the baby due?"

"Gina? Oh, you sent the vegetables to the kitchen last week! The baby is due very soon!" Loveleen beamed as Gina moved forward and gave her a hug. She then turned to Kitt. "And you, my sweet, must be Kitt! It is very nice to meet you. Now come on in. Of course, if Eshaan had bothered to respond to any of my messages, you would be tasting *his* food tonight."

The trio stepped in behind the voluptuous woman and she closed the door. Once inside, the two ladies could not help but gasp. Kitt turned to Eshaan. "Oh, my God. What in the world is this?"

"Sometimes illusion, delusion, reality, and dreams coincide, my friends. And here, at this point, you can dare to believe you can make a difference." With those dramatic words, Gina pulled Eshaan by the arm and led them all into the rather large room.

The garish setting seemed meek in contrast to the even gaudier waitstaff dressed in shocking yellow trousers, matching green shirts, and black turbans. The room was filled with ornate, golden tables, and each table had four or five people seated around it. The brightly lit large room had several large lotus-shaped chandeliers. Silver and gold silk draperies covered every inch of wall, and even hung from the ceilings.

"This looks like a restaurant with a spa complex having an identity crisis," whispered Loveleen.

The loud chatter of the crowd drowned out sounds from a small live band playing soft flute music.

Gina seated the threesome at a table right in the center of the room. The table hosted large copper goblets for each guest, along with flat crystal plates in the shape of a lotus flower. There was no cutlery, but a basket in the center of the table was filled with packaged moist towels. Gina picked up the RESERVED sign placed on the table. "I always save a place for my Eshaan. Never know when you will show up and make this place come alive. Oh, did I tell you? Tonight is the love story of Razia Sultan." Then she signaled for the server to pour drinks into the goblets.

"Loveleen, I will have them bring you something without alcohol. Oh, now I have to go. We are starting." Gina bent down and gave Eshaan another kiss, this time on his forehead, and was reaching for his lips when he gently turned his face so that the kiss landed on his cheek. "I'll be back, Eshaan."

Kitt felt a little twinge of jealousy. *Was Eshaan seeing another woman?*

Before the ladies could ask what exactly was going on, the lights dimmed and conversation hushed. The flute players picked up the tempo, and a small spotlight came up and shone on Gina.

"Welcome, one and all, to our special interactive dinner theatre. As many of you know, we meet once a month to enact a story from the history of our beloved India. But here, fate is not in charge. You are in charge. You get to tell the actors what to do next. Your words shape the story. Tonight, Chef Azad has cooked up delicacies from the Mughal Empire that ruled over our beloved Delhi for so many years. And the story? Here you go."

A screen was lowered down at the far end of the room and the show began. On a background showcasing the old city of Delhi, a deep-voiced narrator spoke: "Tonight, we bring you the love story to beat all love stories. In 1210, Sultan Iltutmish ruled Delhi. A powerful monarch, he believed his daughter, Razia, was qualified to rule Delhi, and he pushed her to the forefront, against the current wisdom of society that only a man could be a ruler. Razia became the first ever woman to rule Delhi. And then, she fell in love. Today, you will hear her tale, and if you don't like it, you will have the power to change the story. Will you change it? How? Should it be changed? What do you think should happen? Let us begin."

The screen disappeared. The room became dark and silent. The only sounds were the muffled movements of the waitstaff. Kitt moved closer to Eshaan and reached over to hold his hand. He turned to her, surprised at the gesture. He could smell her hair. Jasmine. As always.

The mini orchestra began to play a soft, melancholic tune and soft lights came on. A man with a white flowing beard, wide chest, and some serious body armor appeared. The narrator announced, "This is Sultan Iltutmish, Sultan of Delhi, one of the most powerful men of his time."

"I come from slaves, and today I rule the most beautiful place in the world, Delhi. But I fear that my end is near. It is time for me to pick a successor," he said as he walked around the room and began describing his woes, his children, and his need to pick the right person to carry on his legacy.

"Razia, my daughter, is a fierce warrior, the most competent stateswoman, and a true leader. Yet the world says only a man can lead?" he hollered, using commonplace words instead of a strict Urdu dialect, as was spoken at the time. Gina had earlier insisted on using pure languages, and then had given up when the patrons complained they didn't understand.

"Oh, look at the food!" Loveleen exclaimed as the servers quietly brought out an array of kebabs, fragrant saffron rice, and various breads to each table.

"Food? You want to eat with all this going on?" Eshaan joked with his sweet friend.

"You be the intellectual, and I will be the glutton. We will see who has a better and more productive evening," smirked Loveleen as she bit into the glorious chicken kebab laced with cardamom and mint.

The actor moved toward the crowd, and the waiters serving the food moved back into the shadows. A waiter quietly placed a scotch in front of Eshaan, who smiled and said, "Advantages of being the boss's favorite here."

"Who should rule the Sultanate of Delhi? Should it be my incapable sons who are lost in the pleasures of the mind and flesh, or should it be my daughter, Razia? Can a woman rule a country? Should she?" asked the Sultan of Delhi again.

People murmured their responses. The Sultan ignored them all. He walked up to a table in the back of the room and asked an older couple seated there, "Would you make your daughter the head of your empire, or your son? Whom would you pick?"

"My son, of course," responded a lean and dark man sitting at the table. "Sons rule. Daughters are to be pampered. They are just too emotional, and they should not be running anything."

The comment caused expected commotion, with several other diners yelling, "No, no. Don't listen to him. Women rock! Razia should be the Sultana!"

The room went dark.

The audience hushed.

A slim, tall woman appeared from behind one of the silk draperies. Her lavish outfit, a long, flowing satin tunic and dark tights, were accessorized with diamond and silver belts. Around her neck, she was wearing several pearl and gold necklaces, and the large turban on her head was decked out with white feathers.

"I am Razia, and I challenge anyone here to defeat me in a fight. I am capable of ruling. Who says I cannot rule? I will be the next Sultan of Delhi, Razia Sultan!"

"Wait, did she say 'sultan'? This actress doesn't have the right words! If she became the ruler, she would be called Sultana, right? Isn't that the female version of the Sultan?" Loveleen whispered to Eshaan.

"She always maintained she was no less because she was a woman. And wanted to be named Sultan and not Sultana," Eshaan responded.

Kitt's phone buzzed, and Eshaan looked at the screen. *NIKOLAS*. He looked on as Kitt picked up the phone, whispered into it, and then put it back down on the table. This time, screen down. He squeezed her hand tight.

The crowd cheered and called out, "Razia, Razia, Razia—"

The actor playing the Sultan pointed to the actress and spoke,

"The people have spoken. Razia, a Sunni Muslim with a Turkish heritage, finally ascends the throne and becomes the first woman ever to rule Delhi!"

The crowd cheered louder. The music picked up the tempo.

"Aren't you going to eat, Eshaan? You have been pushing your food around on the plate for the past hour," Loveleen said as she picked up the kebabs from his plate and placed them on hers.

Gina came back and sat at the table with Eshaan. Kitt pulled her hand away as she noticed Gina placing a hand on Eshaan's leg. Gina placed a large envelope on the table. "This is your cash for the last few dinners you cooked here. I've been meaning to come by and give it to you in person, but since you are here now—" she said as she gave his leg a gentle squeeze.

The play went into the second act. Three young actors, playing noblemen of the time, showed up and surround Razia. "Marry us, Sultana?" they asked, and she turned them all down.

The spotlight quickly moved across the room, where a tall, young African man stepped out, bare-chested, wearing long, flowing white pants. His chest appeared red with large welts. He smelled of horse manure and the narrator continued, "This is Yakut. History tells us there were strong rumors that Razia fell in love with him."

There are cheers from the women as the handsome man walked up to Razia and said, "I honor you, Sultana, and all your achievements. But what is to become of us?"

As the couple looked into each other's eyes, the actors playing the noblemen drew their swords. "She is in love with a slave! She deserves to die." Commotion ensued as Razia and Yakut tried to defend themselves. Suddenly, all the actors froze in place, the music died down, and the spotlight focused on Yakut and Razia as they held hands and looked skyward for help.

"If you were Razia, what would you do? Would you step down for love, or continue to rule? Are you a woman in love, or are you a role model to be remembered in history as the greatest female ruler of Delhi? Should she remain the Sultan?" the narrator asked.

"Razia, you should no longer be the Sultan of Delhi," Eshaan said as he stood up and called to the actress.

"What? How can you say that, Eshaan?!" Both Kitt and Loveleen were stunned at their friend's comment.

The spotlight shifted to Eshaan. Razia walked over, drew her large gem-studded sword, and waved it toward Eshaan.

"Speak, young man. Speak! I want to know why you think that I, an expert in policy, in sword fighting, a woman who has been educated in all aspects of leadership and politics, should not run the country now because I love a man."

The room was hushed.

Eshaan took the actress by her arm and led her to the other actor on the floor, Yakut, the slave.

"First, tell me, do you love him?" Eshaan asked Razia, who nodded with a triumphant yes.

"We are here today to rewrite history, so we could have it as we wanted, yes?" Eshaan directed his question to the crowd. A loud cheer went up.

"So, here is my rewrite. I am sick and tired of Indian love stories, the great ones, ending up as tragedies. Why must all the Sonis, the Anarkalis, all the beautiful women of Indian love stories, end up either dead or married to men they don't love?" he asked as he looked straight at Kitt. Her face looked pained.

The audience cheered again.

In the meantime, Gina shifted restlessly at the table.

"You girls are his best friends, right? Tell me what I have to do to get him to marry me? I can change his life, give him that kitchen, everything that he wants. But . . . what should I do?" Gina asked Loveleen and Kitt, who were too stunned to answer the question.

The spotlight now shone on Eshaan, Yakut, and Razia.

"You have shown the world there is life beyond the veil. You, the daughter of a slave, ruled one of the most powerful empires in the world. For that, I salute you," Eshaan continued. "But I ask, why must love always take the backseat? Here, today, Yakut is not in a position to make that decision. But you, you are. You have the power to change everything."

There was more cheering from the crowd, but louder jeering from the actors playing the nobility.

"Razia, marry him," someone from the crowd yelled.

Eshaan took Razia's hand and Yakut's hand and placed them together.

"The Sufi saints say you have to drown in love, and it is the ones who drown who make it across. Just once, show us the magic of making it across. Just once show me, I mean us, that not all love stories are destined to end in disaster."

"Fantastic, Eshaan," Gina said as she stood up, clapped her hands, and rushed up to him to give him a hug. He pulled away as gently as he could. The actress playing Razia declared her love for the slave.

"You know, Kitt, he is a catch, and once he becomes a TV star, there will be thousands of Ginas wanting to marry him. I don't know what you think you are doing, but, believe me, he will be gone if you don't take the chance now," Loveleen said to Kitt as she finished her last bite of kebab.

"Love is always the right answer. In fact, I believe it is the only answer," Eshaan said loudly.

"No, don't give up the crown of Delhi! You must continue to rule. All this love nonsense is a waste of time," another woman countered.

Eshaan shrugged his shoulders and returned to his table, not even noticing that Gina was still standing there applauding. A server came over. "Gina, madam, we need you inside."

She nodded to the group, promising to return in a few minutes. "You were awesome, Eshaan!" she said as she left.

He sat down next to Kitt. In the dim light, all he could really sense was her smell. He could feel the warmth of her breath as she nuzzled her head against his shoulder. "I feel guilty when I touch you, and guilty if I don't. I am not an educated man. I haven't traveled the world. I don't know the first thing about love, but I do know I cannot stand to see you with someone else," he said. He paused as he reached out to her and gently lifted her chin so he could look into her eyes. "Tell me the truth. Do you love him?"

"It isn't that simple," she said as she closed her eyes and placed her head back on his shoulder.

"What the hell is that supposed to mean? You are marrying the man! Do you love him or not?"

Silence. The kind that made you want to reach out and shake someone, the kind that meant someone who thinks they are being kind, are actually being quite cruel, the kind that made you question every decision, every breath.

In truth, he felt she had answered his question in silence. Love isn't quiet. Love makes you want to sing out loud, makes you look like a fool in front of learned monks, makes you write poetry, sing sad songs, laugh at yourself, yet never give up on each other. Silence wasn't love, at least not to Eshaan.

"Okay, then answer me this. Are you happy? If you are happier with him, then I will let you go. I promise. Just say the word."

This time, her response was more painful than silence. But it gave him his answer, loud and clear. He felt her warm tears on his shoulder.

He put his arm around her neck, and they sat close and just let the time be. The noise, the music, the food, the people, it was all irrelevant. If she had been happy or indifferent, he would have walked away. But she wasn't. He tugged her closer as though he wanted her to melt in his embrace, to shield her from whatever it was that was hurting her, to tell her he would rip the stars from the sky and lay them at her feet.

"I love you more than I have ever loved anyone," he said in a soft voice.

"Some things are just not meant to be," she finally broke her silence and pulled away.

"Eshaan, come dance with me!" Gina appeared again at their side and she offered him her hand. He took it, and she pulled him toward the floor. Then, gracefully, she turned around to Kitt. "*Tu sei il suo sogno d'amore*," she said. "*Mentre lui è il sogno d'amore mio!*"

"Subtext? What the hell did she just say to you?" Loveleen asked.

You are his dream of love
While he is MY dream of love

Kitt sat there in silence, avoiding eye contact with Loveleen, who was already on her soapbox with her *I told you so* lines. She put a hand on her heart and tried to ignore what it kept repeating: she wasn't worthy of Eshaan. Not now, not ever.

The lights came back on and dessert was served.

Chapter 28

The moonlit sky was tentative. The air was restless; it knew in a matter of hours the scorching sun would return with a vengeance. The night wafted nothingness, as if no spirit lived in this city, as if no soul stirred in its bosom.

"Please, Dad. You have to help me," the pleading voice of a young man made Eshaan stop in his tracks. He did not expect anyone to be out this late.

It was just after three, and Eshaan was standing outside Dr. Sinha's bungalow, waiting for Loveleen to come out. At least once a week, the duo went to the local Sikh temple before dawn. They helped with meal preparations for the devotees for the coming day. It was a ritual they had enjoyed for years, and according to Loveleen, it was this very ritual that earned her the karma to live the glorious life as she did, without doing an honest day's work.

It had been a week since the night of the *Razia Sultan* dinner, and Eshaan had not heard a peep from anyone: Kitt, the reality television show, or any new donors for the kitchen. Each morning seemed like a replica of the day before. "Whoever said you can never breathe in the same air twice must never have been ignored," Eshaan told Tulku Tenzin. Even the lizard on his wall hadn't moved an inch. "It is almost as though the world has decided to pass me by this week," he mentioned at least three times a day, if not more. And now, Tenzin had (purposefully) been hard to find!

Despite the early hour, Eshaan secretly hoped Loveleen had convinced Kitt to join in for the early shift. The chances looked bleak. Nikolas was due to arrive any day now, and Eshaan had heard through the grapevine that Kitt and Dr. Sinha had been talking to florists and caterers for the wedding dinner. Eshaan's thoughts were interrupted again by the quivering, young male voice that said, "Don't turn me away, Dad. You are my only hope."

Eshaan stood quietly in the shadows listening, trying to figure out who was talking and to whom.

"No, I cannot give you any more money. What for? You live in *my* house, so you have to pay no rent. I gave you your Mercedes." The voice that responded, Eshaan recognized it instantly. It belonged to a very angry and agitated Mr. Mehra. In an instant, Eshaan knew the young voice belonged to Mehra's son.

Eshaan quickly took out his mobile phone and sent a message to Loveleen.

DON'T COME OUT. MEHRA IS OUT HERE ARGUING WITH HIS SON. I'LL TEXT YOU WHEN THEY ARE GONE.

The two men continued to argue.

The solar lights that Dr. Sinha installed around the house cast a wicked shadow across the yard.

I AM AT KITT'S. WE CAN HEAR THEM. HE HAS A SON? Loveleen texted.

Eshaan had met Amit Mehra on a few occasions when the young man came to visit Mr. Merry Mehra. Amit, often dressed to the hilt in the latest designer threads, was the polar opposite of his father. He was polite, funny, and very cordial to people around him. Although their brief conversations had rarely wandered away from the weather or cricket, Eshaan had taken an immense liking toward the man, and had even invited him once to a friendly cricket match against the monks.

"Dad, I need cash. You have to trust me. I would not be asking if it was not important. Come on, Dad, please? I don't have much time," the young man was pleading.

"Don't you know that giving of money on a Friday evening is inauspicious? It is considered an offense against Goddess Lakshmi. She will be offended and turn her back on us. Is that what you want?" Merry Mehra responded with his predictable astrology-laden philosophy.

TECHNICALLY, YOU MORON, IT IS EARLY SATURDAY MORNING, Loveleen texted Eshaan, who had to curb the urge to laugh.

"Dad, my ATM card was sucked in by the bank's machine and I cannot draw any money tonight. I know you keep cash at home. Just for the night, Dad. Tomorrow, I will go to the bank and get the cash to pay you back," the son's voice shook.

It was clear to Eshaan that the young man was in a state of panic. He could not understand why Mehra was being such an ass about it. Perhaps the world was right: once a scorpion, always a scorpion.

The son continued to beg.

Then, a sudden sharp noise startled Eshaan. Mr. Mehra had slapped his grown son.

"Amit, I will not offend the Goddess for your silly needs," Eshaan heard Mr. Mehra say, and then heard footsteps.

LOVELEEN, DO NOT *COME OUT. MEHRA IS GOING BACK IN AND UP TO HIS FLOOR,* Eshaan texted her again.

K, she responded.

"Dad, Dad . . . Dad—" Amit called after his father.

"It is bad luck to call someone when their back is turned to you," Mr. Mehra turned around and retorted in a loud and angry voice, and then disappeared into the shadows of the stairwell.

Amit stood there looking uncertain.

"Hi, Amit." Eshaan came out of the darkness. It surprised him to see he was, in fact, crying.

The young man, startled at the sight of another this late, quickly wiped the tears off his face.

"Eshaan, what are you doing here this time of night?" he asked as he tried to hold his hands together to stop them from trembling.

"I'm sorry about how your father behaved. He and his stupid astrologer . . . there has been a lot of trouble here because of that," Eshaan replied, offering him a handshake.

"If I find his astrologer, I will cut his balls off—" Amit's voice trailed off. He stood there helplessly and stared back at his father's house, as if staring hard enough would make his dad reappear.

"How much did you lose in the *satta*? And are the goons already here to take you down?" Eshaan asked.

"Wait, what? *Satta*? You think I gambled and that is why I need cash?"

"Come on, man. Let's look at it logically. What sort of activity requires immediate cash? If it were for a hospital emergency, you would have told your father that. So, yes, I am betting you gambled, lost money, and now the goons are on your case to pay up or they will kill you, rape your wife, and take your Benz."

Amit fidgeted. It was like a scene out of a really bad Bollywood movie: two literal strangers, in the middle of the night, talking about goons and thugs wanting money.

"Okay . . . yes, I lost a gambling debt. They fucking took the Benz and still want cash. They gave me a few hours. I tried the bank, but could not get enough. The fucking car is worth ten times what I owe them, but they are insisting on cash. Fuck," Amit said.

"Why didn't you just tell Mehra the truth?" asked a woman's voice. Amit turned around to see two women coming out of Dr. Sinha's house. The women introduced themselves to a very shaken Amit.

"My father has a big house, no, a *huge* house in Delhi, and yet he lives here. Do you know why? Because a fortuneteller told him that he needed to live in a small rental or he would die young. He won't help me, no matter what. I have one other friend that I can try." Amit turned and began walking to his bike.

"Hey, Amit. Wait. How much do you need?" Eshaan asked.

"Why? Why are you asking?" Amit questioned.

"How much do you need?"

"Four lakhs, but tonight they only want half since they have the car. I have the money in the bank. I just don't have it right this minute," he said.

"Eshaan, *you* are helping Mehra's son?" a stunned Kitt asked him.

"Yes, the man is a bastard, but, you know, the kid shouldn't be punished for his father's fuckups. If the Lama had thought that, I would be in the gutter, dead by now. And besides, I have messed up so many times and people, like you, have always helped me. "

Loveleen chimed in, "I can help as well. I hate Mehra, Kitt, but I know Delhi goons. It isn't that they cannot wait until morning; it's all about teaching him a lesson."

Loveleen went up the stairs and was down in a few minutes with several wads of cash. Amit, still in tears, was on the phone with his wife, reassuring her that he was going to pay the thugs off soon.

"Here, but you will need more?" Loveleen handed the cash to Amit.

Kitt went back into the house too and woke her father up.

Dr. Sinha, even in his sleepy state, was very concerned. "You people need to stay far away from Mehra and his problems. This is going to lead to issues, I tell you. That man is mad."

"Come on, Papa, it is just a loan, and Eshaan thinks it is a gambling debt," Kitt tried to convince her father.

"Kitt, I have never said no to you for anything. But this time, the answer is no. You cannot do this. It will create all kinds of issues if Mehra ever finds out." Dr. Sinha was now wide awake.

His resolve lasted about three seconds when he saw how upset she really was. Without uttering another word, a sleepy Dr. Sinha opened the tiny safe inside his Godrej steel *almirah*. He handed a few large wads of cash to Kitt.

Kitt went back out and noticed that Eshaan was back from the monastery with a few wads as well.

"Here you go. I am giving this to you on one condition: Stop now. The next time this happens, you won't be so lucky," Eshaan said and handed Amit some cash. Kitt followed suit

"Why are you all helping me? I . . . I am not even in a position to say no to your money . . . and from what you are saying, my father has not been kind to you all." Amit wiped his sweat with the back of his hand.

Instead of answering him, the three friends counted the money, which was close to what he needed.

"I have enough in my pocket to make the amount," Amit said with a feeble smile.

"Go, your hour is almost up," Eshaan urged the young man to leave.

Amit called his wife again. "I have it."

He then called another number and muttered, "I have it. I will be there in ten minutes."

"I promise I will pay you back," he said to the three friends as they stood there in silence, hoping they had done the right thing.

"Girls, let's go. We are getting late," Eshaan said, breaking the silence.

"Oh, I forgot the car keys. Let me go get them," Loveleen said and turned to go back into the house. She stopped and let out a small yelp. The lone bulb in the stairwell was now on, filling the entire patio with a sharp white light.

And, standing there, his face scrunched with anger and his nostrils puffed, was a very livid Mr. Merry Mehra.

Chapter 29

Instinctively, Eshaan moved in front of his very pregnant friend to shield her from the venom he knew Merry Mehra was getting ready to spew.

Mehra's stance was one of a wounded animal, getting ready to attack his prey. He was holding his mobile phone in one hand, lips clenched, face scrunched, and his eyes were bloodshot. He was sick and tired of these . . . these worthless, lowlife scoundrels getting into his business. First, that Loveleen with her cat, then Eshaan, with his high and mighty attitude, acting like he was better than everyone else, and now even that white woman, Kitt. She was just as worthless as the other two. He needed to consult the stars again, as he was ready to move or find a way for these three to move out of his life.

"You rascals," he said as he hurled his mobile phone at Loveleen, who ducked to miss it. It fell on the hard concrete and clattered before busting open.

"Mr. Mehra, you should be ashamed. Trying to hit a pregnant woman? What kind of a man are you?" Eshaan asked. "And besides, I am the one who helped Amit. Why are you taking it out on her?"

"Your son is in trouble, and you did not help him. What kind of a father are you?" Loveleen taunted in her loudest voice, and it echoed in the deep night.

The night watchman, who patrolled the streets, stopped to look in, and a few lights turned on in neighboring houses.

"What is going on here?" he asked, and Eshaan shooed him away. No point starting World War Three at three in the morning. Now he just needed to get Loveleen out of here before Mehra got too agitated.

"You think I don't care about my own flesh and blood? How dare you?!" Mehra waved his hands in the dark night air. The stark white light reflected off his face, giving him an almost ghoulish aura. "Do you know we don't give money on Friday night? It is inauspicious. Do you know anything about our religion or our culture? How could you? You are a whore. A whore pregnant with a bastard child," Mr. Mehra was now screaming. In the quiet dead of the night, his angry screams vibrated with a threatening energy.

Before Eshaan even knew what was happening, Loveleen pushed him aside and wobbled forward. Kitt tried to pull her back. But, of course, that was like trying to stop a full-speed train with a small feather.

"You think I am illiterate? I am not, and I have the one thing that you don't seem to possess, COMMON FUCKING SENSE. I always put the needs of my unborn child before my own. Not like you, putting yourself before your son's needs and his life. You are a failure as a father."

"You have no right to judge me. How DARE YOU GIVE MY SON YOUR FILTHY MONEY?"

"My filthy money is saving your son's life. Your precious son just lost a lot of money gambling. Yes, gambling. Don't look so shocked. And the thugs from whom he had taken money are waiting for him to bring the cash NOW. Those thugs, they don't believe in any God or Goddess. They only believe in ONE THING, and no, it is not money. It is power."

Loveleen, out of breath, leaned over to Kitt for support.

"Enough now, Mr. Mehra. If you need to discuss anymore, please go to your son." Eshaan tried to stop the escalating battle.

"I will fix you, Loveleen, and your nonsense. I know all about how to fix the likes of whores like you. And you, Eshaan, I thought you were a good man, but you are just like her, trash," Mehra said in a chilling voice, and turned to go back to his flat.

Kitt looked visibly terrified. "Loveleen, why did we get involved? He is a crazy man. That was a direct threat. Should we go to the police or something?"

"There is no need for that," said Dr. Sinha. He had been unable to fall back to sleep and heard all the commotion. The threats Mehra was making seemed silly, but he knew the man had decreasing common sense, it seemed, by the hour.

Years ago, when Merry Mehra had first moved in, Dr. Sinha used to enjoy speaking with him about the joys of astrology, studying how the movements of the moon affected lives, and how the stars pulled the strings of mere mortals. But over the years, Mehra's astrologer had been gaining ground, and Mehra had gone from a God-fearing man to an obsessive, fearmongering, God-forsaken man. His hatred, strangely, seemed to be very concentrated and directed to Loveleen, and more recently toward Eshaan. Dr. Sinha was determined to speak to Mehra later that day and ask him to vacate the premises. His behavior was getting out of hand.

Suddenly, Loveleen sat down on the ground and clutched her stomach.

"This cannot be happening. The baby is not due for another three months."

Chapter 30

Despite the commotion with Mehra in the early hours, things had settled down. The bright sun was glittering, the sounds of temple bells tolling, and the vendors calling out from their vegetable carts meant the workday was about to begin. Eshaan left to volunteer at the Sikh temple. He wanted to stay with Loveleen, but Dr. Sinha assured him that she would be okay. "I am so sorry to leave you, but I have to go and help. When I asked them to donate the steel plates, the people who volunteer there did not hesitate one second. I have to honor my commitment to keep helping them," he said to Loveleen, who in turn kissed him on his forehead, telling him that was one of the reasons she loved him so much.

As soon as Eshaan left, Dr. Sinha and Kitt helped Loveleen back up to her house and onto her bed. Dr. Sinha insisted she lie down to rest, as she refused to go to the hospital. Her contractions were getting less painful, but they hadn't stopped. Dr. Sinha gave her a quick checkup.

"Listen, child, if you get up and walk around, I will come and handcuff you to this bed," he said after he examined her, and then placed his hand gently on her shoulder. "You need to rest, at least for a week."

"A week? No way! I cannot." She managed a weak smile.

Dr. Sinha shook his head. As much as he found his own daughter to be an enigma, he could not understand Loveleen. She was smart, practical, intelligent, and yet behaved like a stubborn toddler on some days. He stood there waiting for her to confirm that she would take rest, but she just smiled.

"I have to go now, but you just call me if you need anything, okay, child? And for God's sake, Kitt, talk some sense into your friend." Dr. Sinha picked up his medical bag and left. Kitt, who was sitting at the edge of Loveleen's bed, only smiled.

The minute he left, Loveleen sat up on her large bed. She picked up the photo that was on her side table. It showed her and Saachi, dressed in bright red chiffon skirts embroidered with golden flowers. In the photo, there were garlands around their neck and they were holding each other's hennaed hands. Loveleen traced a heart around Saachi's face with her finger.

"I was going to call Saachi to tell her about the contractions. But I decided she would worry too much. I hate it when she worries."

"Loveleen, that picture that you are holding, where . . . ?" Kitt asked, but before she could finish her sentence, Loveleen interrupted, "Yes, it is a wedding photo. We got married in a very small temple, and it was then that I decided to get pregnant. This is as authorized as it gets in India for gay couples. No court of law will marry us."

Kitt smiled, got up, and gave Loveleen a hug.

"No matter how well I think I know you, you always manage

to surprise me. Now, rest up and I will come by later to check in on you."

After Kitt left, Loveleen decided she was too hyped up to sleep. She clicked through the various television channels, killing a couple of hours. Her maid brought her some breakfast. She ate a little, still feeling very uncomfortable with the pain.

She debated a nap, but then texted Kitt instead. *I'M DONE WITH THIS BED REST. I NEED TO TALK TO ESHAAN, AND HE IS NOT ANSWERING HIS STUPID PHONE. I AM GOING TO THE MONASTERY FIRST, AND THEN I WILL COME TO YOUR HOUSE FOR TEA.*

DO NOT COME DOWN. I AM COMING UP. AND YOU WANT TEA? IN THIS BLISTERING HEAT? Kitt texted.

YES, TEA, DAMN IT! was the response. *HEAT KILLS THE HEAT, DARLING!*

Kitt stopped texting, picked up the phone, and called Loveleen.

"Forget the stupid tea. You should be resting. Papa will be furious if he sees you walking around."

Loveleen laughed aloud. "I feel just fine. Please don't worry. Walking out. See you in a few minutes."

Kitt was standing on her patio as she hung up the phone. She saw Eshaan getting into Loveleen's car. She called out to him, but he didn't hear, so she ran out to tell him to wait for Loveleen. She ran so fast that she bumped into the milkman delivering bottled milk. Dr. Sinha hated the new packets of pasteurized milk at the stores, so the whole building now got fresh milk delivered from a nearby dairy. And all that fresh milk was now on the floor of the courtyard intermingled with glass shards from the now broken milk bottles.

The milkman began to scream, "Madam, where are you looking? Can you not see? What will I do now? Madam, Madam?"

Kitt stopped rushing. "Oh, so sorry. I can pay you for this, so sorry," she said. One person's mess is another's miracle. Loveleen's black cat was thrilled at the spilled milk and was licking it furiously.

"What the hell happened here? Oh, let me go get Cat before she cuts herself on the broken glass," Loveleen said as she came down the stairs and moved toward her pet.

"Oooooo . . . madam, what money? Who will clean up this big mess? Where will I get more milk now for my customers? You will give money, but they will be angry with me!" the milkman continued to yell at Kitt.

"She said she would pay you, now take the money and go. What is it you are grumbling about?" Loveleen responded sternly to the man in her native Punjabi.

"Okay, okay, I will take the money, but you have to give double, since now I have lost all this milk."

"Let me go get my purse," Kitt said as she turned to walk back into the house and suddenly came face-to-face Mr. Mehra, who was standing there looking completely aghast.

In front of Merry Mehra, follower of all things inauspicious, were two things that should never happen by themselves much less together: spilled milk and a black cat.

"Oh, Mr. Mehra, this was an accident. We will clean it up," Kitt said, but Mehra was staring straight at Loveleen, who smirked at him as she picked up her black cat and gave it an extra tight hug.

Mr. Mehra turned around and went back to his floor.

Relieved that disaster had been averted again with Mehra, Kitt ran in to get the money for the milkman. By the time she came back, the milkman was calm and joking with Loveleen.

"Kitt, Eshaan just called. I will go up and get some knives and then go to Karma Kitchen. Some rich dude with a conscience is giving the kitchen forty kilos of tomatoes, and Eshaan needs more knives. I will bring some and meet you there," Loveleen said then noted the frown on her friend's face.

"Don't look so worried, darling! I will just sit and do nothing. I promise I will rest!" Loveleen added, and then disappeared up the stairs.

The young maid that Kitt's father employed came out to clear the broken glass. Kitt began to help pick up the larger shards.

Suddenly, there was a shrill scream near the stairs. Kitt turned to see what happened.

Loveleen was lying at the bottom of the stairs.

Before she passed out, she mumbled, "The bastard pushed me."

Chapter 31

Eshaan tried to breathe slowly, one deep breath in, and one deep breath out. He felt his insides trying to squeeze his very soul out of his body. He had confided in Kitt earlier that night that he felt as though his body was being pushed through a juicing machine, like the ones that extract sugarcane juice. The cane goes in whole, filled with riches, and comes out the other side, bare, crushed, and lifeless.

Do we create our demons, or do our demons create us? Eshaan wondered.

The sun was already out, and Eshaan knew that in a few minutes, he would have to be in the kitchen to cook. He sat on the edge of the bed to steady himself. He learned a while ago that the only way to bear the nausea was to run, fast, as fast as he could, so his spirit would become one with the wind and the pain would be lost in the quiet energy swirling around him. But, these days, even running wasn't helping. Instead of strengthening his spirit, the runs seemed to be depleting whatever little was left inside him. The deep, dark truths that haunt lives don't just show up randomly; they show up at the most vulnerable of times.

On top of it all, he missed Loveleen so much and hoped she would recover soon from her nasty fall.

Eshaan wet a towel and covered his face with it. Sometimes that did the trick and toned down the nausea. At some point, he must have put the towel down and passed out on the bed.

He was roused from his sleep by Radio Rani calling out his name outside his window.

"Eshaan, Eshaan, come out here *now*! There are rats in Karma Kitchen."

He got up, still feeling very groggy, opened the door, rushed past her, and into the kitchen. The kitchen hadn't even opened for breakfast yet, and there was a long line of people waiting to get in already.

"What the hell? Where?" Eshaan screamed as he looked around inside the kitchen. He then stopped short, looking very confused and totally embarrassed to be standing there in his pajamas and no shirt.

Several of the monks were standing behind the cooking counters and beaming smiles at him. The air was fragrant with the smell of fried onions and toasted cumin.

"Radio Rani, I don't see any rats. What the heck is going on? What is everyone doing here this early?"

"*Happy Birthday to you*," a sweet voice began to sing.

Eshaan turned around to see Kitt walking in with a large chocolate cake. One large candle adorned the cake and sparked like the sparklers Eshaan loved to play with during Diwali, the festival of lights.

The monks joined in the singing. Out of the corner of his eye, Eshaan saw Gina coming through the door, carrying a rather large gift box. *Who told her?* he wondered.

Birthday? In reality, he did not know which year or which month he was born. This day was the day Lama Dorje had found him and pronounced him "still alive." So it was his birthday, the day he was reborn.

He smiled, trying to put away the memory of the nightmarish week they had all had. Loveleen was still in the hospital after her fall. There had been no news from Merry Mehra or his son Amit. Both seemed to have disappeared into thin air. The police had come in to question Dr. Sinha and Kitt about the incident after a neighbor complained.

Of course, trouble attracts more trouble, and as though on cue, Karma Kitchen began to have serious growing pains. First, as predicted by the Lama, the water in the taps just stopped, and then, the large boxes of spices he had purchased began to reek and little worms started crawling out of them, and as if that wasn't enough, Eshaan noticed the lines to eat free were getting longer, and the kitchen had essentially turned into a free food charity that had very little food to give away.

"Eshaan, we are happy you are a part of our family here," Lama Dorje said as Kitt placed the large cake on one of the tables. The Lama had been away for what seemed like an eternity, helping the Dalai Lama in Dharamsala, but had returned the previous night.

"I have to admit the rats idea was really funny! You should have seen the look on your face!" The Lama chuckled.

"Happy birthday, handsome." Gina handed him his gift and leaned in to kiss him on the lips, but he quickly turned his face and she planted it on his cheek. Not one to give up easily, she moved her hand on his left buttock and gave it a tight squeeze.

"Eshaan, happy birthday! But what happened to your back? It looks like someone scratched you," Tulku Tenzin said as he eyed Eshaan's flesh.

"Oh, Loveleen's black cat paid me a visit last night," Eshaan joked as he tried to pull himself out of Gina's tight grasp. Kitt looked visibly upset and stood next to the cake, her hands folded across her chest.

Everyone laughed. The room filled with chatter, laughter, and serenity as Eshaan went around hugging and thanking everyone. He came to Radio Rani, who was looking at him with a fierce scowl.

"Stop now, Eshaan, or I will tell Lama Dorje. I promise you." Rani's voice was threatening, and this time, he sensed she wasn't making empty threats.

"Come on. It is my birthday today. Be nice," he whispered, and then saw her tears. "I will try. Okay? I will try. I promise." He bent down, wiped her tears, and hugged her. She clutched onto him as though she was trying to contain the energy that was leaking out of his spirit.

Gina gathered the crowd around the cake.

Kitt held up her tablet. "Eshaan, Loveleen is here too on the camera. Say hi!"

"Happy birthday, but, really *jaan*, what the heck are you doing half nude in front of the monks?!" Loveleen teased him. She was smiling, but her face looked drawn, her eyes were swollen, and her voice was slurring.

Eshaan blew her a kiss and said, "I'm coming there after lunch is served here, and I'll bring you cake and a new cricket poster I found."

Loveleen blew him a kiss.

"Everyone, I have an announcement to make. Listen, listen," Eshaan tried to quieten the crowd.

Lama Dorje hushed everyone. The crowd huddled around the cake and Eshaan. Even Potato *Baba* woke up from his sleep, from his quiet corner of the kitchen, to see what the commotion was all about.

Rani invited the people standing outside in the line to come inside and have some cake, as breakfast was still an hour away. Eshaan looked at the beggars coming in and smiled. He recognized most of them. And now, they recognized him. He noticed a couple of them had even washed up before coming in. Oh, and the fact that they washed up meant the water was back in the taps! Maybe this was a sign that, despite all the problems, things would work out for the best.

"Okay, come on, Eshaan, share now. We are waiting. I think this baby will come faster than your announcement," Loveleen's voice boomed over the phone.

"Yes, Eshaan, tell us!" Gina added.

"Yes, yes, we are ready," said Lama Dorje.

"I have a two-part announcement. First, guess who emailed me early this morning?"

"You got in, didn't you? I knew it. The cooking show? You are in? Right?" Kitt could barely contain herself, and the look on his face confirmed to everyone that he had indeed made the next cut.

The crowd broke out into huge cheers. Gina ran up to him and gave him a hug. He thanked her then pulled himself away and walked up to Kitt and hugged her tight. He felt her cool hands on his bare back. He pulled her closer. "Put on a shirt, Eshaan. I cannot believe I did that to your back last night," she whispered then gently pulled herself away. They hadn't planned it. After visiting Loveleen at the hospital, Kitt had accompanied Eshaan back to his room. In less than a minute, they were in bed together. After she left, he felt an emptiness he had never felt before. It was like she had taken his soul with her. His stomach had cramped, his chest tightened but, eventually, he had passed out on the bed.

"Come on, Eshaan, cut the cake," Tenzin called out to him. Reluctantly, Eshaan let Kitt go and noticed Gina looked sad.

"Gina, aren't you going to sing for me?" he called out to her, and she smiled and roused the crowd.

Everyone sang together as he cut the cake. He took a small slice and turned to Kitt. "This is for you. For always making my life sweeter."

"Eshaan, you must win that contest! I would love to go back to Austria and tell everyone that a TV celebrity catered our wedding." The accent was unmistakable. Eshaan looked in the direction of the sound. Nikolas walked into the kitchen, beaming a smile at his bride-to-be, the love of Eshaan's life.

No one remembered that Eshaan had another announcement to make.

Eshaan Veer Singh's Journal

I see her
I hear her
She is here
Yet
She will never be here
I see her tears
I reach out to touch
To drink her pain
To be the one
He reaches her before I do
He wipes her tears
Her tears are her healers
She cries for the couple we will never be
Her tears
Are her shield

Present day

Chapter 32

Eshaan, grateful to be driving Loveleen's car, arrived at the studio two hours before the shoot was to start. He opened the trunk to take out his cooking implements. The cooking show staff had instructed him to bring his favorite utensil, and he had chosen his treasured *sil batta.* "Possibly the parent idea of the modern day mortar and pestle," Lama Dorje had remarked when he presented the gift to him. Eshaan had smiled at the comparison; he loved his tiny mortar and pestle for his spices. But his *sil batta,* flat marble stone with a long bat-like stone for grinding, was perfect for making all the pastes and chutneys he so loved creating.

The sun hadn't risen yet, but the parking lot at the studio was already buzzing. Eshaan recognized a few of the contestants from his first visit, and even saw one of the judges getting out of their car. The wafting aroma of freshly made tea filled the parking lot as a young man, dressed in chef whites, passed out tea-filled terracotta mugs to the very grateful and nervous contestants as they arrived at the studio.

The cooking studio was in an old warehouse right outside

Delhi's city limits. The land had lain barren for years until a producer realized there was big money to be made in reality food shows. In fact, cooking shows were outshining the typical mother-in-law/daughter-in-law soaps that had been popular for years. This was the third season of this particular show, and never had there been more interest. The last season brought in so much endorsement money that the producer was able to refurbish this entire warehouse and create special cooking kitchens for the contestants and the staff. There was even a large tent pitched outside that main studio that housed tables and chairs and a large buffet set-up to provide meals for everyone working on the set.

A guard showed Eshaan to his van. The bright blue makeup van had a large white sheet stuck on the main window. The sheet read CHEF ESHAAN VEER SINGH. Eshaan stood there for a few moments staring at his name. Perhaps his luck was changing.

"You really did not need to come along, Lama Dorje. I know you are busy," Eshaan whispered as they stood outside the sets of *India's Best Home Chef.* With Loveleen still in the hospital and Kitt now busy with Nikolas and her upcoming nuptials, Eshaan was fully prepared to go solo for this next round of competition. Gina had not returned his calls thanking her for his birthday gift. He promised himself he would call her after the day's shoot.

"I'm here because I want to be here. That is it. You just worry about what you will be cooking up," Lama Dorje said. The guard told Eshaan to wait in the van and requested the Lama to follow him onto the set to a special area meant for the families of the contestants.

"Eshaan, sir, the director has requested some individual shots so we will get you dressed for that first," said a young woman, who was in the makeup van waiting for him.

It took a good two hours to get him ready, new haircut, fresh shave, makeup, gel-spiked hair, a deep blue–colored shirt that showed off his tattoos, and snug black jeans.

"I don't recognize this person," Eshaan said as he pointed to the mirror in the van.

"You don't need to. When the show airs, people will be recognizing you as you walk down the street," the young woman said as she opened the van door for the photographer.

"The light is great and good for a shoot. Let's move this along quickly before the light becomes too harsh," one of the senior photographers said as they all began to fire instructions at Eshaan on how he should pose, how he should stand, how he should smile, and more.

During a short break, Eshaan checked his mobile. No texts, nothing from Kitt. Loveleen sent three pictures of her swollen feet. There was one from Gina that read, *LOVE YOU! BREAK A LEG, AS THEY SAY HERE IN THE THEATRE.*

"Take your *sil batta*. We will do a few poses with that over at that kitchen counter." The photographer moved Eshaan a few feet away toward a large makeshift outdoor kitchen.

Twenty minutes later, Eshaan walked onto the set. The crew inside was busy moving tables and dressing up the bronze-plated island that would be used to showcase the final dishes. A few people were stocking the showcase pantry. A couple of men were replacing some bulbs in the main studio. Cuss words were flying around freely.

"Yes! This is the look I wanted for you! But we need to call clothes, call clothes now, and have them give him a bandana.

Who is listening? Did you hear me?" the director said to no one in particular, but pointed at Eshaan and then continued to bark directions to the staff.

As if by magic, a staffer came running in with an electric blue bandana and tied it around Eshaan's head, then told him to head to where all the contestants were waiting.

Suddenly there was a hushing sound on the set, and everyone stopped what they were doing to see what the fuss was all about.

A glowingly beautiful woman, draped in a black chiffon sari, glided onto the main set. There were a few stray whistles from the audience, and then, as was customary for her, thunderous applause. She looked toward the audience and waved as a soft, yet triumphant, smile crossed her lips.

"Rumor has it that she rolls for an hour in white flour to get that bleached white look," Eshaan heard a contestant whisper to the group. The group stifled a laugh.

The elegant Indian woman, almost six feet tall, had wavy black hair that came down to her buttocks, striking black eyes, a figure that most women dieted endlessly for, and yes, skin that was spuriously white.

"Maybe the face-whitening cream she endorses actually works for her," another contestant whispered.

"What is she doing here?" Eshaan asked no one in particular.

"Can you believe that Maneesha Oberoi, the reigning queen of the Indian film industry, is going to be the guest judge today?" another voice replied.

"Yes, it makes complete sense that our cooking skills will be judged by someone who has probably never cooked a single day in her life," someone quipped, and the group laughed aloud, letting off some tension.

Both the chefs who judged Eshaan the last time seemed taken by their guest judge, as they followed her like small puppies to her spot at the Judges' station. Their new bright red, sleek leather chairs were positioned right in front of the bronze island, where the contestants would be sharing their dishes of the day. The minute Maneesha Oberoi sat down, her hair and makeup people rushed to her to freshen her up.

The director called out for an all clear on the set.

The lights turned off.

The contestants stood still, many of them holding hands as the tension returned.

"Contestants, please come onto the set now, single file . . . walk slowly, and don't bump into each other, please," the shrill voice of the director broke the silence on the set.

As the twenty or so contestants walked onto the main stage, a spotlight came on and shone on each one of them. They were each asked to come to center stage and say their name out loud.

The two judges introduced themselves next, praising each other to the sky and back. Then, Bollywood royalty, Maneesha Oberoi, stood up. "I'm here to support all these wonderful people who make terrific food." Her words were drowned out by the star-crazy audience and crew.

"Does anyone know what they will be asking us to make today?" a nervous young contestant whispered to the group as they all crowded together on the stage and tried to smile under the bright light that was now shining on all of them.

"No idea, but I am guessing, since the judge is so glamorous, the dish will have to have some glam take on it. Maybe we will get to cook with liquid nitrogen or something as crazy!" a lanky young man responded.

An assistant director rushed to the set and tried to position the hopefuls in a visually attractive way. "Where is makeup uncle? We need him here now. Please tell him to fix the faces of these three. We have less than ten minutes before we roll."

"It is so hot in here. Can someone please fix that, and I want a glass of chilled *nimbu paani*, lemonade, for all the contestants, *right now*. I don't want a repeat of what happened last time," the director shrieked at his staff. A week ago, two of the contestants had passed out in the hot staging kitchen due to dehydration and the shoot had to be stopped for the entire day.

As the makeup uncle fixed up one of the young female contestants on the set, another production team member brought out the lemonade for the crew.

"We are getting ready for a take. Please look alive, like you want to be here. Come on now, give us a nice smile," the director yelled as the taping began.

Chef Ram Singh, dressed in a loud golden jacket and deep blue pants, stood up and faced the contestants. He began by thanking the sponsors then introduced the guest judge.

"All of you know who Maneesha Oberoi is. She needs no introduction. We are all delighted and privileged that she has chosen to be with us for this episode as we pick the final ten. You are all here, because we believe you all have what it takes to move forward. But today, today is a big test. We will not be judging you; *she* will," he said, and then for added drama, he swung around and pointed a finger at the movie star.

"Madulika Oberoi, the superstar, will be the judge. She has

traveled the world and eaten in the best of the best places. Oh shit! Sorry!" Judge Chef Ram said as he heard boos from the live audience.

The furious director stared at Chef Ram Singh and spoke into the microphone that was connected to the earpieces the judges were wearing. "Not Madulika, Maneesha. Let's do this again. This time, with the right name, please. She will walk off if you do this again."

The introduction was shot again, this time with the correct name, and the audience screamed adulations, the contestants clapped, and the camera panned to Maneesha, who beamed her best smile to show off her newly capped and polished pearly whites.

"Thank you for the nice welcome," she said then stood up and faced the contestants.

"So before I tell you what the theme is, let me explain why I picked it. As an actress, I have to watch every single calorie, and sometimes that means I don't get to eat what I want. And really, truly, sometimes I just crave flaky, warm, potato-stuffed bread *paranthas,* loaded with homemade white butter—just like my mom used to make. So that, friends, is the theme: a memorable taste from your childhood," she said, and then glided back onto the chair and asked for a glass of water and some green tea, as she was feeling faint in the heat.

The camera moved off Maneesha and onto Chef Ram Singh again. "You can use anything from the pantry. You will have to prepare three servings of your completed dish, one for each judge. You will have an hour, and your time starts . . . now!"

The camera zoomed in on the contestants running back to

the pantry and staging kitchen.

"Cut!" the director announced.

"We need four portions. Three for tasting, and one for the glamour shot. When the glamour shot serving is ready, please call one of the assistants in yellow. They will move the dish to the bronze island for shooting," the director was screaming as the contestants were still rummaging through the pantry, trying to find the perfect ingredients for their dish.

"Listen up. When you get to your cooking stations, we will bring the camera in front of you. You will look up and tell us what you are cooking and why. You have ten minutes to get all your ingredients to your counter. And then *that is it*. You will have fifty minutes to cook and present."

The staging kitchen buzzed as contestants whizzed past each other like aspiring dancers, trying not to collide. The graceless waltz of the bright-eyed, food-loving contestants continued until they heard the director again. "I want everyone at their stations and ready to go in two minutes."

Two contestants crashed into each other, dropped all their ingredients, and began bickering with foul language and impolite hand gestures. The camera, as always, loved the chaos, and was almost orgasmic when a fight broke out over the only blender in the kitchen. A weary assistant promised to get another one as soon as possible.

The director called time and all the contestants ran back to their stations.

The makeup man was called once again to give them all a touch-up, and the camera began to roll.

The cameraman careful moved up to the first contestant in

the line, and Chef Ram Singh followed closely behind him. Slowly, the cameraman moved his hand to indicate he was ready. "So, Ms. Mina, what are you making? Remember the theme is the taste of childhood," Chef Singh asked the tiny woman behind the counter. "I am making a *parantha* that my mother would make me when I was very hungry. I know Maneesha *ji* likes *paranthas,* so she will like this. Her *parantha* was stuffed with potatoes, but my mother made mine sweet, so mine has jaggery, saffron, and crushed cardamom. There was not enough time to make the butter, so I am using this store butter."

Chef Ram Singh shook his head in a peculiar way, and it was hard to determine if he was saying he liked or didn't like what the young woman had to say.

He went from station to station asking each contestant the same question, and gave strange looks in response to their answers.

Eshaan braced for his turn, and when Chef Ram Singh arrived, Eshaan explained he was making a simple version of the Tibetan *thupka,* a soup with vegetables and meats. "As I recall, you made a soup last time as well. This is not very creative, but if it is the memory, it is the memory." Chef Singh shook his head and moved on to the next contestant.

For a minute, Eshaan debated if the soup was the right way to go then decided to trust his gut feeling. He placed three pieces of chicken thighs into a large pot, filled it with water, added sliced onions, fresh minced cilantro, and a slew of spices then set it on medium heat to boil. Once the broth was done, the rest, he knew would just be assembly.

Eshaan brought out his *sil batta* and prepared a thick paste of onions, green chilies, garlic, fresh turmeric root, and a tiny speck of asafetida. The thick stone assaulted the tender ingredients, forcing them to share their spectacular aromas. Typically, he would add noodles to the soup, but he had none at the moment. There was only one package of egg noodles, and the girl next to him had picked that up earlier. To improvise, he began to create curls from the carrots and the radish he had picked up. *They will have to do,* he thought.

"Fifteen minutes! Be sure to create a dish that impresses our taste buds!" Chef Ram Singh called out.

Eshaan skimmed the foam off the gently boiling broth and used a ladle to remove the pieces of chicken to set them aside. Then he sautéed the spice paste in a large pan. He strained the broth over the paste, and almost immediately, the two melded as though they were meant to be together forever. Moving faster, he shredded the cooked chicken and added it and the vegetable curls to the broth. He moved his nose close to the pot and took a deep inhale. It was usually at this point, he recalled, that Lama Dorje would express gratitude for the ingredients that were going to nurture him and thank nature for its amazing bounty. The smell always reminded him of his early nights at the monastery as a terrified young child, trembling at the sight of strangers, weeping in the presence of the Lama, and begging God/Buddha/Allah/any God who would listen, to bring his mother back.

The contestants rushed to meet the approaching deadline, stopping to help each other get the dishes portioned and plated. The large kitchen was filled with smells of toasting cinnamon, frying onions, and fresh lemons.

"It is nice to see you all helping each other, but don't forget to get your own work finished. You will be judged on how you did, not how you helped someone else," Chef Ram Singh said, pointing a finger at Eshaan, who, having finished his own dish, was helping a lady plate hers.

"Five minutes! Get your dishes ready *now*." Chef Ram Singh was loud and stern.

The fanatical chaos got worse. There were tears, screams, shrieks, name calling, and muffled laughter as one contestant stood at her station, lit an incense stick, and prayed over her dish.

Eshaan stood tall as he spooned his fragrant soup into four large colorful bowls. He remembered Dorje feeding him this soup with a spoon and constantly saying, "This will help you heal. Your spirit and your heart will soon rejoice." The soup, at first, tasted bizarre to Eshaan. His mother had never cooked anything like that. But slowly, he became more comfortable with the light broth and the savory pieces of chicken and vegetables that came with each spoonful.

The countdown began.

"Hands off the table," Chef Ram Singh announced, and all the contestants moved away from their stations.

"Be sure to send out the dish for the shots *right now*," the director screamed.

Maneesha Oberoi was now in the staging kitchen and left a pong of perfume behind her as she walked toward the cooking stations. The camera was whirring. While the contestants were cooking, the production team had removed the sliding wall that separated the main set from the staging kitchen. Now the audience could see all the contestants at their stations and the judges walking around tasting and offering instant feedback. The contestants were told on the spot if they were in or out.

The first three had already been told to pack up their spice boxes and leave.

"Too much salt." Maneesha grimaced at one, and too much butter was her complaint with the next one.

"You made a fried egg? I do understand that this is the taste of your childhood, but could you not have been a little creative? Maybe deep-fried it and served it over some potato chips? Oh, this is just unacceptable. At this level, you are expected to do more," Maneesha told contestant number three. The contestant protested and wailed about the unfairness of the judging. Then, as would happen in any soap opera, the contestant began to cry and was escorted out by the production staff.

Cameras kept rolling and the director was clearly thrilled. Tears, mean words, and unfairness assured great ratings.

"So, soup man, are you ready for us?" Chef Ram Singh asked as he led the actress to Eshaan's station.

"Tell us what you have made and why," prompted Maneesha in a rather condescending tone as she sized up the young man, then smiled provocatively at him.

"I love the aroma of ginger and cilantro," said Chef Navin Patel, picking up one of the bowls and smelling it. He then placed it back down and waited for Eshaan to explain.

The camera zoomed in on the soup then panned up to Eshaan's face. He simply stood there staring at the bowls of soup on his counter.

"Oh, come on now, young man. Where is your tongue? Speak! Tell us about your dish!" said Chef Ram Singh.

Eshaan brought the palms of his hands together then looked up. "I was rescued from poverty when I was a child. The monk who rescued me, Lama Dorje, the monk seated there in the audience, prepared this soup and fed it to me for months on end. It is this soup that saved my life . . . but . . . but . . . but—"

"It saved your life? So what is the *but*?" asked Maneesha in a sharp voice.

Eshaan bent down, picked up each bowl of soup, and threw the contents into a large trashcan that was placed right by the cooking station.

There was a stunned gasp from the audience.

A couple of people screamed out, "WHAT ARE YOU DOING?"

"Wait, wait . . . why the heck did you do that? We haven't even tasted it yet!" Chef Ram Singh's eyes were ablaze with anger. He turned to the director and shrugged his shoulders. The director signaled the cameraman to keep filming—nothing better than an on-air disaster.

"Are you listening to me, young man? This is very disrespectful," Chef Ram Singh's voice quivered with anger, and he waved his hands in the air as a dramatic display of displeasure.

Eshaan picked up the empty bowl. His voice was soft and cracked when he spoke. "I am sorry . . . I just could not do it."

The audience was still gasping and screaming questions at Eshaan.

The director spoke up, "Quiet, please. Let the young man say what he wants to say."

"You asked us to share the taste of our childhood. This . . . this empty bowl . . . is all that I really remember about my childhood, constant hunger and empty utensils."

With that, Eshaan removed his apron, wiped his tears, and walked off the set of the show that could have changed his life.

Eshaan Veer Singh's Journal

I stare at the bowl
It reminds me of days
Filled with vegetables and worry
With cilantro and the fears of a heartbroken child
I stare at the bowl
The noodles float free
In a broth that was, in my childhood, seasoned with hints of misery
It was said to heal
And I thought - the taste that defined
An innocent childhood time
But that…that childhood?
That truly never was mine
I lift up this broth to serve it to you
And then I realize what I am about to do
I cannot feed you my fears
I hesitate no more
As I decide
The broth and the lies
Must not have a life
You stare at me for the fool you think I am
But you don't understand…
The reality inside

My bowl
You see
Needs to symbolize
Truth…not lies

Chapter 33

"It has taken me two hours to find you, child. Had it not been for Raju and his dogs guiding me here, I would never have found you! You aren't answering your phone," Lama Dorje said as he sat down next to Eshaan. Raju waved to them and retreated back into the depths of the garden.

Both men were seated inside the ruins of an ancient house in the city of Mehrauli, one of the seven old cities that made up Delhi. These ruins, inside a large archeological park, were just a stone's throw away from the monastery. Eshaan often came here when he needed some time to think. During the days, it was filled with kite-flyers, picnickers, lovers, and kids playing cricket. But at this time of the evening, only the darker elements dared come into the park that turned from interesting to haunting as the light gave way to darkness.

The sun, distancing itself from the world, was covering up for the night, blanketed by large, dark rainclouds. The air was thick with the pungent stink of vomit and failure.

Eshaan sat still and said nothing. He stared straight ahead into the impending shadows, a broken man with his broken spirit. His hands clutched his legs to his chest.

"I am sorry, Lama. Starvation was the taste of my childhood. My childhood ended the day my mother died," he said as he wiped his tears.

Lama Dorje placed his hand on Eshaan's back as the young man sobbed. The Lama had not seen Eshaan cry like this in years. In fact, he had been convinced Eshaan was on the road to recovery when his nightmares about chasing his mother but never catching her had stopped a year or so ago. Today, after watching Eshaan at the studio, the truth had dawned on the Lama: Eshaan's problems with his health had started right around the time the nightmares stopped.

Several crows were now pecking at an enormous dead rat that had been baking for the day in the hot sun. A gentle wind brought the lurid smell of decaying flesh to the nostrils of the two men. Eshaan flinched and covered his face.

"You spoke your truth, and that is what matters," Lama Dorje said softly.

"I let you down. I let Kitt down, Loveleen . . . all of them. Rani, Om, they were all relying on this to be our way to run a successful kitchen. Now, now what will I do? I have failed, again." Eshaan's body jerked as he wept.

"I am not let down. I did not come here to tell you that I am upset with you about the cooking show," Lama Dorje said as he folded his hands across his chest.

"You are not? I guess you are a monk, so you are extra kind," Eshaan said.

Eshaan's naïveté never failed to make the Lama smile, but not today. Today, he had decided he was going to confront him.

"Eshaan, I know," the Lama said in a firm voice as he stared straight at the setting sun.

"What do you mean, you know? You know what?" Eshaan was clearly startled. "I don't understand. I don't know what you are talking about."

"You are dying in installments," Lama Dorje said.

"What? Dying? I am not dying! Who told you that?" Eshaan tried to change the mood and wished the monk would just stop talking.

Had Radio Rani revealed his secret to the Lama? Eshaan waited tentatively for the monk to continue speaking.

The old monk removed his glasses. "A long time ago, when I was a young man, our senior teacher liked to tell us about a house burning down."

"Don't do this, Lama. Not today. I can barely understand your stories when I am feeling good." Eshaan shook his head and looked pleadingly at the monk.

Of course, the Lama would not let go. "Answer me this question, child. Imagine you are inside a house that is burning. What would you do?"

"I know this is a trick question." Eshaan was glum.

"Just answer it. It is a simple question. If you are inside a burning house, what would you do?"

"I would try to save who or what I could, and then I would try to save myself by running out. That is it," Eshaan said listlessly as he kicked the ground below with his feet, causing dust clouds to appear, making him cough.

"Yes, that is it. But what would you be doing a year later?" the Lama Dorje asked.

Eshaan blurted out, “A year later? Well, I would hope I had a new house to live in.”

“So you would have left the burning house and tried to find and settle in a new place, yes?” the old monk repeated, and Eshaan nodded.

The monk looked straight into Eshaan’s eyes. “Your past is gone. It influenced you, and it made you who you are, but it is gone,” the Lama said.

“But I am responsible. I could not save her, Lama. She loved me so much. I could not save her,” Eshaan wept as he had when he was a child on that first night, when the Lama had found him.

“Eshaan, living in the past is not going to help you. You were a mere child. You did what you could. Today, life is offering you such riches, but your heart and mind, they . . . they still believe your house is burning. Until you take actions to heal, you will not be able to move forward with anything.”

The shadows of both men lengthened as the sun went lower, hiding, recovering, resting before another dawn.

The Lama, taking advantage of Eshaan’s silence, spoke again. “Eshaan, when we pray and meditate, which you do with me every day, all our ancestors are by our side. By not eating, by punishing yourself and throwing up the food you eat as a reprimand to yourself, you are dishonoring your mother and her spirit.” the Lama’s voice was strong, unwavering yet compassionate.

Eshaan stood up. He could not believe the monk knew what he had been doing.

“Did Radio Rani tell you?” Eshaan turned his face away from the monk.

"No one told me. I've suspected it for a while now. Your penance is not going to bring back your mother." The monk placed his hand on Eshaan's back.

"The universe is offering you a chance to make a difference with many people, and you are throwing it away because of your guilt. Hurting yourself will not bring her back or heal her spirit."

Eshaan instinctively moved his hand to the tattoo on his arm. *Rab Rakha*, protected by God.

A couple of street kids came running up to the two men and held out their hands, begging. Lama Dorje told them to go to the monastery and ask for Tulku Tenzin. He assured them that the young monk would feed them dinner.

"See these children? They are perfect for your kitchen. The mistake you are making is that you are worrying about who should be fed and who should not. Do you know what you should be doing instead?"

Eshaan shook his head.

The sun had done its job for the day. The air was now cooler. The clouds were getting darker as the rain began, tiny drops washing away the burden of the day. The sweet smell of the drops merging into the dry, parched earth offered relief to the men, who had been smelling dead rats and vomit for the past hour.

"If you want to feed the world, you first have to feed yourself, your stomach and your soul. Then focus on those who want to be helped. Make them your helpers. If someone wants to eat and leave, let them go. Don't judge them. You can only help those who want to be helped."

The monk remained quiet for a moment and then added, "You cannot starve yourself on purpose. You must not. Do you understand what I am telling you?"

Before Eshaan could answer, his phone began to beep. It was a text from Tulku Tenzin. *ONLY THE ASHES REMAIN.*

Eshaan Veer Singh's Journal

Those smells
Of sizzled cumin
Of roasted mustard
Of charred eggplant
Of boiled rice
Of sweet puddings
Of pungent garlic
Those smells
Assault my nose
Seep into my skin
Bleed out as my sweat
Those scents
I pretend to respect them
I pretend to adore them
I lie
Those scents
Make me weak
Drain my resolve
Those scents
Make the bile rise up
I try to stop
I beg it to stop
I pray it stops

It isn't the smells, he tells me
It is you
How does he know, how does he see
that
I am a prisoner of my own memories

Chapter 34

Eshaan and Lama Dorje raced toward the monastery. Their feet barely touched the ground as they ran, defying the wind, defying the traffic, defying all laws of the universe. Eshaan had not even texted back to ask what had happened, but his heart told him that text was not sent lightly.

Even before they reached the monastery, they saw smoke billowing from the building.

Eshaan stopped in his tracks, covered his mouth with his hands, and let out a pain-filled howl.

Lama Dorje turned to him. "We must go to see if they need help. Having a breakdown will not do anyone any good. Now *move*."

The two men rushed toward the monastery. The elaborate wrought-iron security gate was wide open. The guard was sitting down on his broken plastic stool. He stood as soon as he saw Lama Dorje. His face had a few small cuts on one side.

"I am so sorry. I tried to stop them," he said.

The men ran toward the smoke that appeared to be coming from the back of the monastery.

"It's gone," Eshaan said as soon as he reached the back.

A shadowy skeleton of Karma Kitchen stood where the dream kitchen used to be. The building, while still standing, had been ravaged by the fire.

Eshaan walked up to the entrance of the kitchen. All the lovingly crafted tables, chairs, the old A/C and the new one, the bamboo bowl outside, all burnt, charred to bits. The new fans were still smoldering in the fire. The sweet smell of sizzling spices had been replaced by the sour stench of destruction. There were pieces of broken sticks on the ground, at least one large bloody knife, and several broken glass bottles.

Eshaan picked up the knife with his trembling hands and looked at Lama Dorje. "This is blood. What in God's name happened here? Is everyone okay? This is horrible."

"We tried to stop them, but we could not," Tulku Tenzin murmured. He had been sitting on the grass in front of the kitchen.

"Tenzin, my friend. Are you okay? Is everyone okay?" Eshaan walked over to him and placed his hand gently on his shoulder, and then noticed Tenzin's back was bleeding.

"Oh, my God. You need a doctor. What the hell happened here? Where is Om? Where is Radio Rani?"

Tenzin shook his head. "I'm okay. It is just a small cut." He went on to explain that earlier that morning, Om had refused to let some of the local thugs, who repeatedly came in for free food, into Karma Kitchen.

"It was the same thugs. You remember; they came in last week and you told them to work and they just laughed. Do you remember that?" he said.

Eshaan nodded his head. Those guys were trouble.

The first time they came in, Eshaan had signaled to Om to just let them come in to see what would transpire. They had been obnoxious but harmless at that time. They ate and left without saying a word to the monks or Eshaan. The second time they came in, Eshaan had asked them to help out. "Work for what? You are in our area. Understand?" had been their threatening response. They ate, made a huge ruckus, and left.

"Yes, those same guys came in earlier this morning. There was already a long line and they pushed and shoved everyone so they could come in first," Tenzin continued. Om pushed them away and told them to leave, and one of them punched him. Not one to back out of a fight, Om had returned the punch. Several of the people in line stepped in and beat up that thug. "The thug was wailing on the ground. Om was letting the people back in to eat and I thought it would all be fine . . . but—" Tulku Tenzin's voice cracked.

While all this was happening, two of the thugs left and returned with large sticks, knives, and a huge can of petrol. But this time, they weren't alone. They had come in with some group that was carrying banners. All of them had black headbands around their foreheads.

Tenzin was sobbing as he explained the people waiting for food in the lines ran away, and the ones eating in the kitchen ran out as well. Om never knew what hit him. His screaming caused many of the monks to come running out into the yard. In a split second, one young thug threw the can of petrol into Karma Kitchen and then threw a lit cigarette.

"Where is he? Where is Om? And where is Radio Rani?"

Eshaan's voice was strained, controlled.

"They are both alive. Dr. Sinha took them to the hospital. Om's nose is broken, and one of the thugs slashed Radio Rani's back," Tenzin said softly.

The others in the group, the ones with the headbands, also threw in a couple of cans and matches. Tenzin said they were screaming about morality and how people who helped the immoral, who went against the laws of God and the land, did not deserve to have a business.

"What? They were yelling about what?" Eshaan was confused for just a second and then it clicked. The local thugs had never been this violent. This was the work of the bigger hate group.

"Lama, I think this group he is describing sounds like the right-wing haters. The morality comment makes me wonder if they were talking about us helping Mehra's son?"

Tulku Tenzin described the banners that the group was carrying. They read, SINNERS AGAINST GOD; SINNERS CAUSE HIV; SINNERS DESTROY MARRIAGE.

Eshaan put his hand on his heart in a feeble attempt to calm himself down. He stood and stared at the smoldering kitchen. "Lama, look, my house is still burning."

Chapter 35

Loveleen stared listlessly at the children who were playing outside the window of her hospital room. Despite the sweltering Delhi heat, the children were absorbed in their game. They would make a short tower of stones and then take a ball and hit the tower in a way that all the stones tumbled down. The thick air was filled with the soot from trash fires burning nearby, but that didn't bother them. Her tears had stopped.

In all her dreams, even in her worst nightmares, she had never thought it would come to this. Now, everything seems ludicrous How could she ever have believed she could have the impossible dream? Her hand touched her belly as she tried to calm herself down.

Loveleen and Saachi had married quietly at a small temple in the hills of Dharamsala, as far away as they could get from Delhi. The only witness had been Eshaan. At the first temple, the young priest asked where the two grooms were. When they explained that there was no groom, he looked repulsed. Loveleen was ready to tell him to go to hell, but Saachi had spoken with such love and tenderness that the priest had calmed down. He still refused to marry the two women. Not sure what to do next, the trio decided to try one more temple before quitting. It worked; at the next temple they visited, a much older priest had not thrown them out. He said there was too much hate in this world and he refused to be a part of it. "Who am I to judge who someone loves?" he had said. Then he had proceeded to give them a lecture about what it meant to take sacred vows, and married them according to Hindu rites. He reminded them the only way to honor God was through love and kindness to each other and to the world.

Just a few weeks after the wedding, Saachi had wanted a baby. Loveleen and Saachi had bribed their way into a fertility clinic, and despite the odds, the laws of the country, and everything else under the sun that was against them, Loveleen had become pregnant in the first try. Everything had worked out a bit too smoothly. Of course, now here she was, paying for being too happy, too soon.

"Child, you need to eat something. You have to eat. Just one bite?" the elderly nurse tried to convince Loveleen to take a small bite of buttered toast. Instead, Loveleen began to cry again as she tightly clutched a piece of paper.

"Why are you crying? Does something hurt? Are you cramping?" The nurse waited patiently for an answer, but there was none.

The experienced nurse was clearly worried. The child in front of her was hurting, but she couldn't find a way to soothe the pain. It was usually not hard. A pregnant woman was easy to guilt into good health by gently reminding her that her behavior would hurt the baby. But there were days she would have to care for ones like Loveleen, whose pain seemed too deep, the despair too strong.

"Let me turn the TV on for you. Maybe something fun will cheer you up? Do you like to cook? You know, if I wasn't a nurse, I would be a chef somewhere," the nurse said, turning on the small television set as she tried hard to distract the pregnant woman.

Loveleen just stared at the screen. The nurse went to the bathroom and returned a minute later with a wet towel she used to gently wipe Loveleen's face.

"Hi, darling! Look what we brought you!" boomed a male voice.

Loveleen turned toward the door of her room and saw Nikolas and Kitt walking in. Nicholas walked over and handed Loveleen a box filled with *jalebi,* a gooey, syrupy, crunchy dessert, a large bouquet of yellow roses, and a few balloons with the words GET WELL SOON printed on them.

Kitt rushed to her side. "Loveleen, what happened? Is everything okay? Is the . . . the baby—"

The nurse answered, "They did a sonogram this morning. The baby is fine. But something is wrong. She isn't eating and has been crying all day." Loveleen closed her eyes. "Are you her relative?" the nurse asked the new arrivals.

Kitt shook her head then gently tapped on Loveleen's shoulder, asking her again what was wrong.

"Hey, Kitt! Look, you are on TV." Nikolas pointed to the television set that was mounted on the wall just across from Loveleen's bed. It was a commercial for *India's Best Home Chef* showing the winners of the first round. On the screen, Eshaan and Kitt hugged as an audience member shouted, "Lucky guy, he is going to the next round and he gets a great girl."

Kitt stared up at the screen and then at a visibly upset Nikolas, but the nurse intervened before any words are exchanged. "Can I please see you both outside the room? The patient needs rest."

With that, she marched both of them out of the room and shut the door behind her.

Loveleen opened her eyes and looked again at the card in her hand. It was from Sacchi, her lover, her wife, the same lover who was to move in with her just after the baby arrived. The same lover who had said, "Yes. You get pregnant, and I promise you that we will be together. We will be a family. I promise."

After her fall, Loveleen had not informed Saachi, as she knew Saachi had a tendency to worry. But once the doctor gave her the green light that the baby was safe, she sent a text to Sacchi telling her what had happened and asked her to come visit. There was no response. Loveleen sent three more text messages, even called several times, but there was no response.

Then, twenty-four hours after her last text message had been sent, there was a knock on the door of Loveleen's hospital room. A delivery boy had come with a fiery red bouquet of water lilies. As beautiful as red water lilies were, the message on the note could not have been uglier: GOOD LUCK WITH EVERYTHING AND GOODBYE, SACCHI.

Chapter 36

The elderly nurse, obviously unnerved, told Kitt and Nikolas that Loveleen had asked for sleeping pills three times already within the past few hours.

"Sleeping pills? She cannot take those. She is about to give birth," Kitt said, and then realized that is, of course, why the nurse looked so worried.

"I am not supposed to share anything with anyone who is not legally her next of kin, but you know, no one other than you and that other young man has come to see her. Where is her husband?"

Kitt looked to Nikolas, unsure of how much to share. She had never seen him look like this. His face had turned beet red and he was pushing down on his cane.

"She is not married," Kitt finally said to the nurse.

"Widowed? It doesn't make any difference to me, but it seems to me that she is waiting for someone who hasn't come," the insightful nurse said.

The activity in the hospital corridor suddenly jumped as an orderly pushed a gurney just in front of Kitt.

"Move please, side please . . . move!" he shouted, and Kitt and Nikolas moved back.

There was a policeman walking right behind the gurney. Kitt thought he was going to go along with the orderly, but he stopped at Loveleen's door.

"How is she?" the rotund police officer, dressed in a traditional khaki outfit, asked the nurse.

"Why is the police here? What is going on?" the nurse asked as she tapped her foot on the floor.

"I am here for her safety. Now, please answer my question. Is she okay?"

The nurse nodded. This was getting more bizarre by the moment.

"Please do not let anyone into this room. I will stay here for the day, and then another officer will cover this door by night," he said, and then asked them to move away to finish their conversation.

"What is this about? What the heck is going on? Is her life in danger?" Nikolas realized the sensitivity of the moment. India never ceased to surprise him since the day he had landed, his Indian wife-to-be did not want a traditional wedding, her best friend was a lesbian, he saw her hugging a monk-to-be on a stupid reality cooking show, and now here he was, in the middle of a hospital, with a senior officer guarding a woman who had been pushed down the stairs by a superstitious man claiming a black cat sipping spilled milk would ruin his life.

"I will go check with the administrator to see what is going on with the policeman. Will you wait here?" the nurse asked then disappeared into the chaos of the hospital.

Nikolas and Kitt just stood there, in the middle of the hospital floor, as a harsh tube-light provided a deeply depressing white light that covered the entire area. The area buzzed with people rushing, the sound system constantly paging doctors. The smell of antiseptic mixed with a citrusy orange scent filled their nostrils as an orderly mopped the floor next to them.

"Kitt, we need to talk," Nikolas said softly. "I realize now is not the time, but if there is something going on, I need to know about it."

"No, nothing is going on," Kitt was a little too quick to respond.

Nikolas moved aside as another orderly appeared, pushing an elderly man in a wheelchair. The police officer at Loveleen's door was speaking into this phone and looked increasing worried. "Would you like a coffee?" Nikolas changed the topic as they waited for the nurse to return. She nodded, but before he could leave, the nurse came back.

"No one knows why this officer is here or who sent him. All I can tell you is I think she is suicidal. Can you give me your mobile numbers in case we need to reach you?" The nurse noted Kitt's phone number.

"Can we see her?" Kitt asked, worried about her friend, and wondered what happened to cause such emotional pain. She knew it had nothing to do with Mehra and the fall. As bad as it was, it had not harmed Loveleen or the baby.

"Well, there is no point now. I will send you a message if . . . God forbid—" the nurse's voice trailed off.

Nikolas put his arm around Kitt. "Don't cry. We will be here for her. Don't cry. Come on. Let's go home now, and we can come back in a few hours. There is no point standing around here."

As they got into a taxi, Nikolas directed the driver to take them to the nearest hotel. "I think we could both use a drink," he said as Kitt just sat there quietly with her hands folded in her lap.

"Kitt, there is something I've been meaning to ask you. That . . . that scene on the TV . . . should I be worried?" Nikolas asked as softly as he could. He knew in his heart this was neither the time nor the place, but he couldn't help himself. He needed to know. The first time he landed in Delhi, he had sensed Eshaan may have had feelings for Kitt, but she had appeared very cool toward him, and Nikolas thought perhaps he had been overreacting. Then, the second time he had arrived, she was hugging him at his birthday party. It didn't seem to be a particularly platonic hug, and he had brushed it off as jealousy. After all, Eshaan was a handsome man.

But today, on TV, that was something totally different. The way she looked into his eyes when he hugged her. And, even more painful, the way she hugged him back.

"Kitt, have you heard a word I've said?" Nikolas asked, really annoyed she was on her phone and texting instead of answering his really important question.

"Where are we? What is this location? Tell me fast," Kitt asked the taxi driver, who gave her the name of the street.

"Hang on," she said to Nikolas and made a call on her phone.

"Yes, Eshaan, we are near the Marriott in the city. Where exactly do you need us to go?"

"Wait, I am asking you about him, and you are ignoring me

and talking to him on the phone? What the fuck?" Nikolas was seething.

"Stop, Nikolas, this isn't about us. There is serious trouble," she said then gave the taxi driver a new address to go to and told him she'd pay double if he got them there as fast as he could.

Chapter 37

"I am taking her, and there is nothing you can do about it," Eshaan's voice was loud and determined as he argued with a young doctor assigned to care for Loveleen. He was standing just outside Loveleen's hospital room. An orderly was rolling the lunch tray out of her room. Eshaan caught a glimpse of the tray. Untouched.

The policeman, who had just stepped out for a quick smoke, was back and looked quite troubled.

"Who are you? What is the purpose of your visit here?" he asked Eshaan.

Eshaan eyed him with suspicion. What the hell was a police officer doing at Loveleen's door? Was he too late?

"I am her friend," he told the policeman, who just smirked and tapped his foot.

"You have a name, young man? I don't have all day. There is going to be trouble here soon." He looked stern and quite angry.

"My name is Eshaan Singh," he replied.

"Why didn't you just say that sooner? Yes, you need to take her. Lama Dorje texted me this morning and told me what was going on," the officer said as he began to open the door.

Of course, now the police presence made sense. The Lama had been the one to get the news that Loveleen was in danger, and he told Eshaan to get her out of the hospital as fast as he could. In the meantime, he must have called his officer friend to come and stand guard.

"I am sorry, sir, but I cannot advise you to take her. She has not eaten for two days, as you can see from that tray. I have her on a glucose IV, but she is weak," the doctor tried to reason with Eshaan.

"I have to take her. It is not a matter of choice at this point." Eshaan's tone was now gentler, but still as firm.

The officer reasoned with the doctor, letting him in on the situation at hand. The doctor stepped aside.

Eshaan opened the door and went inside. Loveleen was sitting up on the bed with her hands clasped in front of her, staring at the television mounted on the wall. He picked up the remote control and turned it off.

"Eshaan, what—?" She asked softly.

He told her to get dressed. "We are leaving now. I've lost everything, and I will be damned if I lose you, too. Get up. We are leaving."

"What do you mean lost everything?" she asked.

Eshaan was already rifling through the plastic bags next to her bed. He picked out a shirt and skirt then placed them on her bed.

"Get dressed or, I swear to you, I will pick you up in that stupid gown and carry you down this fucking hall." He turned around and walked out, banging the door closed behind him.

The doctor was waiting, along with Loveleen's elderly nurse and the policeman. Before the doctor said another a word, the nurse spoke, "Child, is she your wife? She needs care—"

"Please, let me take her. I am not her husband. I can tell you this though: if she stays here, she will not make it. Please, I beg you to understand," Eshaan said, and the officer, again, added his support.

"Will you please bring her for a checkup tomorrow? Or take her to a clinic near you? She is still really weak."

Eshaan nodded.

The doctor told Eshaan to go to the payment counter. "To check her out without arousing any suspicious, just go to the counter. It will be the best way. Otherwise, we will have to report you, and that will cause a slew of issues."

Eshaan hesitated then checked his phone. There was a text from Kitt. *WE ARE THERE AND SAFE. LOVELEEN OKAY?*

"You go, Eshaan. I will wait here," the policeman said. "But hurry, please. Trouble is on the way."

Eshaan ran toward the payment counter on the other side of the building. Time was running out. There was a long line at the counter, and he tried to cajole people into letting him go first. Most everyone said no, but then an older gentleman finally allowed him to take his spot.

"I am paying the bills for my dead son. But it seems like you still have someone alive that you need to rescue," the old man said as he moved aside.

Eshaan bent down and touched the man's feet. "I am so sorry about your son, but yes, this is a matter of life and death. Thank you, sir."

The man at the counter pulled out some paperwork then told Eshaan to sign it. "A Mr. Amit Mehra has paid for everything up front, so there are no extra charges. In fact, you may be getting some money back. Let me check," the man said.

Eshaan signed, turned, and ran as fast as he could. "Sir, sir, sir, you have a large amount refunded," the man called out to Eshaan, but he was already gone.

"You need to leave now. My junior officer informs me the group is on its way here. He spotted them about two kilometers from the hospital," the officer informed him.

They both let themselves inside Loveleen's room. She was sitting on the bed, staring out the window. "Saachi left me, Eshaan. Can you believe it?" she mumbled as he entered. "Wait, what is the officer doing here?" she asked, a bit bewildered. "Is everything okay?"

Eshaan listened, but offered no sympathy or words. He simply picked up her packed bag and slung it onto his back. Then he went up to her and took her hand. "Can you stand?"

The friends walked together slowly toward the exit of the hospital, accompanied by the officer.

Loveleen, stubborn as always, had refused the wheelchair.

Eshaan, in addition to carrying her bags, was also carrying the box of sweets and fruits Nikolas had brought in. As he exited the hospital, he handed over the food to some street kids playing nearby.

"Why do we have a policeman with us? What is going on? Why aren't you speaking with me?" Loveleen asked.

He said nothing as he gently guided her into her car.

He had driven her to the hospital when she took that nasty

fall, a place meant to heal her. And now, here he was, taking her away from that very place, as it would soon be worse than hell for her there.

"Go now," the officer commanded, and they drove off.

"Mehra is going to jail for what he did to you. Kitt and Dr. Sinha went and filed a complaint that night. I hope he rots in that prison," Eshaan told her as he maneuvered the car through the maze of cars, cyclists, vans, and pedestrians encircling the exit of the hospital.

Loveleen stared out the window, and then slowly whispered, "No, he won't. His son came by to see me this morning. He was on his knees apologizing. He was crying and telling me how sorry he was for what his father had done. I think he even paid the hospital bill, or at least he told me he would. Then the police came by to take my statement. I told them I tripped."

Eshaan slammed the brakes. "What the fuck is the matter with you? Why in the hell would you do that? He needs to be taught a lesson. This is not right. You should have let him go to prison. 'Specially for what he has done now!"

Loveleen began to cry again. "What is the point of all this anyway? He is a foolish old man. Besides, all is gone now. What will revenge get me?"

For the next hour, both of them sat quietly as Eshaan navigated the car through the old Delhi streets. Old Bollywood songs played on the car radio, and the air conditioning worked hard to keep the car cool. Loveleen closed her eyes and fell asleep. Eshaan pulled the car to the side and called Kitt.

"We should be there in ten minutes. Are you all there?" he whispered into the phone so Loveleen could not hear him.

"Yes, we are here, and don't worry. Everything is fine," Kitt responded.

Eshaan quickly got off the phone and accelerated to get to the destination. In his heart, he knew they would be safe now, but he needed to get her away just in case. He made doubly sure they were not being followed. He let out a small sigh of relief. Perhaps it was all going to be fine now. Rani and Om were, thankfully, back to the monastery as well, healing.

He could not believe how quickly things had gone from bad to worse. Early this morning, he had been cleaning the burned kitchen. Gina had heard about the fire through some friends and had come to help. He had hoped Kitt would stop by, but she never came. Rani had been helping despite her injuries, but Om, heartbroken that his behavior had caused the fire, would not move from his position outside the kitchen.

Eshaan and Gina were cleaning when one of the monks came in and asked them to come to the monastery's library to take a look at the breaking news on the TV. They had rushed inside to see what was going on and stood there, stunned and amazed, that one man could unleash so much cruelty against love.

"Don't tell her anything. Just get her out of the hospital," had been the Lama's advice after seeing the horror show on TV.

"Don't bring her back here, Eshaan. Bring her to my farmhouse," Gina had said.

Now, Eshaan looked at his friend sleeping quietly in the car. Thank God he had reached her in time.

He braked suddenly for a truck cutting him off, waking Loveleen.

"I cannot believe she left me." Loveleen started to cry again.

"She didn't," Eshaan replied.

As gently as he could, he went on to explain Saachi's brother, an extreme right-wing homophobe, had read Loveleen's text messages and confronted Saachi, who admitted everything and hoped her family would understand. Instead, they beat her black and blue. She sent the flowers and the note to keep Loveleen away so she could be safe.

"What the hell? Where is she? Is she okay? Eshaan Veer Singh, you better tell me now what the hell is going on. Where are we going?"

"She is fine," he said.

"Why are we here?" she asked as he stopped the car in front of a sprawling bungalow on the other side of town. Loveleen assumed he was taking her home.

He rushed out of the car and opened the door to let her step out. A gentleman dressed in a police uniform, who had been waiting at the footpath outside the bungalow, moved forward to lend her a hand.

"Please, come in," he said, and held out his hand for her to take.

"What is going on?" she asked again as they entered Gina's farmhouse. Loveleen was stunned to see a very battered but smiling Saachi sitting on the couch, along with Kitt, Nikolas, and Gina.

Saachi got up, rushed to Loveleen, and hugged and kissed her. "Are you okay?" they asked each other at the same time then started laughing.

Eshaan finally spoke. "Loveleen, I am sorry I didn't tell you anything, but your insistence of playing the warrior queen worried me, and I was really concerned that if I told you the truth, you would stay to face the crazies who were coming, instead of walking way."

He finally sat down and explained that Saachi's brother, violently furious that his sister had a gay companion, had come to Dr. Sinha's building looking for Loveleen. Instead, he had found Merry Mehra. Mehra had been surprised but then told the young man all about Loveleen and about Eshaan, who "enabled" Loveleen. The two of them went to a local hate group that claimed to fight for the purity of Hinduism and incited them about the gay couple. The organization immediately called the local TV station to talk about this illegal couple and their illegal marriage, and, of course, the illegal child.

The hate group had started a parade to protest the gay couple and was on their way to the hospital. Lama Dorje had heard through the grapevine that several local thugs had been included in the parade to "take care of the situation."

"Kitt came just in time to my house. We left the house and saw the big Jeeps of that organization arriving just behind us," Saachi added.

"Loveleen, there is more," Eshaan said as tears began to roll down his cheeks.

"The hate group burned Karma Kitchen to ashes," he said quietly.

"*No*," came the stunned response. "This is all my fault. I am so sorry, Eshaan. I should have never fought with Mehra."

Loveleen began to cry and he rushed to her and put his arms around her. "It is no more your fault than mine. This was meant to be. And so it happened," he said.

Eshaan's phone buzzed. "Can I speak with you?" It was Mehra's son, Amit Mehra, the gambler whose life they had saved and whose father returned the favor by burning down the kitchen and shoving a pregnant lady down the stairs.

"Let me talk to him." Loveleen stood up and nearly pulled the phone out of Eshaan's hand.

"No, no. I will talk to him."

"Is she okay? I heard what my father did. I am so sorry. All I could do was pay her bills. She saved my life," Amit said before Eshaan could utter a word.

"How did Mehra manage to have a son as kind as you?" Eshaan asked.

"I don't even know where he is, Eshaan. He hasn't been around since that night," the son said. Eshaan explained to him how the kitchen had burned down and how Loveleen and Saachi were now essentially in hiding.

"I just cannot believe my father would stoop so low. I am ashamed to be his son. Please, can you find it in your heart to forgive me? If I hadn't gambled, none of this would have happened." Amit sounded genuinely remorseful.

Eshaan spoke gently into the phone. "It is no one's fault. Now we just need to figure out a way forward."

The group sat in silence as Gina served some tea and cake. She told the girls they could stay with her as long as they wanted, and that this house was very safe for them, especially since she had called a private service to place an armed guard outside.

Eshaan got busy on the phone, trying to figure out what to do next. Gina got up to show the girls to their rooms.

Kitt was trying to figure out what to do, when Nikolas spoke up. "I'm glad you all are okay. I really need to leave now." He got up and looked at Kitt. "Are you coming with me, or shall I go alone?"

Chapter 38

"Sometimes, it is hard to tell the calm from the storm," Loveleen whispered to Kitt as they lay in bed at Gina's house and stared at the ceiling fan above.

"I . . . I doubted her love for me. Now, I feel like a fool . . . and I am still stunned that Karma Kitchen burned down. Why didn't you call and tell me this when I was in the hospital?"

Kitt turned to her friend, propping herself up on one elbow. "It is over now. We need to move forward."

They had been together pretty much every single moment after the hospital incident. Eshaan had also been sleeping on the couch and refusing to leave Loveleen alone for any stretch of time. The threat of Mehra was still there, even though Dr. Sinha had padlocked the door to Mehra's flat.

Saachi had to be admitted again for her injuries, but was healing well. To be sure no one would know where she was, Dr. Sinha had admitted her to his friend's private hospital under an assumed name. Loveleen also had a checkup, and the doctor had given her an all-clear, but insisted she still needed to take it easy.

Things were stabilizing . . . until Nikolas gave Kitt an

ultimatum the night they had brought Loveleen back from the hospital. "Marry me this week, or I am leaving. I don't care if there is one person at the wedding, or six hundred. If you love me, we do this now and we leave. I cannot stay here any longer."

It had been three days now, and her father was already going overboard with preparations. Nikolas, while pissed that Kitt wasn't there helping as much as he liked, understood her need to be with Loveleen.

"So you are going to marry him, Kitt? Why?" Loveleen asked as Kitt spoke to her father for the sixth time that morning about the florist.

Before she could answer, Loveleen almost screamed as she pointed to the television. "What the hell? Kitt, look!" Loveleen stared at Saachi's damaged face on the screen.

"This is Saachi, who was accused of being gay by her brother and almost beaten to death by her family. After being interrogated by the local police for a few hours, her brother has retracted his story. His sister is not gay, he says. Her brother, after some pressure from the local police, added that he was misled by another man named Merry Mehra," the young reporter spoke in English mixed in with several Hindi words.

The news anchor went on to interview the hate group that had marched to the hospital, and they blamed everything on Saachi's brother, saying he incited them and they were sorry and would leave these young women alone.

The story continued to unfold as Saachi's family members admitted that while they did beat her, it was only to teach her a lesson about going against nature. It was clear they did not want to give the interview, but were being pressured to do so.

There was no mention of the hate group's burning down the kitchen.

"Only in India. I wonder what the hell happened," Kitt said as she smiled.

"I know exactly what happened!" Loveleen exclaimed. This had to be the work of Amit Mehra paying her back for helping him. She knew it in her heart. When he begged her to help him, he had promised to help her in return. She knew he was the only one capable of doing such a thing. He had the resources to pull something like this off.

Both women sat and drank tea as they watched the circus on TV and nervously laughed at the travesty of justice, or injustice, as the case maybe.

KITT, MY LOVE, ARE YOU STILL WITH LOVELEEN? LUNCH AT 1:30 PM? I MADE RESERVATIONS AT INDIAN ACCENT. WILL SEE YOU THERE. I HAVE A SURPRISE, came a text from Nikolas. Kitt read it and sighed.

I CANNOT MAKE IT. HELPING LOVELEEN. I AM SURE YOU UNDERSTAND, Kitt texted Nikolas back. He didn't respond.

Chapter 39

Kitt counted ten guards earnestly guarding the gates to the monastery. The special guards were all four-legged and extremely loyal to the man who had been helping feed them. Raju the Dogman, along with his dogs, stood tall as Kitt approached them.

"Raju, Eshaan must be so happy you are here!" she said to the man, who looked too young to be able to handle so many dogs, and yet too old to be standing all day.

Raju nodded. He had lost his ability to speak years ago, but his heart overflowed with gratitude toward Eshaan, who was possibly the only human who had ever interacted with him in a positive way. He moved his dogs aside and let Kitt go through the gates.

Kitt walked onto the monastery grounds and smiled as she heard the chants coming from the main prayer hall. The monastery was humming. Despite the chaos of the past few days, the calm had returned.

The soothing sounds of the chants echoed and bounced off every inch of the monastery gardens. The breeze, sweetened with the smell of jasmine, caused Kitt to just stand and take it all in. It was as though nature was saying that all was as it should be, in harmony. There was a time she used to hate walking into any religious building, but this last trip had softened her dislike.

As she walked toward the back of the monastery, she spotted Om and Radio Rani sitting on one of the benches. He had his arm around her shoulders, and they appeared deep in discussion.

She smiled and walked past them toward Karma Kitchen. Although she had seen the burned down kitchen before, the sight still made her stomach turn. The once beautiful kitchen was now a symbol of all that was wrong with the world: greed, vengeance, violence, and ignorance.

Kitt knew the police had come by several times to question Eshaan and the monks about the damage caused in Karma Kitchen. Eshaan had absolutely refused to file a complaint.

"If I file a complaint, the thugs who did this will go to jail and come out worse than when they went in. Perhaps this was the karma of the kitchen," he kept repeating.

Kitt tried to make him change his mind, but he was adamant. "If you are worried about retaliation, we can get some guards here," she had tried to reason with him every which way, but he stood firm.

"You are being unreasonable. How will you fulfill your dream to feed people if you don't have a kitchen? And now we have no money to build a new one." When he refused to listen to her, Kitt had even asked her father to intervene.

Dr. Sinha tried hard to convince Eshaan that thugs should not be allowed to get away with this kind of behavior. It made them feel like they had power and it would get worse.

"Dr. Sinha, you know how much I respect you. But . . . but Lama Dorje once told me that the lessons I need to learn will keep haunting me until I learn them. There is something here that I need to learn. Until that happens, this kitchen will keep burning."

Dr. Sinha had hugged him and offered the only piece of wisdom he truly believed in. "Eshaan, an old friend of mine once told me, '*Trust Allah, but tie your camel.*' So, you just figure out what your lesson is, but in the meantime, get some security for this place . . . okay?"

As though on cue, Raju and his dogs had arrived, and so far, at least over the past couple of days, they had succeeded in keeping any unwanted elements away from the monastery grounds.

"Eshaan? Eshaan?" Kitt called. He was inside the kitchen, helping remove some of the burnt furniture. The black soot covering the floor now covered Eshaan's white shirt and most of his jeans. His hands were coal-black as he picked up pieces of what used to be chairs and hurled them into a large heap of junk just outside the kitchen's door.

"Eshaan, I want you to come with me right now," Kitt said adamantly.

"Kitt, I am surprised to see you here. Is everything okay? In any case, I cannot go anywhere. Look at this mess." Eshaan pointed to the kitchen.

"Look, an hour won't make a difference. Please, this is important. I get married in a day. If not now, I will never have another chance," she pleaded.

Eshaan clenched his fists and tried hard not to let any

emotion show. Did she not realize how much it hurt him when she talked about her impending nuptials? Perhaps just as he had made peace with his burned-down dreams, she had made peace with her fate.

She asked him again and he finally agreed, shouted out instructions to the various people in the kitchen who were cleaning, washed his hands and his face, and then walked up to Kitt. "Okay. Here I am. Now what?"

She walked with him to the car outside. Loveleen was already inside, waiting in the passenger seat. "Did she tell you where she is taking us? No? She hasn't told me either. Maybe she is kidnapping us and taking us to a nice resort for a week?" she said as he entered the car.

"Here is where we are going." Kitt handed Eshaan a list of directions, but no final destination.

They crisscrossed through old lanes and by-lanes and arrived at their destination, but not before making two bathroom stops for Loveleen and one stop to pick up some frankies for lunch.

Eshaan parked the car in a large dusty parking lot and opened the door for Loveleen to step out. Kitt was already outside and holding onto the small plastic bag carrying their lunch and a few bottles of chilled soda.

"Okay, now can you tell us what in the world we are doing here?" Eshaan pretended to be annoyed, but in his heart, he was thrilled.

Kitt had been supportive of the kitchen, but very aloof since Nikolas had seen the TV commercial. Rightly so, he guessed. But now he wondered what was so important that she had to drag them all out here. But she was already walking a hundred feet ahead, calling out to them to walk faster.

"Don't act like you don't like it, Eshaan. You are thrilled she is giving you so much attention," Loveleen pinched his side and joked.

The sun, hiding behind the clouds, seemed calmer today than in previous days. Several kids were playing cricket in the small garden that lined the path the two friends were walking on.

They walked a touch faster to keep up with the fast-moving Kitt. She weaved through tiny lanes hosting small houses, a tiny shop selling butter, bread, and tea, and several vendors selling grilled corn. A few stray cows walked around as flies buzzed over their dung.

Kitt looked back to make sure they were still following her, and then she turned the corner and stopped. It was here, just as she remembered it.

She was standing in front of a very large, ancient well. The well, the size of a large park, had over three hundred steps leading down into its center. These types of wells, called step-wells, were very common in old Delhi. They were built to provide travelers with a place to bathe, meet people, and rest before continuing their journey. Many wells had religious buildings built right beside them, so the weary travelers could also say a prayer before continuing their journey.

The unseasonable rains of the past few days had filled the well with some water, but the stairs that led into the large water pool were still visible. Surrounding the well were large gulmohar trees in full bloom, making it appear as though it was wearing a garland of orange flowers.

"Oh, this is so beautiful. I know this area so well and I did not know this was here," Eshaan said as he and Loveleen caught up with Kitt.

The three friends walked up to the well and stared into the water below. The water was mesmerizing as a gentle ray of sunlight danced on the quiet, still surface. A few people were seated along the sides. One woman was reading a book, another sitting in meditation, and a couple was snuggling as they threw small pebbles into the water.

Kitt pointed to a spot under a flaming orange gulmohar tree. "That looks like it has a nice shade. Maybe we can sit there for a bit. This is where my father brought me after my mother left us," Kitt said as she continued to stare at the water.

"He told me the water here is sacred and healing. They say whoever bathes in this is healed of pain forever. I don't know about forever, but I just . . . I have been feeling so helpless watching the two of you go through so much lately that I thought . . . perhaps—" Kitt trailed off as she pointed to the water.

The water was cool as the three friends dipped their toes in, then walked down a few steps so the water came up to their waist.

"Oh, this feels good." Eshaan smiled as they all held hands.

As they walked deeper into the water, Eshaan remembered the night when Kitt, nestled in his arms and sleeping, began to call out, "Don't go, Mama, don't leave, Mama!" Her words had shaken Eshaan out of his own peaceful sleep. He had reached out to wake her up but, thinking better of it, only hugged her closer. Tears rolled down his cheeks as he cried for what had been taken from them both.

How ironic it was that what tied him to Kitt was loss—their

mutual fear of being abandoned, even more than what he saw as their romantic, Bollywood-style love. More than anyone, he knew Kitt understood the gut-wrenching loss of his mother, just as he could relate to her hopelessness when her mother deliberately left her.

"You're a regular knight in shining armor and she's the perfect damsel in distress," Loveleen had said, rolling her eyes. He'd said nothing then, but in his heart he knew it was really the other way around: Kitt had saved him from drowning in the abyss of abandonment.

"You know I cannot swim, so don't let go!" Loveleen laughed, breaking in to Eshaan's reverie.

"They say these waters heal because of their sulfur content, but I don't think that is why," Kitt offered. "They heal, because they somehow give us the power to accept the truth. Perhaps the truth mingles with the water and becomes tolerable."

They allowed the water to wash all over their feet and their spirits.

Kitt finally broke the silence.

"I owe you both an explanation . . . about Nikolas," she said as she scooped up some water in her hands then poured it back out.

Loveleen looked at Eshaan and mouthed, *Tell her now. This is the time. Tell her.*

He stayed quiet.

Kitt admitted, for the first time since he had seen her this trip, that she was not in love with Nikolas.

Kitt hugged her body with her arms. She had hoped that of all people, Eshaan would understand. How could she abandon the man who helped her so much? Good people did not abandon those who loved them just because circumstances changed. They just didn't. Kitt was determined not to repeat the pattern and abandon Nikolas as her mother had abandoned her father.

Loveleen tugged on Eshaan's hand, but he stayed quiet and listened intently.

Kitt became quiet for a few moments and then began to explain that when she and Eshaan first got together, she was already going out with Nikolas.

"I wasn't really in love with him. But Eshaan, after . . . after us, I decided to go back to Austria and break up with Nikolas so I could be with you."

She explained that when she arrived back in Austria, Nikolas was at the airport with flowers. She wanted to tell him right then, but it seemed like a horrible thing to do to someone. So she kept quiet. He drove her to his apartment. When they entered the dark apartment and flipped on the switch, a large shout of "Happy birthday, Kitt," greeted them. He had arranged for a surprise birthday party for her with all her friends. She had hugged everyone, cut the cake, and had a bit too much to drink. She went to find him to tell him the truth. As she approached him, he turned to her and said in a loud voice, "Everyone, can I have your attention please?"

"He proposed to me. In front of all our friends. He put the ring on my finger. I just froze. I should have said no. I could barely open my mouth," she said as she fought her tears.

Kitt went on to explain the disaster that struck within minutes of the engagement. She said she ran out of the apartment, part jetlagged, part drunk, and got into her car to go for a drive. Not realizing what she was doing, she put the car in reverse instead of drive. Nikolas had followed her out of the apartment and was behind the car when she pushed the gas.

"I damaged his legs. Forever. I . . . I was so frightened by his screams that I put the car in drive and smashed into the cars in front of me. We both landed in the hospital. I had a few broken ribs. He . . . he cared for me, despite the damage I did to his legs."

Kitt began to weep hysterically.

"Don't cry, Kitt . . . please," Eshaan said.

She heaved and cried and cried.

"He is fine. Right? His leg? I know he is walking with a limp, but is there any other serious damage?" Loveleen asked as gently as she could.

"Isn't the limp enough? I have scarred him physically, and now . . . now I cannot give him another emotional scar," Kitt responded.

She then turned to Eshaan. "I hope you will forgive me, Eshaan. I have to marry him."

"Look on the bright side. Maybe I will be the hot affair you have after you get married," he joked as he attempted a feeble smile.

Kitt managed a weak smile.

"This is just stupid, Kitt." Loveleen was getting tired of her two friends acting like wimpy idiots. "You love him, and he loves you. I don't see what the bloody problem is. You do know that people break off engagements all the time. Wait, I know you know that . . . so what the hell is the problem?"

"I . . . I . . . after the engagement, I was going to tell him that

I did not want to marry him, but then . . . Eshaan, that photo you sent—" Kitt began to weep.

"Wait . . . wait . . . what photograph? What are you talking about?" Loveleen looked questioningly at Eshaan. He shrugged his shoulders.

"The one . . . that photo . . . you were wearing the . . . you were dressed like a monk."

It took a second, and then he remembered what she was referring to. He, along with Lama Dorje, Tenzin Tulku, and a few others had gone to Dharamsala. The Dalai Lama was there to speak privately to the monks. Eshaan really wanted to hear what he had to say, so he borrowed Tenzin's clothes to dress like a monk so he could sneak into the meeting. They had taken a few pictures before the meeting. It was at that moment that Eshaan, desperate to hear from Kitt, who hadn't been responding to any of his messages, sent her a picture with a caption: *HEARTBROKEN SINCE YOU'VE LEFT, SO NOW PLANNING ON JOINING THE MONASTERY.*

"Kitt, that was a stupid joke. All you had to do was ask me. You are basing your entire decision on a stupid prank photograph?" Eshaan shook his head, angry, disappointed, and heartbroken.

Kitt began to cry.

Eshaan placed his arm around her. "You know I love you. I love you more than I have ever loved anyone in my life. Don't cry."

Kitt continued to weep as she pushed herself closer to the true love of her life.

A lifetime seemed to pass in the next hour.

"Nikolas has set the wedding date for next Monday. I could not get him to push it out anymore. I have to marry him. He is a kind and good man, and he should not suffer because I made a stupid mistake," Kitt whispered as she stood to leave. "That is the truth I need to learn to tolerate."

Loveleen decided she had had enough and spoke up.

"I think you are wrong, Kitt. Don't fool yourself. You are not marrying Nikolas out of obligation. You are marrying him because he is less risky. After your mother left you, don't you think in your heart you are wondering if you marry Eshaan, he may leave you and join that monastery? Nikolas is a sure thing. Eshaan isn't. And that, my friend, is the truth you need to tolerate."

Chapter 40

The burned kitchen was now, finally, all clean.

Cart loads of burnt pieces of wood, plastic, and plates had been hauled off to a dump about a kilometer away. The last remaining telltales of the disaster—cooking oil containers, which had aided the fire—had been stuck to the floor, but Om managed to even clean those up.

Eshaan had just returned from a mandatory counseling session that Lama Dorje insisted he register for. Telling a complete stranger about his innate fear of food, about the bile rising in his stomach when he attempted to eat, about how the haunting smells of baking bread and toasting spices made him break out in a nasty sweat, was very hard for Eshaan. But he had promised the Lama that he would at least make an attempt.

"This is going to take a long time, Eshaan. Are you sure you are up for it?" The counselor, a young man, had been kind but firm. The counselor insisted Eshaan have a full physical, even though the initial exam concluded that Eshaan's body had not yet been destroyed. "Just understand that if you don't change your ways, destruction is already dancing on the horizon," the counselor warned him again and again that the journey to healing was going to be long and painful.

Eshaan had not been keen to talk to the counselor, but the young man did not seem to mind. Instead, he encouraged Eshaan to just sit quietly if it helped him.

"The demons that limit us," he had said, "have a lot of power." He proceeded to give him two different types of exercises to begin immediately to stop himself from throwing up at each bite. "It will be very hard, but you will literally have to take your power back, one bite at a time," the counselor advised.

It was at the end of the session that Eshaan had finally felt comfortable enough to say he would indeed come back again in a couple of days for the next session.

Now, back from the meeting, Eshaan hesitated accepting a cup of tea and a slice of toast from Radio Rani, who stood watch to make sure he ate it.

"You know, I am going to try and eat. I promise," Eshaan said to her.

"Hey, I heard the advice Dr. Sinha gave you that day. 'I trust Allah, but I tie my camels.' I am going to stick with you to make sure you don't do anything stupid!"

They had both laughed. A much needed relief from all the tension of the past few days.

Eshaan took a sip of the tea then immediately called a meeting in the monastery gardens to talk about the next steps for Karma Kitchen.

"So, we are here now to decide the future of this, well, what remains of this kitchen. I am open to all suggestions," Eshaan said to his small crew.

The looks on their faces startled Eshaan. Tenzin, Om, and Rani looked forlorn. Their eyes stared at the devastated building, and he knew what they were thinking.

"Come on, guys! It is not over yet," he said to them, but they simply shook their heads.

"How will this ever be rebuilt? This needs a lot of money now," Rani said in a soft tone. Om nodded. Even Tenzin, who was usually balanced, just sat there and shook his head.

"Hey, now! You guys are beginning to sound like me. I used to be this negative, and it was because of your faith we got the kitchen up and running. And now, when I need you all the most, you cannot back out!" Eshaan tried to pump them up.

He realized in an instant what he was seeing: that feeling of helplessness, that feeling that every route had closed, that feeling it was all over.

"I am *not* going to let them give up on this. We cannot give up on people who depend on us. I am *not* going to give up," he mumbled under his breath.

"So we should just let this die? Our story will end like this? We will tell people that we tried hard, but when it got really difficult, we gave up?" Eshaan searched deep in his heart to pull out the words his mind was trying to put together.

"It is not that. How will we ever do this? Who will help us?" Rani, ever practical, tried to get him to stop being so idealistic and emotional.

He sat down on the grass and crossed his arms over his chest. "Fine, humor me, then. Let's say we have the money to redo this kitchen. Then what would we do differently?" He hoped against hope this would be the bait they would take. Getting them excited was critical, not just to get the kitchen back up, but in truth, to help him in not giving up.

Om piped up, "I think we should *not* invite people into this space to eat. This is a sacred kitchen."

Rani nodded in agreement and added, "Yes, no throngs of people outside who are neither grateful nor deserving."

Eshaan shot them a hurt look.

"I am not saying we should not feed them . . . just that they should not be in here if they are looking for a free meal. This is a sacred kitchen. The focus should be on those who want to learn so they can pull themselves out of poverty," Rani said.

Eshaan touched his arm. Rab Rakha. *Yes, they're getting their spirit back*, he prayed in his heart. *I cannot do this without them. Please bring them back to the spirit of this kitchen.*

"I do have an idea, Eshaan," Tenzin, who had been very quiet for the last few days, finally spoke up.

"Yes?" Eshaan looked over and smiled at the gentle monk.

"What if . . . what if we take the food to the hungry? I mean, we could easily get some of these food carts outside to sell food to those who need it," Tenzin said, and then quickly added, "I know you don't want to have a restaurant model, so let people buy the food with whatever little money they can. Then, it is not begging and they are earning their meal."

Om and Rani both chimed in that they loved the idea.

"And then in here, we can focus this kitchen on training those who want to work," Eshaan added to Tenzin's idea, and said the monk's solution would solve a lot of issues. The food cart vendors were excellent at handling the beggars and the crowds. The thugs generally did not bother with them. Apparently the same food on the cart was much less appealing. The kitchen could work on its mission to help those with a desire to improve.

Everyone nodded.

"Also, friends, I do have some news. The cooking show people? They invited me back. I guess my walking off the set was great for their ratings," Eshaan said as he smiled for the second time that day.

"Now, the question is how to get everything back so we can achieve our new plans," Tenzin spoke again.

The four of them looked at each other, but no one had a clue as to what the immediate next steps should be.

"Eshaan, why don't you go get the pot, and I will get the vegetables," he heard an old voice calling out to him.

He got up and turned around to see who was talking. A group of beggars from the street had come into the monastery. Potato *Baba*, the man who had sat quietly for days in one corner of Karma Kitchen peeling potatoes, was leading the group. He was pointing toward a few of the utensils that had barely survived the fire.

"There is nothing for you all here," Om said in a very matter-of-fact way to the beggars. "How did Raju let you all come in here?"

Eshaan placed his finger on his lips, signaling Om to be quiet.

Then, another beggar spoke up, "Eshaan, you fed me, do you remember? I know you wanted me to do some work when I first came here, that first day. That was the first full meal I had in months."

There was silence as the beggar stepped forward toward him. He placed his hand on Eshaan's head. "You fed us twice a day without asking anything of us, and now . . . now, maybe we can help." The beggar wiped his tears.

"Look at me," Potato *Baba* added. "I am actually standing and not passing out due to thirst, because of you. We will help you restart this magical kitchen."

Before Eshaan could say anything, Radio Rani directed the man and his little troupe to the vegetable garden in the back to see what they could find, and she herself rushed into the main kitchen to see if she could borrow some additional pots, oil, and some spices.

Tenzin raced into the monastery and came back with a large portable stove the monastery often used during big outdoor events.

Eshaan felt his heart racing. This was it; this was what he had wanted all along. The entire group was smiling, encouraging each other, joking around, and asking if the beggars even knew how to cook!

No one noticed that Nikolas was standing behind the group, frantically taking pictures. He snapped away at the cleaning, the beggars cooking, the monks sweeping, and Eshaan laughing and talking with everyone.

Chapter 41

Truth be told, Nikolas had just come out for some air. It was sheer curiosity that led him to go inside the monastery. The sight of ten small dogs guarding a massive building made him smile. He wasn't intending to see Eshaan, but when he heard him talking to his little group, he just stood in the back and listened. A part of him wanted to see what it was about Eshaan that was so special that Kitt would be willing to leave it all for him.

Although Kitt had agreed to marry him, in his heart he could not help but feel he was perhaps pressuring her. He had asked her about it again at breakfast.

"I am a grown woman. If I did not want to marry you, I would tell you, right?' she had said then gave him a kiss. It had caught him by surprise. They hadn't been intimate since they had arrived here. Her excuse, as always, had been to wait until after the wedding. Her display of affection this morning had assuaged his worries a little. In fact, he had noticed that even Dr. Sinha looked a little relieved.

To be fair to her, Nikolas reminded himself he hadn't been around much, either. This new deal, crucial to the success of his company and financially for them as a couple, had pulled him away a lot. Kitt hadn't complained once about his leaving suddenly. *Most women*, he told himself, *would have had a coronary*. Besides, he had heard Kitt talking to one of her friends in Austria this morning and she was telling her that they would be celebrating their wedding reception in Vienna soon.

He had sipped his coffee, considerably calmer than before. They had been discussing the details of the simple ceremony at the breakfast table, when Loveleen had stopped by to say hello. It didn't surprise Nikolas, but it did annoy him that within minutes of her arrival, the conversation shifted to Eshaan, his kitchen, and the disaster. But Kitt was sitting next to him, holding his hand, so he decided then and there to let his suspicions go and joined in the conversation.

"He needs money. I've tried to give him some, but he refuses to take anything from me now," Loveleen was saying.

"Yes, I've tried as well," Dr. Sinha added.

"Wait, I don't understand. If he needs help, why doesn't he just accept the help you are offering? Seems to me that he is being stubborn for no reason," Nikolas offered.

Loveleen and Dr. Sinha exchanged looks and smiled.

"You would think so, right? He feels he is responsible for the kitchen burning down and all of us losing what we invested into it. Guilt is a terrible emotion, because in its back pocket it carries shame," Kitt said.

"So he is going to let his dream fail, because he feels guilty that he failed?" Nikolas shook his head. He could not understand how failure could be a virtue in anyone's eyes.

"He will eventually work it out, I think. Sometimes, I want

to hit him over the head with the truth that people *want* to help him. I have never seen anyone stand in his own way as much as Eshaan does," Loveleen had said.

After the animated discussion at breakfast, Loveleen had gone off to see Saachi at the hospital.

"Oh, and Kitt, Kimi *Bua* is arriving this evening. She will be here just in time for the wedding," Dr. Sinha had announced after checking his buzzing phone.

For the first time since arriving, Nikolas noticed Kitt had actually responded with a positive statement related to the wedding. "I am so glad she will be here, Papa. I know how you love your sister, and it is wonderful she'll be here for the wedding!"

Dr. Sinha had then insisted that Kitt go with him to order some dessert-filled boxes that would be distributed to friends and family to commemorate the wedding, and Nikolas had decided he needed some air.

So now, here he was, trying to capture what was going on in front of a burnt-out kitchen in a monastery.

Nikolas was taken aback at Eshaan's compassion. Never in his life had he seen a man so gentle and considerate of those deemed to be the children of a lesser universe. The beggars, in their tattered and torn clothing, with their filthy feet and smelly hands, cooked as Eshaan stood close by. He hugged them, laughed with them, and guided their shaking hands as they stirred the food in the pots.

Kitt was wrong in her assessment of Eshaan; Nikolas was sure of that. The Eshaan he was seeing here would never have felt guilty for letting the investors down. He would only have felt guilty for letting the hungry down.

Nikolas felt his heart well up. God had guided his steps well today, and he was glad he was here taking pictures.

He continued to take a few more pictures, then went back to Dr. Sinha's house.

Kitt was on her way out with her father, but Nikolas pleaded with her to stay back. "I have a way to help Eshaan," he said, and Dr. Sinha left on his own.

"How?" Kitt asked.

Nikolas didn't answer, but instead handed her a thumb drive and a piece of paper with some notes scribbled on it.

"Go ahead and crop all these images to these sizes then load them on this USB. I am going to go shoot some quick videos and I will be back in an hour or so, and yes, *then* we will be able to help. Also, call Loveleen and tell her to come over here right now. Oh, and tell her to bring Gina as well. We need all hands on deck. *Now*!"

He frantically looked around the room and finally found what he was looking for, his new video camera.

"Nikolas, I am so grateful you are helping him, but . . . but why? How?" Kitt asked quizzically. He had been so unhappy for the past couple of days.

"Do you know what people want for the people they love the most?" Nikolas asked Kitt.

"No, but I have a feeling you are going to tell me," she said, and smiled.

"People want the ones they love to be happy. I love you, and I know you want to help them. If I can help them and make you happy, well then it is the least I can do. Oh, and in the bargain, I may earn some good karma too!" Nikolas beamed, and then was gone again.

Chapter 42

"This is so delicious," Eshaan smiled as he took a small bite of the curried potatoes the beggars had cooked up. The potato dish prepared with tomatoes looked lackluster, but tasted of fresh cilantro and sharp ginger. Everyone around him nodded in agreement.

Lama Dorje had joined the group a few minutes ago and beamed with pride at the sight of the group. He sat down and began to eat along with the rest of them.

Eshaan hesitatingly took another bite of the *roti* and curry and swallowed slowly. "I had forgotten what real food tastes like, Lama Dorje," he whispered.

Radio Rani, who had been watching Eshaan intently, rushed to the rescue and took his small plate away from him.

The beggars looked confused. "Is our food not good enough?" Potato *Baba* asked.

"No, no, it is not that. I think he is full and I want to eat this." She smiled playfully and began to eat from the plate. Eshaan looked relieved. It was going to be a while before he could eat anything. He could still feel the bile rising in his throat.

"This reminds me of how my mother used to make potatoes," Om chimed in as he licked the curry off his fingers.

Nikolas was in the back, filming quietly. The group called out to him, but he simply smiled and waved them off. "I am just capturing a little bit of Delhi to take back with me," he said.

You are taking everything back with you, not just a little bit, Eshaan wanted to say, but instead got up and walked to Nikolas.

"I hope you will come and taste the food they have prepared. It would mean the world to them," Eshaan said as he brought his palms together. Then, in a softer voice, he added, "I wanted to apologize to you for any hurt I may have caused. Sometimes my eyes have dreams bigger than my means. I am sorry, so please forgive me."

Nikolas put his camera down and held Eshaan's hands.

"I am happy to join your group, and all is forgiven. We all have dreams that are bigger than us, right? That is what hope is all about, and that is what keeps us moving forward."

"Do you like it? Is it too spicy for you?" Potato *Baba* was curious to see Nikolas's reaction as he bit into a large piece of potato.

"It is just as it should be, delicious!" Nikolas smiled at the old man, but was grateful when a large glass of chilled water appeared in front of him, thanks to Tenzin.

The whole crew seated in the large lawn of the monastery was laughing and eating together. This was the energy that had been missing from the kitchen, Eshaan realized. *It had always been us and them,* he thought. But really, this was what it was all about, all of them together and what they create together.

Since almost all the plates and spoons were gone, Potato

Baba, making the dish, served it to everyone on a piece of roti, Indian griddle bread.

One of the old woman beggars, a regular to the kitchen, was passing the potato-topped *rotis* to a few new beggars who had come in and sat down with the rest of the group.

As she delicately picked up each *roti* and handed it over to each person, Eshaan noticed she was crying.

"Are you tired, *Mataji*?" he said, addressing her with a respectful word, Mother. "If you are tired, sit down and eat. I am almost finished. I can hand these out."

The old lady shook her head and sat down next to Eshaan. She spoke slowly, savoring each word, each pause, each minute of attention from another human. "You, child, are too young to know what happy tears are," she said as she wiped her face. "Let me tell you a story."

There was pin-drop silence. Nikolas stopped eating, picked up his camera, and zoomed the camera in on the woman.

"I used to sell handmade wooden toys on the beach to make my living. I made enough money to educate my two boys, who got jobs as clerks with the water department. I was so happy. Then, as if overnight, my luck changed. The kids who used to buy my toys became more interested in fancier toys . . . toys that needed batteries. My business died, and then my husband died, too."

The woman paused, used her dirty sari to wipe her tears, and then continued. "When I could no longer sell toys, you see, I became a burden to my children. They never mistreated me. I raised them well that way. Yet, each night at dinner, each son would remind me of the price of everything: the onion I was eating, the incense I was lighting, the broom I used to clean the floor. I cooked and cared for them my whole life and never told them the price of anything. They were living under my roof, and yet, I was the one to hold the burden. So I decided to leave. I could not bear the indignity." Tears rolled down her cheeks. "Don't be sorry for me. I have survived five years on the street. I am crying today, because, suddenly, I feel empowered again, because I worked here. I cooked and fed the hungry. I am no longer unworthy because I don't have money. Thank you for giving me this gift," the old woman said, and kissed Eshaan on his forehead.

Om, Rani, Lama Dorje, and Tenzin all stood up and clapped. Nikolas called out to the Lama to ask him to translate what the woman had just said.

After hearing the story, Nikolas knew he had what he needed, so he said goodbye to the group and rushed off.

For the first time in his life, Eshaan realized what it was he had really been trying to do. He had mistaken his goal. It wasn't just about feeding hungry people. He now knew his desire. It was to never, ever let another human being feel so helpless and so humiliated that they gave up on themselves. He finally understood his mission was to give the less fortunate what they needed to gain back their self-worth, their self-respect, and the ability to stand on their own and earn their keep.

He felt his eyes moisten and smiled. *I guess I am old enough. I do know what happy tears are.*

Chapter 43

"No, no . . . no camera allowed in the monastery. Please, no publicity. No press. Please go." The security guard outside the monastery was fighting a losing battle, as a horde of TV reporters shoved their cameras and mics into his face and asked him to open the gate so they could go in.

The security guard wished that Raju the Dogman and his dogs would arrive already. He pushed and shoved to keep them outside until one person finally said, "We want to speak with Eshaan Veer Singh! Does he still live here?"

"What are you people doing here?" the guard asked, but no one would answer. It was afternoon prayer time at the monastery, and the guard was annoyed at all the noise these people were making.

He put his hands in the air. "Listen, listen, yes, Eshaan lives here. I will get him. But please, can you all just calm down? I am not allowed to let anyone into the monastery, but I will call and ask him to come out!"

Even as he said it, he wondered if he was doing the right thing. Then he saw Kitt, Nikolas, Gina, and Loveleen all walking toward him, and all of them were smiling. He went back to his security booth and dialed Eshaan's mobile number.

When the guard came back out, he announced, with some authority, that Eshaan was coming out in a minute, and that seemed to settle the media for a minute or two.

As was customary, every single passerby stopped to see what was going on—people coming out of their houses, the food cart vendors, the thugs (yes, the same ones who had burned the kitchen down)—were all there, along with their theories of what was going to happen.

Eshaan walked up to the gate, curious to see what was going on and a bit tentative. *What are all these TV and satellite vans doing here?* he wondered.

The reporters saw him and began to scream out their questions.

"Chef Eshaan, here, please! Can you tell us exactly who burned down the kitchen?"

"Is it true they beat you up?"

"We heard the beggars are becoming cooks here. Is that true? If so, how are you making sure the food is hygienic?"

"What the hell are these people doing here?" Eshaan asked the guard, who shrugged his shoulders and pointed to Kitt and the others, who were waving wildly to Eshaan. Kitt pointed to her phone. Eshaan looked at his and saw Loveleen was calling him.

He was about to answer, when the media roared again, this time even louder. Then he saw her, the famous Bollywood star Mancesha Oberoi. She had just stepped out of her car and was standing with her back to the monastery gate. "I will answer your questions one at a time. Please. Yes, you with IndiaTV4. Ask."

Eshaan answered Loveleen's call. "What the heck is going on?"

"You are about to become a star," Loveleen said.

"Come on, this is no time for pranks. What the hell is going on?" he said, trying to keep his voice down.

"Eshaan, Nikolas created an online campaign for you to help fund Buddha's Karma Kitchen. I called the cooking show to tell them, and they were all over it. Gina, here, called everyone she knew to contribute. The number of donations on that page is climbing as we speak. He put up the video of the beggars cooking for you! It has gone viral," Loveleen said, and Eshaan stood there, stunned.

All this time, he believed Nikolas hated him because of his relationship with Kitt. But here he was, saving Eshaan's dream. People never ceased to surprise him. He lifted his face to the sky. He was learning, it seemed, a new lesson a minute.

Loveleen had a tendency to stretch the truth, but Eshaan also knew that unless it was a big event, Bollywood hotshot Maneesha Oberoi would not be there with her minions in tow.

Eshaan slipped out of the gate and pushed his way to the movie star. "Maneesha *Ji*, it is me, Eshaan," he called to her over the cacophony of screaming reporters, shrieking fans, the several monks now standing behind him, and the security guard still yelling for everyone to settle down.

"Eshaan, come over here." Maneesha finally heard him and turned her dazzling smile on. "Here is Eshaan. He is the one responsible for this kitchen, and we are going to do all that we can to rebuild. If you want to help, donate money to his

KARMIC PAY page that is set up. You can get details from my manager here. That is it. No more comments."

The photographers went crazy as she placed one hand behind his waist and waved to them with the other hand. He tried to move away, but her grip was solid. "Eshaan, you want money to run this operation? Then look up and smile."

Eshaan was overwhelmed as the photographers closed in. He recognized some of the anchors. He had only seen them on TV, and now here they were. "Please, can we have some group shots? We want to see the team behind Buddha's Karma Kitchen," yelled out a tall, lanky man with a camera.

Before Eshaan could respond, Maneesha turned to the security guard and told him to bring the team out now. At a loss for words, in front of his favorite Bollywood movie star, he simply opened the gate and motioned for Lama Dorje and the rest of them to come out.

"Nothing like having a monk on your side to create sympathy," Maneesha whispered.

Lama Dorje, Radio Rani, Om, Tulku Tenzin, and Eshaan all stood behind Maneesha as she loudly introduced them as "workers in the kitchen."

"Please wait. There are more who are part of this group," Eshaan called out, and then turned toward the open gate and signaled for the two beggars who had cooked the meal the previous afternoon to come join them.

Eshaan then called out to the thugs, "You gave this place a new life and new meaning. Please come."

And finally, he looked to Kitt, Loveleen, Gina, and Nikolas. He folded his hands in prayer and bowed his head. "This, today, is your creation. Please join us."

The beggars and thugs stood there frozen. Eshaan walked over, took the old woman and Potato *Baba* by their hands, and led them toward the waiting group.

"They cooked for us here. These are the people we were feeding, and now, they are feeding us," he said as he gently moved them to stand next to Lama Dorje. The media applauded.

"Wait for me!" Dr. Sinha walked as fast as he could to join in. He had been watching from the patio, and of course, this was his tribe, so he had to be in the photograph.

The thugs, unsure at first, joined in the photo opportunity.

"Keep the enemy closer. I like that," Loveleen, who had now joined in the group photo as well, whispered to her friend.

"This is Buddha's Karma Kitchen," Eshaan said, beaming with pride as he pointed to the group.

"Eshaan, darling, you just became, what they call in this business, an overnight sensation," Maneesha Oberoi said as she pulled him to stand by her side. She was glad she had listened when the cooking show producer called and told her what was going on. Her recent films had received a lukewarm reception, but this? This would change all that. Now, here she was, a savior of the poor. And the fact that Eshaan was young, handsome, and by her side was just icing on the cake.

The group huddled together as the reporters pressed on with questions.

Lama Dorje offered a statement on behalf of the monastery, and everyone clapped.

"This is going live at eight this evening," one of the reporters informed them. "What would you like to ask the public to do?"

Before anyone else could answer, Maneesha moved to the front. "We need donors. We need money to help rebuild this kitchen. Then, we need food—vegetables, rice, wheat, *chai*—to set the kitchen up so it can function and feed people. Right?" She looked to Eshaan. He nodded. Maneesha kept talking, and Eshaan stole a look at Kitt, who gave him a thumbs-up. Her other hand was holding onto Nikolas's hand.

He smiled. This was it. Not everyone got everything they want.

He shifted his attention to the camera. "Yes, as Maneesha *Ji* said, we need that, but we need cooks who can train these folks to cook, so they can get jobs. We need restaurant owners, *dhaba* owners . . . we need you all to come out and help us train and employ these people. Yesterday, without any training, these two made some of the best food I have ever tasted." The words just flowed from Eshaan's heart.

"This is not an easy task. This city is filled with people who need help. But I encourage you to join us and help Eshaan. And yes, of course, don't forget to watch me this week on *India's Best Home Chef*, as I judge the show." Maneesha beamed her smile then stared at her manager and signaled to him that this show was over.

Chapter 44

"Children these days. I just don't understand all this modern romance and all that. She does not even have a wedding sari on! You have totally spoiled her and this is unacceptable." The sharp, almost shrill voice belonged to Dr. Sinha's older sister, who everyone called Kimi *Bua.*

And today, Kimi *Bua* was on a rampage and was fuming mad. She had just returned from her month-long spa adventure, and here this girl was getting married, *married*, with no wedding outfit.

Dr. Sinha shook his head at his sister. "I told you they both didn't want to do anything that is wasteful or showy. I think it is fine for them to have a court marriage, and then we are having the entire family here for dinner afterward. Didn't you see the flower arrangements in the living room? And a famous chef is doing the dinner, a *ten-course* dinner!"

Dr. Sinha and Kimi *Bua* were seated in the tiny patio of the Sinha residence.

A calm, cool sky soothed many a frayed nerve, as the heat index was the lowest it had been all summer.

"Good morning, Dr. Sinha. You ordered these? I have brought them for you," a young man came in the main gate and to the patio. In his hands, he was holding two wedding garlands made with white and red roses and a touch of fragrant jasmine.

"Oh, good. Can you take them inside? The maid will pay you," Dr. Sinha told the delivery boy.

Kimi *Bua* was not impressed.

"No henna? No music? No rituals? What are you doing with your daughter? This is no way to get married. And the groom? He is living here? Staying here with her before marriage? You allowed this? It is shameful."

"Kimi, you are being old-fashioned. Where does it say that every Indian wedding has to be a Bollywood movie–style event? Besides, all the money I would have spent at the wedding is now my gift to her and sitting in her checking account."

A very loud clapping noise startled both Dr. Sinha and Kimi *Bua*. They looked toward the patio to see what was going on. The *hijras*, transgenders who invited themselves to come bless auspicious occasions for a small fee, had arrived.

"We were told there is a wedding here, but maybe that is not true?" the leading *hijra*, dressed in a shocking blue sari, said as she surveyed the house.

"No flowers, no tent, no music, no guests?" muttered another one dressed in a golden sari. "Sorry we trouble you. Why did they tell us there is marriage here?" She placed both her hands on her hips and cocked her head when she spoke. "Anyway, there is nothing here. Let's go," she told her crew and they left.

Kimi *Bua* was now seething. "This is a bad omen. These *hijras* will curse Kitt and you. You say the marriage is in one hour at the court? I've seen funerals that are more cheerful." Kimi *Bua* shook her head then stood up to go back inside. In addition to all this bad news, the mosquitoes had made quite a feast of her toes.

Dr. Sinha ignored his sister then turned his attention to his buzzing mobile phone.

Kimi *Bua* entered the house and ran straight into Nikolas, who was dressed in dark blue trousers and a starched white shirt.

"Good morning!" he said cheerfully. She eyed him skeptically from top to bottom, rolled her eyes, muttered a hello, and continued on to Kitt's room.

"Kitt, at least wear something that is colorful. Why this white dress? We Hindus wear white at cremations, not marriages," she said when she noticed the young girl was wearing a long white gown of sorts.

Kitt was brushing her golden hair and simply smiled at the old lady. "Nikolas gave me this as a present, so I am going to wear it." She pointed to a large gift box lying on her bed. It was filled with makeup items, a large bottle of her favorite perfume, Obsession, a few silk scarves, a set of beautiful freshwater pearl earrings and necklace, and a large rose. Nikolas had given it to her the previous night.

Kimi went to the closet and pulled out a long, silk, beaded red scarf and draped it over her niece. "At least a touch of color. You are getting married, not going to a funeral! Now, let me help brush your hair." She made Kitt sit on a small chair and furiously attempted to knot the young girl's hair into a bun. Then she turned the chair around to look Kitt in the face.

"What are you so sad about? See, if this was a proper

marriage, with music and food and guests, you would not look so sad. Oh, and I saw the boy, your fiancé. He is young. If you don't take care of yourself, you will look like his mother in a year."

"Oh, God, that is funny!"

Kimi *Bua* turned to see Loveleen standing at the entrance to the room. She was holding a small pink gift bag.

"And you. You are a bad influence on Kitt. Pregnant without a husband? You are watching too many TV shows. All these Indian shows are now just as bad as the western ones. Now, help her finish her makeup. If this is what she wants—" She stomped out of the room in a huff.

Chapter 45

The steps of the old courthouse were broken, which was to be expected. However, what was not expected were the small flowers pushing out through the cracks providing cheerful color.

The small group, Dr. Sinha, Loveleen, Kitt, Nikolas, and Kimi *Bua* (under protest), were all headed into the main clerk's office for the signing of the wedding papers, and in Nikolas's words, "Finally making this woman my bride."

"Where are your friends from the Kitchen?" Kimi enquired earlier as everyone was getting into the car to leave for the courthouse.

"Oh, Eshaan is competing today to get into the finals. Radio Rani, Lama Dorje, and all are there with him. I—" Loveleen had begun to explain, but then the look on Kitt's face made her quiet down.

The wooden benches outside the clerk's office were rotting and stained. "What is that red color?" asked Nikolas, pointing to the red patches on the wooden chair.

"People used to spit out their paan, you know, betel leaf. I think now they've banned eating it here, but I guess they still haven't cleaned up the mess," Dr. Sinha replied.

Kimi, burdened with the two garlands and a box of sweets, sat down on the bench and sighed. There were at least four couples ahead of them, and it looked like it was going to be a really long morning.

"It is a text from Eshaan. He is wishing you well and says to thank Nikolas. He was almost mobbed by fans outside the studio." Loveleen read some of the lines from her phone, but no one except Kitt was listening.

"I am just going to go freshen up," Kitt said out loud, and pulled Loveleen's hand so they could both go together. "Really? He was mobbed? Show me the message," she demanded as soon as they reached the bathroom door.

Kitt took Loveleen's phone and read the message: *IS THE CEREMONY OVER? SHE MUST LOOK AMAZING, RIGHT? HE IS LUCKY. I WILL ALWAYS LOVE HER, LOVELEEN. TELL NIKOLAS THE SOCIAL MEDIA THING WORKED LIKE MAGIC. I WAS MOBBED COMING IN AND THERE IS A LINE OF PEOPLE OUTSIDE THIS VAN WAITING TO INVEST IN KARMA KITCHEN. CAN YOU BELIEVE THAT? AT LEAST THAT WORKED OUT, RIGHT?*

WE ARE WAITING FOR THE CLERK. GLAD TO HEAR THE NEWS, AND YES, SHE LOOKS BEAUTIFUL, Loveleen had texted back.

IT IS TRUE WHAT THEY SAY, THEN, ISN'T IT? NO ONE GETS EVERYTHING. TELL HER I LOVE HER. WAIT…NO, DON'T TELL HER THAT. I GOTTA GO.

Kitt handed the phone back to Loveleen.

"You are making a big mistake. You need to walk out of here now," Loveleen told her friend. "You will not get this chance again. Go. I will manage your family. Go to him. He needs you.

This is his final audition. If he wins this, he will be able to create these kitchens around the world . . . and he will need you by his side. I have known him a lot longer than you have. He is a good man. He loves you. He will—"

Kitt looked at her friend, her own eyes brimming with tears. "You think I don't know that? I love him, but I owe Nikolas too much. I just cannot. And he is right—no one gets everything." With that, she wiped her tears and adjusted her red silk scarf. She opened the small purse she was carrying and refreshed her lipstick and her perfume. Then she looked at Loveleen and said, "Come on now. I am getting married, and you have to support me!"

The two friends returned hand in hand to the clerk's office.

"Ready? Some more officers arrived, so it looks like we don't have to wait anymore." Nikolas beamed at his beautiful bride-to-be. He held out his hand and she took it, and they all walked into the clerk's office.

The old clerk, Mr. Sharma, looked up and smiled. "Oh, welcome, welcome. Do you have the witnesses? Also, I need the no objection forms from your embassy, as I am guessing you are not Indian?"

Kitt nodded just as the rest of the group walked in. Then she opened her purse and handed him an official application, embassy certificates, and the check, as requested by the government. Before they had even come to India, Kitt had checked online to see what was required and had sent in some paperwork already, per the country's thirty-day notice requirement. Everything was now set for the wedding.

The clerk smiled and accepted then put on his reading glasses to check the application.

The office was clean compared to the corridor. A sizeable picture of the Indian Prime Minister Modi hung on the wall behind the desk. A large round table on the left side of the well-lit room was filled with bouquets of flowers.

The clerk instructed Dr. Sinha, Kimi *Bua*, and Loveleen to sit on the small green sofa in the room, and then turned to the couple. “People these days want to say their own words, you know, promises to each other and all that. So you want that? You can do that, and then we do the garlands and then we sign. Simple, simple.”

Nikolas took Kitt by the hand and turned his head to the clerk. “Mr. Sharma, we are ready. Kitt, do you want to go first, or shall I?”

Kitt looked visibly disconcerted. “I did not know we were supposed to write vows . . . since this is India. I just thought—”

"Please, no getting upset. This is the happiest day of our lives! Just tell me what you feel. That is it."

Kitt cleared her throat and looked at Loveleen, who discretely pointed to the exit door.

“I . . . I . . . I think you are the kindest, sweetest man I know. I am just so honored to be your wife, and I promise to dedicate my life to caring for you,” Kitt said slowly, then smiled and squeezed Nikolas’ hand.

“I think you are the most beautiful and kind woman I have ever met, and I promise to love you and care for you ’til the day I die,” Nikolas said then bent forward to kiss Kitt on her forehead.

Dr. Sinha walked over and handed them the garlands.

Nikolas placed his around the neck of his fiancée, and she did the same for him. Dr. Sinha and the clerk clapped. Kimi *Bua* just winced, and Loveleen managed a feeble smile.

"Now, sir, you must sign here, and madam, you must sign here." The clerk pointed to a large paper on his desk.

Nikolas picked up the pen on the clerk's table and signed his name on the document.

"Perfect, sir, and now, madam, it is your turn." The clerk looked at Kitt.

She picked up the pen slowly, and then bent down to sign her name.

"I must say, madam, and I hope you don't mind my saying so, that scent . . . it smells so earthy, so marvelous!" Mr. Sharma said as he smiled at her.

"Wait, Kitt, before you sign . . . I have to ask. Do you know what *petrichor* is?" Nikolas asked suddenly.

Eshaan Veer Singh's Journal

Keep being you
She says
With a bright smile
Simple words
Be me?
Who am I supposed to be?
With her marrying another man
How will I ever be me?
Who am I?
A broken heart
A fearless warrior
A friendless loner
Be you
She says again
This time no smile
Her eyes are stern
Filled with confidence
Be you
Soar high
Be you
Fortune awaits
As you fulfill your destiny
I look into her eyes

Deep into her soul
I decide to leap
To leave her
For this new destiny
Why?
Why now?
I saw myself in her eyes

Chapter 46

The crowd outside the studio was animated, loud, and cheerful.

"Eshaan, Eshaan—"

The chanting got louder and louder when they saw their new hero on screen, ready to take on the cooking challenge.

A large movie screen had been set up just outside the studio, so the crowds could see what was happening inside, live. Scores of young women, men, and children were watching closely.

"This is all thanks to Nikolas," Eshaan had remarked before entering the studio. Nikolas, who was a sheer genius at social media, had combined forces with Gina, her contacts, and the cooking show, and created nothing short of a miracle.

"We want to go in and see him. He is family," Dr. Sinha tried to convince the guards at the main entrance of the studio.

"Sir, they are shooting live right now. I am not allowed to open the door. The director will fire me. *No one* is allowed to go in or out."

Dr. Sinha shrugged his shoulders and looked at his family.

"Come on, we can watch him on the screen," said Loveleen as she pulled Kitt with one hand and Dr. Sinha with the other toward the large outdoor movie screen.

The audience became very quiet as they heard the judge call on Eshaan to come forward and bring his dish to the tasting table.

"This is to remind our audience that the final challenge before going to the Super Finals is this: each contestant must prepare a dish that to them defines hope. And they must use our one special ingredient, King Butter. So now, let us welcome our final contestant for the day, a fan favorite, Chef Eshaan!"

Eshaan's shy smile made the crowd break out into a loud applause again. Loveleen clapped as loud as she could. "Go, Eshaan!" she screamed as Kitt stared at the screen, her fingers playing with the garland around her neck. Nikolas cheered him on as well, clapping and screaming as loud as he could. From the corner of her eye, Kitt saw Gina standing tall right in front, clapping and cheering loudly. Gina saw her as well.

I'm coming over! she mouthed as she walked over to Kitt. "You are here?" Gina questioned then looked at Nikolas. "I thought you were getting married today?"

"That was this morning, and now we are here," Loveleen answered, and then told them to be quiet so she could hear what was going on on the screen.

"So, Chef Eshaan, the last time you were here, well, we did not taste your food because you threw it in the trashcan! I hope that is not the plan this time." The judge's words were dripping with sarcasm.

Eshaan nodded gently. "I am sorry about that. But, yes, this time, I do have a dish—"

Before he could finish, the camera careened over to the

celebrity judge, Maneesha Oberoi. "Yes, we are looking forward to tasting your dish. And let me remind our viewers here that our sponsors have promised an extra payment of ten lakhs toward his Karma Kitchen *if*—and that is a *big* if—he manages to win the judges over in this round. Sorry, Eshaan! More pressure for you."

The drums rolled, and the judges walked toward Eshaan's counter where his dish, individually plated for the three judges, awaited their judgment.

"So, Chef Eshaan, what have you prepared for us today? And I am reminding you again that the theme for this episode is hope."

"Yes, sir. I thank you again for inviting me back. I am very grateful."

Kitt's eyes widened as she looked at him on screen getting ready to describe his dish. He picked up the plate. It looked like it had some kind of red sauce. A red curry? The crowd began to throw out guesses. He must have made *sambar*, a south Indian curry. No, no, that looks like a red curry. Was it red kidney beans?

It was hard to tell what the dish was from the screen.

Please, Eshaan, don't throw it in the trash this time! Come on, do it for your mom, do it for yourself, and do it for Karma Kitchen, Kitt's mind screamed. She reached out and held Loveleen's hand, and both friends closed their eyes in a moment of quiet prayer.

"Over the few days, as the public has come out to support me, I realized that my mother's death, as horrible as it was, was destined. If she had not died the way she did, I would never have made it my life's mission to help people. Even in her death, she taught me an important lesson," Eshaan said before he described the actual dish.

"This dish . . . my mother cooked at the home of a local landowner when I was a child. It is a simple butter, cream, and tomato dish she often cooked for their kids. Every once in a while, she would bring a little home for me. She said that poverty did not mean we were not entitled to good things. It just meant we had to work harder than others to get them. Now, with your permission, I would like to take a bite before sharing this with you. I haven't tasted it in twenty years."

Only a handful of people watching Eshaan take that first bite understood the significance. It was a rebirth; the son had found his mother again. His house was no longer burning. In his memory's kitchen, she was alive, well, and had just blessed him with success. He put down his tasting spoon then handed each judge a small bowl of the butter chicken: a luxurious dish of spiced chicken in a butter-tomato sauce.

"This, to me, is the dish of hope, because it promises better things ahead and that there is always a way forward. Always."

"We will be right back after a word from our sponsors," the ad cut into the screen time and the crowd howled. The screen began to have issues and suddenly went dark. The crowd, now annoyed, began to scream out, "What happened? We want to see our hero!"

Some people turned to their phones to see if they could catch the live feed, and others went on to social media platforms to see what was going on.

The screen came back on. "Sorry for the delay, folks! We have a result."

The crowd went crazy.

Eshaan was standing center stage, along with six other

candidates. Only three would be moving forward. The camera panned the audience, and Dr. Sinha clapped when he saw Om, Radio Rani, Lama Dorje, the two old beggars, and Tenzin sitting in the stands.

Three contestants were axed.

"Eshaan Veer Singh, this dish is so simple. It is so easy to make. We would have thought you would have made something more, you know, complex! Like that soup you made when you first came on board." Judge Chef Ram Singh was smirking. The second judge nodded, as did Maneesha Oberoi.

"No, no, no—" Kitt chanted as she squeezed Loveleen's hand. This couldn't be happening.

"The test of a good chef is not how complicated a dish he can make. But how he can make the dish sing with simple flavors and simple ingredients," Judge Singh said, "However, we were looking for something more aspirational, more luxurious. To win this contest, you had to stand out more."

There was pin drop silence on the set. The movie star was stunned. What were these idiot chefs doing? Eshaan was a hero in the eyes of the public and could make the ratings of their show soar.

Suddenly, Maneesha Oberio realized what was happening: They were going to cut Eshaan from the show. The public would protest, loudly and fervently. If the outcry was loud enough, they would then admit their "mistakes" and bring him back. As a result, of course, their ratings would soar.

"Eshaan Veer Singh, you are out of the show."

The words, those words suddenly made everyone angry. The audience inside, the folks watching outside.

This was a disaster.

The crowd began to clear, and an hour later, the doors of the studio opened. Eshaan emerged with Lama Dorje by his side as the rest of the group followed closely behind. He was telling the Lama how he could not believe what had just happened. The security folks led him to his van. Loveleen, Kitt, Dr. Sinha, Nikolas, and Gina were already there waiting for him. A kind assistant had finally listened to Dr. Sinha and moved them all to the van, away from the loud crowds.

"Eshaan, I am so sorry!" Loveleen rushed to him.

"Don't be! I feel like I won! I have been running away from my mother for so long. I stopped today. I caught up with her again. Everything is fine." He beamed.

Eshaan then noticed Kitt. "Oh, congratulations on your wedding!" he said hesitantly to her, and extended his hand out to Nikolas.

"And to you. A loss in the show, but you won the bride's hand," said Nikolas as he reached out and placed Kitt's hand in Eshaan's.

Eshaan looked at them, totally confused.

"I thought Kitt was over you, you know. But, today . . . there were three of us at the wedding registry—you, me, and her. I knew then I had lost." Nikolas smiled.

Eshaan noticed Gina wiping away a tear. She, then, blew him a kiss and shrugged her shoulders and mouthed, "Next life, you are mine!"

He turned back to Nikolas.

"I don't understand. I was not at your wedding. I was here," Eshaan said, holding on hard and strong to Kitt's trembling hand.

"Ah, yes, my friend. But you were. Kitt made sure you came with us," he said.

Petrichor, that is what Nikolas had asked her when she was about to sign the registry. He made her look up the meaning on her phone, right there at the clerk's office, right as she was about to sign the papers.

Petrichor, the smell of the ground after it rains. That was the perfume she was wearing. It was what Loveleen had given her as a wedding gift, *soundha itar*, the perfume Eshaan wore everyday. It was the only way Kitt could take Eshaan with her to the wedding.

Eshaan Veer Singh's Journal

The rain is here
After the long drought
I used to resent it
I identify with it now
It has a purpose
As does the grass, the lotus, and even the bee
I walk in the rain
It drenches my clothes
I watch the rain
As it hugs the earth
Behind the tall columns of grief and anguish
I see the brightness of the new dawn
I place my hand on my heart
I close my eyes
The wind is cool
Or is it the rain
That soothes the earth
That soothes my pain
The drops, they cease
And then I smell
The scent of the earth
The scent of hope
My tears roll down

My mother whispers gently to my soul
No hunger
No more

THE END

Actually,
this is just the beginning.

Bonus: Head over to monicabhide.com for a free eCookbook specially designed and developed for the readers of this book! The book has dishes Eshaan (and other contestants) may have cooked for the various cooking contests: roasted beet soup, Mango salsa and calamari, Scallops with coconut curry dip. And the book provides a simple recipe for Butter Chicken!

Love Eshaan?

Then you don't want to miss the sequel to *Karma and the Art of Butter Chicken*:

Kismet and the Art of Redemption

"Sometimes the things we want the most aren't right for us," Eshaan tells Loveleen as his wedding day goes from bad to worse. Now, with a broken heart, Eshaan wonders if he really is a doomed soul. He immerses himself in making Karma Kitchen come alive but his loneliness finds no solution. He stops writing poetry, and Lama Dorje worries that Eshaan will slip and stop eating again. His friends gather around to try and help him, but he refuses. Will he find the strength to move forward again and revive his love of life and giving, or will his broken heart break his spirit?

Coming soon!

Acknowledgments

This book is dedicated to my dearest father, Dina Saigal. I learned to make butter chicken from him and I am happy to say that my dish comes nowhere near his version! He is just amazing and has been a guiding light for me.

A special thanks to my husband and guru, Sameer Bhide, for keeping me motivated!

A huge thank you to Simi Jois for the beautiful cover photograph. A special thanks to our hand model who wishes to remain anonymous!

A few years ago, world famous Chef José Andrés came to my house to eat butter chicken. I had written a story how I fell in love with the dish because of my father. Chef José loved the story so much he wanted to try the dish! I credit the inspiration of this novel to him. He has toiled tirelessly for charity kitchens here in D.C. and overseas.

A big, heartfelt thanks to my amazing muses who have kept me on the straight and narrow: Luca Marchiori, Popsy Kanagaratnam, Betty Ann Besa-Quirino, Ana Di, Deepa Patke, Linda Whittig, Amy Riolo, Niv Mani, Aviva Goldfarb, Mollie

Cox Bryan, Sangeeta Bongmom, Andrea Lynn, Alka Keswani, Shirley Taur, Alison Stein, and Stephanie Caruso.

Thank you to the Karmapa International Buddhist Institute (kibi-edu.org) for their advice.

Thanks also to Ramin Ganeshram for all her structural and editing help.

To Mike and Kathleen Flinn Kozar for helping with the description of this work.

I want to thank my family and dear friends who encourage me and my crazy dreams.

To Valerie Murphy for her honest feedback, and Sandra Beckwith for encouraging me throughout the writing of this book.

To James aka Humble Nations for the cover design, Suzanne Fass and Jason Anderson for book design.

About the Author

Monica Bhide is an internationally renowned writer known for sharing food, culture, mystery, love, and life in a lyrical voice. Having roots and experience in many places, Monica is now based in the Washington, D.C. area. She has built a diverse and solid audience through the publication of three cookbooks, a book of essays and one of short stories, a collection of interviews with exceptional women in food, her website, *MonicaBhide.com*, and articles in top-tier media including *Food & Wine*, *Bon Appétit*, *Saveur*, *The Washington Post*, *Health*, the *New York Times*, *Ladies Home Journal*, *AARP The Magazine*, and *Parents*. Her books have been published by Simon & Schuster and Random House (India). Monica released her debut short story collection, *The Devil in Us*, in October 2014. Her sixth book, *A Life of Spice*, a collection of food essays, was released on April 27, 2015.

An engaging story teller, informed educator, and popular lecturer, Monica has taught writing and social media workshops around the world, at Food Bloggers Connect (London), Association of Food Journalists (Salt Lake City), Eat Write

Retreat (DC and Philadelphia), Food and Wine Conference (Orlando), Georgetown University and Yale University (as a guest speaker), and elsewhere. She frequently teaches writing classes for Smithsonian Associates in Washington, DC. Monica is also a frequent presence on NPR.

Monica has given keynote speeches at various organizations for the past several years. Her topics have included finding your creative self and renewing your creative strength in an ever-changing world.

Monica's food writing has garnered numerous accolades and been included in four *Best Food Writing* anthologies (2005, 2009, 2010, and 2014). The *Chicago Tribune* named her one of seven food writers to watch in 2012. In April 2012, *Mashable.com* picked her as one of the top 10 food writers on Twitter. Monica has a growing audience of thousands of engaged followers on Twitter, Facebook, and *MonicaBhide.com.*

Monica is a graduate of The George Washington University, Washington, DC. She holds a master's degree from Lynchburg College, Lynchburg, VA, and a bachelor's degree from Bangalore University in Bangalore, India. She feels fortunate for her rich education and enjoys giving back to the global community by serving on committees and volunteering for Les Dames d' Escoffier, the International Association of Culinary Professionals, and other organizations.

About Simi Jois

The beautiful cover photograph for this book was shot by Simi Jois.

Simi uses photographic images as her canvas and the lens as her brush. Her passion for creating flavors in the kitchen provided her with infinite permutations of expression. Painting with ingredients, pairing exotic spices for mutual enhancement and richness of flavor, Simi narrates her stories through the play of light and bold strokes of color.

Simi's portfolio : http://www.simijois.com
Simi's blog : http://www.turmericnspice.com

Praise for Monica Bhide's *The Devil In Us*

"Monica Bhide's short story collection isn't impressive because it's a first-timer's effort—it's impressive, period. The stories, each filled with strong, feisty characters and exquisite details of people, places, and things, will keep you riveted. There are plenty of Indian Americans writing novels these days, but far too few writing short stories and even fewer writing stories of this caliber."

Sree Sreenivasan, co-founder of the South Asian Journalists Association and Chief Digital Officer at The Metropolitan Museum of Art

"Monica Bhide's excellent collection will transport you to unexpected places, moving you between America and India, hospitals, college campuses, ancient temples, a devastated train station. You will be entranced by the wide spectrum of characters she has created--a newlywed doctor learning to love his wife, a cancer survivor hoping for a second chance, a dying old man

40947490R00203

Made in the USA
Middletown, DE
28 February 2017

ıate, a transsexual who adopts a young orphan. Filled rises and heart, this book will pull you in and not let

ıtra Banerjee Divakaruni, author of Oleander Girl *and* The Mistress of Spices

This book and its characters will haunt you long after you finish reading it."

Kathleen Flinn, author of the New York Times *bestseller* The Sharper Your Knife, the Less You Cry

"Monica Bhide's wonderful, internationally flavored collection is full of spice and life. The beguiling voice of a true storyteller will lure you out of your self into her intriguing, fictional world. Enjoy!"

Diana Abu-Jaber, author of Crescent *and* Birds of Paradise

"Monica Bhide beguiling writing takes us into the rich tapestry within private, intimate worlds that we don't want to leave."

Shoba Narayan, James Beard Award finalist, author of the memoirs Monsoon Diary *and* Return to India